His Clandestine Bride

by

Tora Williams

His Clandestine Bride

Cover Art by *Abigail Owen*

The Wild Rose Press, Inc.
PO Box 708
Adams Basin, NY 14410-0708
Visit us at www.thewildrosepress.com

Publishing History
First Tea Rose Edition, 2019
Print ISBN 978-1-5092-2507-1
Digital ISBN 978-1-5092-2508-8

Published in the United States of America

The last time Edmund had seen such challenge in another's eyes, he'd had a Saracen's sword at his throat. Every fiber of his being screamed to press forward. Was it true? Did he have an heir, hiding here in Molbren? But his instincts told him pushing Isobel would only send her fleeing. Besides, she had the answers he'd craved for five years. He mustn't let this chance slip away.

"I did come for you. Although I can't believe you'd call your message 'begging'."

"What do you mean?"

"You said you were betrothed to another, so I should forget you. Which part of that was the begging?"

"I never—" Isobel thumped her goblet upon the table, slopping crimson wine upon the white cloth. She regarded him with narrowed eyes. "You're a bold liar, for someone once so obsessed with honor."

"It's no lie. I remember what the messenger said, word for word. He gave me your ring to prove you'd sent him. The same ring I put on your finger after you vowed to take me as your husband. Then he gave me your message: *Forget me, Edmund. I never loved you, and I'm to marry another.* Tell me, Isobel, how else should I have interpreted that? It doesn't sound like begging to me."

Dedication

To my amazing nieces, Emma and Elena.
Will wouldn't have been the same without you.

Chapter One

The Welsh Marches, January 1139

The clatter of iron-shod hooves upon the bailey cobbles distracted Isobel from her steward's rambling monologue. She cut him off with a slice of the hand and rose from the desk.

"We weren't expecting visitors, were we?"

"None, my lady."

Strange. Molbren Castle was the most isolated of her late husband's holdings and saw few visitors. That was why she liked it; even without the warfare raging between King Stephen and Empress Maude, she had reasons of her own for wanting seclusion.

She opened the shutters, and an icy blast tore through the barred window. It whipped her veil across her face and scattered the steward's parchments around his cramped chamber. While he gathered them, muttering under his breath, Isobel leaned across the sill and peered out into the bailey to see the castle gates swing shut behind three horsemen. The leader sat tall in the saddle, the fine cut of his knee-length gambeson emphasizing his broad shoulders and powerful frame. There was no mistaking the challenge in the arrogant tilt of the chin, how one hand rested on the pommel of his sword: *cross me at your peril.*

She tightened her grip on the shutters. Who was it?

Why was he here? She strained her eyes in vain to make out any identifying badge. Shivering, she slammed the shutters shut, smoothed her veil, and composed her features. She would greet the man civilly, show him there was nothing here to interest him, and pray he left at the earliest opportunity.

Out in the passageway, she was poised with one hand upon the newel of the spiral staircase when the solar door flew open and her young son dashed out. He ran up to her and tugged her skirt. "Are you going to see the visitors, Mama? Can I come? I want to see the horses." Will turned pleading eyes to Isobel.

She paused and tousled the mousy brown curls so like her own. "Not this time, my heart." It wouldn't do for strangers to see how young and vulnerable the new lord of Molbren was. "Stay here and be good. We'll look at the horses later."

Will's face fell. "Very well." He shuffled back to the solar.

Praying Will would have the sense to stay out of the way, Isobel hurried down the stairs and into the guard room; the two men on duty sprang to their feet. Summoning one, she ordered him to follow. To the other she said, "Don't let any strangers in without my permission." Then she lifted the trailing hem of her bliaut and swept through the main door and down the steps to the courtyard.

The visitors, accompanied by three of her guards, were walking their horses toward the stables. The leader, a head taller than his companions, had his back to her. Something about the set of his shoulders, his upright posture, struck a chord in her memory. As did the shock of raven hair. She'd run her fingers through hair just like that, while smiling at promises that had proved to be naught but empty words. It couldn't be him, though; Edmund Granville was in the Holy Land, and she prayed he would stay there.

Nevertheless, as she approached the group, the blood beat in her ears. She couldn't drag her eyes from the stranger. Dear God, let it be a stranger! If he would only turn, she would see her eyes played tricks on her, and it wasn't the one man who could destroy her peace, take away the only joy in her life.

Then the man turned, and the world went gray.

"Edmund," she whispered, hugging her arms to her chest. How was this possible?

Edmund's eyes locked with hers, and for the merest instant they widened, then his features settled in a calm mask. But she knew what she had seen, and it gave her a measure of hope: he hadn't known she was here.

He hadn't come for Will.

If she hadn't seen his momentary lapse of control, she would never have guessed his shock at seeing her. When he replied, his voice was smooth, with a mocking edge that made her clench her teeth. "Lady Isobel. I see the years haven't changed you."

In all honesty she couldn't say the same about him. Edmund Granville was not the same man she had known five years ago. The Edmund of her memory had eyes alight with warmth and laughter and a mouth forever quirked in a smile. But appearances could be deceptive; the face before her was surely a closer picture of his true self—the man who had abandoned her to an unhappy marriage. A puckered scar now scored his right cheekbone, his mouth turned down, and his brow was creased with frown lines. Worst of all, the slate blue eyes that had once regarded her with love were cold flints.

She clasped her hands behind her back to hide their trembling. "Why are you here?"

He raised an eyebrow. "What, no tender greeting?"

Ice cold fear settled in the pit of her stomach. Would he shame her—announce the truth in front of her men? She drew a shaky breath. Surely not, for it would shame him also. No, for some reason he was trying to goad her, although she couldn't imagine why. She was the one wronged. She was the one who had lain awake night after night, blinking dry eyed into the darkness, ears straining for any signal from him, her faith in him leaching away with every weary dawn. What right had he to be angry? He was the one who had seized freedom and abandoned her without so much as a message.

Still, she mustn't let him provoke her. The sooner she discovered his purpose the sooner he would be gone and away from here. Away from Will. "I am merely trying my best to aid you in whatever way I can," she said. "The nearest town is Ludlow, ten miles away, so I suggest you hurry if you don't wish to find yourself benighted in the forest."

Edmund frowned. "My business is with Sir Roger de Stanton's widow. I will speak with her and no other."

"*I* am Sir Roger's widow. Your business is with me."

To give him his due, only the merest twitch at the corner of his eye revealed his surprise. "My condolences. Forgive my confusion; widows don't

4

usually wear crimson."

The heat of a blush crept up her face. "These are troubled times," she said. "I've spent almost every mark in my possession protecting my people from outlaws and provisioning the castle in case of siege. The expense of black cloth would have been wasteful." As true as that was, she had also refused to go into mourning for a man who had caused her such misery.

Edmund waved the guards back. When they obeyed without question, she narrowed her eyes. Later she would remind them who paid and sheltered them. "It's one outlaw in particular that brings me here," he said. "Cannington Castle recently fell to the king, but The Earl of Cannington escaped. According to our spies, he hasn't reached Maude's territory, so he must still be at large. King Stephen thinks he's trying to reach kin in Wales. The king has ordered me to find him before he's safely across this part of the Marches and into Welsh territory."

"And he thinks I might be sheltering him?" Icy fingers stroked the nape of her neck. If the king suspected she still held sympathies for the empress, her seclusion in Molbren could be at an end. Rather than risk losing her support, and hence her knights, he might well order her to marry one of his allies, and so cement his hold on Molbren. "I can assure you I'm loyal to the king."

"Then you'll have no objection to my search."

"I won't have my loyalty questioned. I took an oath of fealty to the king when Sir Roger died." Only one thought hammered through her mind: *Will*. If Edmund searched the castle, he couldn't fail to meet him.

"You'll forgive me if I don't take your word for it."

He lowered his voice to a pitch meant only for her ears. "I've already experienced how lightly you take your vows."

A wave of dizziness rolled over her, and she reached out to the stable wall to steady herself. It was a vicious lie! He was the one who had broken his vows, forcing her to marry Sir Roger.

"After all," Edmund continued, "only six months ago, Molbren was known to hold for the empress."

Was that all he meant—the change in Molbren's loyalties? Then maybe she could persuade him of her loyalty. "Sir Roger was the one who supported the empress." It was the one decision of his she'd agreed with. Before King Henry had died, he'd made his nobles vow to take his daughter as their queen. The speed with which many of them had abandoned their oaths on his death and upheld Stephen of Blois's claim to the crown only went to show how much they resented being ruled by a woman. She could have pointed out that Edmund's father had been among the first to abandon his oath, but she held her tongue. Edmund had always gone oddly silent when it came to his parents.

Despite her belief in the empress's right, after Shrewsbury had fallen into Stephen's hands and Sir Roger killed, she'd been forced into a difficult decision. Molbren had become almost an island, surrounded by Stephen's territory on all sides bar the west where her lands bordered with Welsh-held lands. "*I* made no promise to the empress, and when I was faced with the choice of giving my loyalty to Stephen or seeing Molbren razed to the ground and my people killed in a futile fight, there was only one rational option." She raised her chin and looked him straight in the eye. "But when *I* give my word, I keep it."

A muscle in Edmund's jaw flinched, and she regretted the barb. She should have held silent; she didn't want to antagonize him, just see him leave.

He made an abrupt sweep of the hand. "In that case you can have no objection to my search." He signaled to his men. "You start in the outhouses; I'll search the donjon."

"No!" She summoned her guards, and they formed a circle round Edmund and his men. Whatever the risk of disobeying an order from the king, she wouldn't let Edmund within sight of her son. Images of Edmund carrying Will away from her tore at her soul. Without him, all the light would be quenched from her life.

"I forbid you entry. Leave now."

****

Even when Isobel nodded to her men and snapped, "Escort these men to the road and make sure they leave," Edmund couldn't take in what was happening. He'd had fever dreams that made more sense. First he'd been hit with the revelation that Isobel de Brockton, the woman who'd cast him off without so much as a goodbye, was in fact the woman he was here to see, and now she was ordering him off her land, her eyes narrowed in challenge as though he were the one in the wrong.

He stepped closer, ignoring the whisper of steel as her men drew their swords. "I am here at the king's command. Think carefully before you turn me away." He was close enough to see the garnet cross at her throat quiver in time with her pulse, to catch the same scent of rosewater that had always clung to her skin.

He clenched his fist around the hilt of his sword until the pommel dug into his palm. He could do this. He didn't desire her. Not anymore. She was merely someone who stood between him and his promised reward. The fact that she had once been the only prize he'd desired was irrelevant. Five years of heat, toil, and blood had swept away all but his need to carve out a place for himself. If he captured the Earl of Cannington, the king's reward would make him one of the most powerful men of England. Whatever Isobel had been to him in the past, he wouldn't allow her to stop him.

She gave a smile that failed to reach her eyes. "I have only your word that you're here at the king's command. As you place so little faith in my word, you'll forgive me for not accepting yours."

She would regret that. "Hand me my saddle bag, Joscelyn." He didn't turn to his squire but kept his eyes fixed on Isobel's. It was a good thing he felt nothing for her, or he might be tempted to pity her. Ripping open the bag's leather ties, he pulled out the roll of parchment and thrust it into her face. "This is a royal writ, granting me authority to search any property. If you turn me off your land, I'll be forced to report your defiance to the king."

Isobel blanched. She took the parchment and examined the seal. "I…the seal seems genuine, but I must have my steward read this for me." She turned to her guards. "Keep them here until I return."

The quiver in her voice set his battle-honed instincts on alert. What was she hiding? No one else had dared question the writ. He watched her return to the donjon, back straight, head held high, but fists clenched so tight she crumpled the parchment in her right hand. Yes, she was definitely hiding something. His pulse quickened. Could his search truly be over so soon after it had begun? Was Isobel harboring Cannington? Maybe he was closer to gaining his reward than he'd thought.

His squires' voices caught his attention. "It will be no hardship to pass a night under the same roof as her."

"None at all. I wager any widow who dresses in a crimson gown wouldn't be averse to letting me warm her bed."

Edmund whipped around and flung the saddle bag into the arms of the lad who had just spoken, making him stagger. "Guard your tongue, Joss. Never speak of a lady in such terms again, either in or out of my hearing."

Joscelyn's face turned the same shade as Isobel's gown. He raised his brows, looking almost as shocked as Edmund felt. In Heaven's name, where had that burst of anger come from? After all, he'd hardly shown her much respect; he couldn't blame his squires for imitating their master. A nagging voice in the back of his mind whispered that it wasn't so much his squire's disrespect that had earned his ire, more the thought of Isobel taking another man to her bed.

"Now, see to refastening my bag securely before you scatter my belongings across the bailey," he said. "And don't plan on a night in Molbren. God willing, we'll be in Ludlow well before nightfall."

He glanced up at the donjon. What was keeping her? It shouldn't take this long for her steward to confirm the document was valid. If she didn't return soon, he would order his men to search the castle without her permission. He couldn't risk being benighted here. He had no intention of spending a moment longer than necessary in her company.

He paced in front of the stables, buffing his chilled hands, plumes of mist twining through the air with every breath. God's blood, did Isobel intend him to freeze to death out here? She'd had enough time for every servant in this God-forsaken place to read the writ. Well, he refused to wait a moment longer.

He glanced over his shoulder at his squires. "Await me here." Then he marched across the bailey.

One of Isobel's guards dashed after him, drawing his sword. "My lord, Lady Isobel said—"

Edmund rounded on him. "A pox on what she said. If you have the stomach to raise your sword against the king's man, then do your worst. Otherwise leave me. Your lady has had more than enough time to read my writ. I won't be played for a fool any longer."

He strode on. *A fool.* She had played him for a fool once before, and that was one time too many.

He clenched his jaw. The day Isobel had walked away from him, he had learned a painful lesson: a woman could be plotting to wound you, even while whispering honeyed words. He would never trust a woman again, especially not one with hair like tawny silk and full, sensual lips that begged to be kissed.

Isobel de Brockton was hiding something, and he was going to find out what it was.

****

Isobel ran up the stairs, heart pounding. Unless there was a problem with the writ, Edmund had a perfect right to enter every chamber in the castle. Dear God, that must never happen! He'd be bound to see Will. Yet how could she deny him without defying the king? Going against Stephen's orders could result in the loss of Molbren and the peaceful life she had built up in the six months since Sir Roger died. The only life she wanted.

As for the light at its center… Stephen would never allow a woman of suspect loyalty to raise the heir to Molbren. He'd foster Will to another lord, and years might pass before she saw him again.

Either way, she stood to lose her son unless the writ was false. Would Edmund stoop to fabricating a document? Before he'd deserted her, she'd have refused to believe it, but now, after his broken vows had forced her into an unhappy marriage, she could believe anything of him.

There came a swift patter of footsteps upon the stone stairs above her, then Will flew round the bend.

"Mama!" He barreled into her, flinging his arms around her legs. "Can we look at the horses now?"

She hugged him tightly until he squirmed in her arms. "Not now, my heart." She thought fast. Part of her wanted to keep Will by her side and never let him out of her sight, but that wasn't an option. She released him and took his hand. "Let's go up to your chamber."

"I don't want to." Will tried to wriggle his hand free, but Isobel gripped it tighter and marched them up the steps.

"Do as you're told, Will. I don't have time for this."

She hurried through the solar and into the passageway beyond, then shoved Will's door open and hustled him inside. Three wooden horses lay scattered upon the floor; she picked them up and thrust them into his hands. "Be a good boy and play with your horses while I talk to the visitors."

Will knelt and peered under the bed. "But where's my soldier? I want to play with him, too."

Isobel pressed her hands to her churning stomach and took three measured deep breaths. Then she knelt next to Will. "I can't look now. I'm too busy." Inspiration struck. "But these horses are just like the visitors' ones. Why don't you make a stable for them? I'll come back as soon as I can and if you've looked after them well, I'll take you to see the real horses."

Will's face brightened, and Isobel kissed the top of his head before leaving. Her last glimpse of him before closing the door showed him draping a blanket over a stool. One problem solved. If only the other proved as easy to handle. She hurried down to her steward's office and slapped the document upon the desk.

"What does this say?"

Simon Fitzgifford unrolled the parchment and squinted at the text. Isobel sank onto a chair and tapped her fingers upon the wooden arm while Simon ran a bony finger along each line of script, his lips forming silent words.

"It's a writ authorizing a search on any property the bearer sees fit," he said at last. He inspected the seal. "This is the king's seal, my lady." His tone implied she would be foolish to defy anyone bearing the writ. Foolish to defy her king.

She closed her eyes briefly and prayed for inspiration. "Is there no way I can refuse?"

"I'm sorry, my lady, but the wording is clear. These orders come direct from the king. If you bar the Earl of Redmarch, there could be serious consequences."

"The Earl of Redmarch?" Isobel snatched the parchment from Simon's hand. She studied the document, catching her breath in sudden hope. However, she only knew enough letters to print her name, and the curling script of the writ swam before her eyes making no sense at all. "It definitely names the Earl of Redmarch, not Edmund Granville?"

"That's right, my lady. Why—?"

She was out of the door before he could finish. The writ in her clenched fist, she dashed down the steps, only to stop short in the donjon doorway when she came face to face with Edmund. He was climbing the outer steps, a black scowl marring his handsome features even more than his scar.

"I've waited long enough." He tried to step past her, but she remained in the doorway, blocking his way. "The writ is valid. Let me pass."

"Indeed." She raised her chin. "It is valid, but not for you. It's for the Earl of Redmarch. Your father is more than welcome to come and search Molbren, but I'd like you to leave. Now." She flung the writ at his feet, enjoying her moment of triumph. By the time the earl arrived, Will would be safely hidden in one of her more distant manors.

Edmund stooped to pick up the parchment. When he straightened, his face was an expressionless mask and he spoke in a tone that lacked all emotion. "This writ is for me. My father and brothers are dead—killed in ambush near Worcester. *I* am the Earl of Redmarch."

Isobel crossed herself, an automatic gesture. "God rest their souls," she whispered through dry lips. Now what was she to do? She said the first thing that came into her head, all the while grappling for some plan...*any* plan...to protect Will. "My condolences. I had no idea. News takes a long time to reach me here."

His lips twisted in a mirthless smile. "Spare me your empty words. Your only regret is not knowing that I would be raised to the heights of earl before choosing a Marcher Lord over me. That's why you did it, isn't it? You wanted more wealth than a third son could hope to aspire to."

Did what? Isobel couldn't make sense of what was happening. What could he possibly blame her for? She could think of nothing to say in her confusion, and before she could get out any words, Edmund marched up the steps. Now he towered over her.

Lowering his voice, he said, "You realized you couldn't hope to live in the luxury you desired if you were married to me. That's why you abandoned me and chose your Marcher Lord. That's why you broke our wedding vows."

Chapter Two

The blatant lie punched the air from her lungs. What was he talking about? Luxury had meant nothing to her. Back then she would willingly have slept in a byre if she could only share it with Edmund. She had clung to her vows, holding out against her father's fury and her mother's tirades for as long as possible. Night after night she had knelt by the window, certain he would come for her, release her from confinement and take her away. She had even endured the humiliation of having her mother rip off her veil and hack off her hair, hissing that she might as well look like a whore as she was so determined to behave like one. Her faith in Edmund's fidelity had remained unshaken right until her cousin had been allowed to visit and had broken the news of Edmund's departure for the Holy Land. She hadn't believed her parents, but her cousin had no reason to lie.

"How dare you?" She scarcely had the breath to speak. "That's not—"

He cut her off with a slice of the hand. "Spare me your excuses. The past is dead. All I care about is finding the king's enemies. Stand aside."

Heart hammering, she forced herself to look him in the eye. Holy Mother, don't let him see her fear. "Send one of your squires to search the donjon. You may search the great hall or the outbuildings, or anywhere else you please, but I won't allow you into the family chambers." It wasn't just that she feared to let him close to Will. She didn't want him in her private rooms. It was too intimate and risked stirring up old feelings. After five years of heartbreak and suffering—all at the hands of men—she had finally earned a peaceful life. She would allow nothing to shake it.

Edmund gave her a long, level look that set her insides fluttering. It was fear for Will, she told herself. Nothing more than that.

"As you wish," he said finally. He turned away and beckoned to his squires.

That one, tiny victory gave her courage. She caught his arm, preventing him from descending the steps. "One more thing," she said. "Allow enough time to reach Ludlow today. Don't expect me to give you shelter, because you're not welcome here." It helped if she stoked the anger. It masked her hurt and prevented the blossoming of desire. No matter that she had broken all the laws of hospitality; she wanted Edmund out of Molbren before nightfall. Out of her life for good.

Edmund's brows drew together, and he dropped his gaze to where her hand still rested on his arm.

She jerked her hand away, only now registering the hard ridges of solid muscle her fingers had encountered.

"Have no fear, my lady. I'm just as anxious to leave as you are to see me gone." He stalked down the steps, snapping orders to his men as he went.

What had caused his antagonism? While she had a justification for her anger, he could have none. Unless it was a guilty conscience at work. It was the only explanation she could come up with. Besides, it didn't really matter. She had no wish to marry any man, let alone one who had hurt her so badly. He would soon be gone, and if she remained in the solar until then, she needn't see him again.

And she must forget the bliss of lying wrapped in the circle of those powerful arms.

On the point of turning to go back through the door, she caught sight of a mass of slate-gray clouds massing above the western hills. Blessed saints preserve her, in these icy temperatures they surely carried snow. Only yesterday she'd longed for a snowfall heavy enough to protect Molbren from outlaws and the raiding Welsh. But now... She clutched the cross at her throat and prayed it would hold off until Edmund was safely away.

The freckle-faced lad sent by Edmund to search the donjon was unable to meet her eyes when he entered the solar, clearly embarrassed at searching a noblewoman's private chambers. Nevertheless, he was thorough, even going so far as to inspect the garderobe chute. Edmund had obviously impressed upon him the import of his task. Isobel bore it quietly, relieved it was this unknown squire and not Edmund now pulling back the heavily embroidered bed hangings in her chamber. However, when he put his hand to the latch of Will's bedchamber door, she spoke without thinking.

"Must you go in there? That's my son's chamber, and I don't want you to frighten him." It was a senseless fear, she knew. If Edmund saw Will, his suspicions might be raised by Will's age; if he then examined Will for any likeness he wouldn't fail to see it, for Will's eyes and face were all Edmund. However, as far as anyone else was concerned, she was merely Sir Roger's widow, and they wouldn't think to question

Will's parentage.

"You know I must," the squire replied. "Come with me, if you wish to reassure him."

Her heart melted when she stepped into the room. Will was curled up inside his "stable"—constructed from a blanket stretched between his clothes chest and a stool—fast asleep with a wooden horse clutched in his hand. She knelt beside him and swept the hair back from his brow while the squire searched the room. In fact, Edmund's man didn't move from the doorway, only glancing inside briefly; the chamber was so cramped there was only space for Will's bed, besides the furniture he'd used for his stable. It was obvious no grown man could be concealed within.

"That's all, then, my lady. I'll leave you in peace." The man gave an awkward bow and left.

The moment she heard his booted feet descend the staircase, she blew out a shaky breath, then seeing Will stir and blink awake, she took his hand. "Bring your horses out into the solar. You can play there until the men have gone. How would you like a pony ride around the courtyard after the meal?" The poor boy deserved a treat for being so good, even if it did mean standing out in the icy wind instead of staying in the warmth of the solar.

"Thank you, Mama!" Will galloped into the solar and climbed onto the window seat, lining his horses upon the stone ledge above the cushioned seat.

Isobel watched him for a while, a smile on her lips, breathing deep while the knot of tension in her stomach slowly unwound. She sat down at her tapestry frame and picked up her needle, threading it with a blood-red yarn. She could do this. She could sew holly berries on her tapestry and make Will believe all was well. Edmund would soon be finished. As soon as her steward sent word of his departure, she would even play the dutiful hostess and bid him a courteous farewell, assured he knew nothing of Will's existence. He wouldn't take Will away.

A whisper in the back of her mind pricked her conscience. Didn't Edmund deserve to know he had a son? But it didn't trouble her for long. He had abandoned her when he must have known there was a chance she had conceived. He'd not only abandoned her, he'd abandoned Will. Therefore, he had no claim on his son now.

"Mama, can ponies walk in the snow?"

Isobel didn't look up from her work, used to Will's endless questions on a wide range of subjects. "That depends how deep it is. Why do you ask?"

"Because it's snowing, but I still want to go for a ride this afternoon."

Isobel dropped her needle and strode to the window. Dry mouthed, she lifted Will aside and peered through the gap where Will had pulled aside one of the horn panes. Holy Mother, help her: thick flakes swirled in the air, so dense she could only catch glimpses of the wall on the far side of the bailey.

She tugged the pane back into place and gave Will a hug. "I'm sorry, my heart. You won't be able to ride in this."

And if it didn't stop soon, neither would Edmund.

****

Edmund kicked the door to the undercroft, slamming it against the wall. An hour spent searching the great hall and connecting chambers wasn't nearly long enough to cool his ire. How did she have the gall to even look him in the eye, let alone deny him shelter? Anyone would think *he'd* been the faithless one. Not only had there not been the faintest flicker of remorse when he'd accused her of breaking her marriage vows, she'd actually denied it. If he'd let her, she'd probably have tried to feed him some feeble excuse.

And if she offered the truth—what then? Would it change anything?

He paused in the act of pulling aside a bale of wool and released a long, shaky breath. Of course it wouldn't. Getting answers would only be important if he wanted her back, and he didn't. Couldn't risk getting close to her, or anyone, again. Letting a person into your heart only gave them the weapons to betray you. He would never make that mistake again.

"My lord?" The voice of his young cousin and squire echoed down the stairwell.

"Down here, Joss. What have you found?"

There followed the scuff of boots upon stone and Joscelyn appeared in the doorway. "Nothing in the donjon, my lord, but you should know it's started to snow."

"God's breath, that's the last thing we need." Edmund sprang up the steps to see for himself. Snowflakes whirled in his face the moment he stepped into the courtyard. There was only a light covering on the ground, but the sting of snow lashing his eyes made it impossible to see the extent of the cloud cover. There was a flight of steps leading up onto the walls behind him, so he leapt up and scanned the skies, praying this was no more than a passing flurry. A momentary easing of the snow allowed him to see out across the westward hills. Thank the saints—only the lightest speckling of snow dusted the rocks and heather upon the hilltops. There were heavy clouds in the distance, but as long as they completed their search and were on the Ludlow road within the hour, they should avoid the worst.

Huddling in his cloak, he ran back down to the courtyard and summoned his squires. "Joss, you say the donjon is clear. What about you, Ancel?"

"No sign of anyone in the stables, my lord, and nothing in any of the outhouses on the north side. I've yet to search the chapel."

A fierce wind blasted over the walls, bringing a fresh flurry of snow. Edmund bowed against the onslaught, tempted to order their departure; in his heart he couldn't see Isobel harboring fugitives. However, there was still that nagging feeling she was hiding something. Letting Cannington slip from his grasp for want of a more thorough search was hardly the way to gain the king's favor and certainly wouldn't earn him his promised prize—Redmarch elevated to a county palatine and acceptance into the king's inner circle.

A far cry from how he had grown up—the unwanted third son, born years after his older brothers.

"There's not much left to search. If we're quick we can still make Ludlow before the worst of the snow hits. I've already covered everywhere on this side of the castle apart from the undercroft, so it's just there and the chapel left. Ancel, take the chapel. If you finish before us, ready the horses."

Ancel hurried off to do his bidding and Edmund returned to the undercroft with Joscelyn.

Joscelyn whistled as he looked around him. "It's bigger than I realized. I didn't see that archway before."

Edmund cursed under his breath when he looked where Joscelyn was pointing. Sure enough, in the shadows beyond a stack of barrels was another doorway in what he had taken to be the back wall. If the new chamber had as many hiding places to search as this one, they would be making the journey to Ludlow with the storm whipping at their heels.

"I've already looked behind the wool bales and grain jars," he said. 'Shift those barrels over there while I search the other room."

He picked up a lantern from one of the wall niches and used it to light his way; the windows high up in the vaulting were definitely admitting less light now, even though it was approaching noon. The storm must be worsening.

The further chamber contained more wine barrels. None of them were large enough for a man to hide inside, but it took longer than he liked to inspect all the dark crannies in the spaces behind. He threw frequent glances up at the windows as he worked, the knot in his gut tightening as each look revealed the sky darkening.

A soft step alerted him to Joscelyn's entry when he was hauling aside several large crates in the last corner that remained unsearched. He straightened and cocked an eyebrow. "Anything?"

"Not unless you count this." Joscelyn held up a wooden soldier. "I expect it belongs to the widow's son."

Edmund froze, his fingers clenched around the corner of a crate. "She has a son?"

"Yes, he was in the lady's apartments."

Edmund swallowed, tasting bile. So she had a son. That was something he hadn't expected. It shouldn't have surprised him, though—she'd been married to Sir Roger for over four years. More than enough time to... He tightened his grip, splinters jabbing his palm. It was one thing to know she was Sir Roger's widow, but to be confronted with the evidence of her sharing his bed was far more painful.

"Come, we're finished here. Cannington is obviously elsewhere, and we must leave if we're to make Ludlow before nightfall." Even more reason to leave Molbren now. He had no wish to come face to face with Isobel's son and see her features blended with those of another man.

He strode up to the courtyard door and stopped short. In the time they had been in the undercroft, the world had transformed. What had been a light snow flurry was now a blizzard. The folk crossing the bailey huddled beneath their capes, any footprints quickly becoming blurred as more snow filled the indentations. Already the cobbles lay beneath a good finger's width of snow and more was falling. Even worse than the snow was the wind that howled around the walls, whipping at his cloak. He tugged it around him and spat out a Saracen oath.

Joscelyn ran up behind him. "Holy mother of God," he muttered. "We'll never make it to Ludlow in this."

"I'll see about that." Edmund jogged toward the stables, where he could just make out Ancel, gesticulating wildly at the stable master.

The stable master ran up to him and had to shout to be heard above the wind. "My lord, it's madness to ride out in this. The road's already covered, and it's drifting. Even if you don't freeze to death, you risk your horse falling into a concealed ditch."

Even so, Edmund was sorely tempted to make the journey. The thought of spending time in Isobel's company, forced to see all that had been denied him, was too much to bear. But then he saw the anxious faces of Joscelyn and Ancel and knew he couldn't risk their lives too.

"Very well. We stay until the way is clear." God's blood, now he had to ask Isobel for shelter. And prepare himself for his first sight of her son.

A boy old enough to play with toy soldiers. He swallowed against a sudden tightening of the throat. No…surely not.

He turned to his squires. "Joss, how old was the lady's son?"

His squire shrugged. "I never can tell with children. Three or four, maybe."

Blessed saints, it couldn't be. The howl of the wind, the shouts of the people hastening across the bailey, all faded to silence. The only thing he could hear was the blood roaring in his ears. It was possible. They'd wed in secret three weeks before it had ended and snatched several trysts in that time. What he couldn't understand now was why it hadn't occurred to him before.

If it was true, it changed everything. He had to know for sure.

Taking the toy from Joscelyn, he marched to the donjon.

Chapter Three

Isobel paced the length of the solar, pausing every now and then to peer into the bailey. Before long, snow shrouded the courtyard, and drifts piled up against the walls and doors. Blessed Mother, please don't let it be as deep as it looked from here.

A servant entered. "The Earl of Redmarch is asking to see you, my lady."

This was it, then. Edmund had left it too late, and now he needed shelter. All her prayers had been in vain. "Very well," she replied, surprised at her untroubled tone when her mind was in such turmoil. "Tell him to await me in the great hall."

The servant curtsied and left. Isobel joined Will on his window seat.

"Stay here, Will, and I'll have Agnes bring you some food," she said, wondering how best to phrase her instructions without alarming her young son. "I must go and speak with the earl and then dine with him, but I'd rather he didn't see you."

"Why not?" Will looked up at her with wide eyes. *Edmund's eyes.*

"I…just do as I say. I don't have time to explain."

She pulled on her cloak and left. She had always promised herself she'd give Will reasons for her instructions. Edmund had only been in the castle a few short hours, and already he'd caused her to abandon her good intentions. She could only pray the bad weather would pass, allowing Edmund to leave on the morrow, or who knew what effect he might have on her life?

The moment she stepped outside, she knew her hope was in vain. Snow stung her eyes, and drifts piled up against the donjon steps. She clung to the wooden handrail as she descended, probing for every stair. Any thought of sending Edmund away faded. Unless she offered him shelter, she would have his death on her conscience. What was more, any fool could see he'd be trapped here for days. She'd lived in these hills for five years and knew all too well how snow could linger for days, cutting Molbren off from its neighboring towns.

The peace of the hall came as a shock after the howling wind. Even the bustle of the servants setting up the boards for the noon meal was calm compared with the violence of the storm outside. She wove around the men and women carrying trestles and boards and sought out Edmund.

She found him beside the central hearth, scowling at the blazing logs. One fist was closed around something, but she couldn't see what. "You wished to see me?" It might be childish, but she couldn't bring herself to anticipate his request and freely offer him shelter. He would have to ask.

His scowl deepened. "I require accommodation for myself and my squires."

She rubbed her temples. Of course he wouldn't lower himself to ask. "Your squires can bed down in here. I'll have the guest quarters readied for you. They adjoin the hall, so there will be no call for you to intrude upon the family rooms. Would you like a servant to show you the way?"

"I know where they are. I did search them, after all."

"Good. The noon meal is almost ready. I'll see you there."

She turned to leave, but he seized her arm. "Isobel, tell me—"

She jerked her arm free. "Whatever it is must wait until the meal." Blessed Mother, she could still feel his fingers, burning her flesh through her sleeve. She had to get away. Now. "Excuse me. I'm…I'm very busy."

She strode away, scarcely knowing where she was going. Only that she must find space to think and work out exactly what she was going to do about Will. Not to mention how she was to survive the Lord knew how many days with a man whose very presence stirred memories she preferred to forget. Memories of shared glances…whispered confidences…the silken slide of flesh upon flesh.

Blessed Mary, save me! She raised her hands to her heated cheeks. Now was not the time for such thoughts.

The open door of a store room beckoned, and she tumbled inside, slamming the door behind her. She slumped against the wall and closed her eyes, praying for guidance. Whether it was an answer to prayer, or just the stone wall against her back cooling her, she didn't know, but calm certainty crystallized in her mind. She could keep Will in the solar today; Edmund had no reason to go there. That gave her time to decide what was best in the long term. Her first priority was discovering the cause of Edmund's anger toward her, what false belief he held. In his present mood, she feared he would tell the king she was unfit to govern Molbren. In that case she stood the risk of being married off to one of the king's loyal men, or seeing Will taken away as hostage for her good behavior. Neither option was acceptable.

No, as much as she dreaded it, she must face the issue. She had to bring about some measure of truce.

And what then? What if he saw his error and begged her forgiveness? Would she want him back in her life—a true father for Will?

No. She prayed there could be peace between them, but the more she allowed herself to remember the agony of the days following his departure, one memory—one pain—stood out, and the ache lingered, never to be truly healed. Even if he had been fed a falsehood compelling him to leave, one fact remained: he had believed it. He hadn't fought for her love. Which only led her to suppose his love hadn't been strong enough to begin with.

She didn't want a man like that in Will's life. Will had suffered enough at the hands of Sir Roger. While she knew Edmund would never harm him physically, Will could still be hurt by a father who didn't love him enough. A father who couldn't be trusted not to walk away again when it suited him.

Men weren't to be trusted—bitter experience had taught her that. She was now in the fortunate position of not needing another husband. She had a comfortable home, and her people were loyal to her. Why risk losing all that by placing her fate in another man's hands? It was far better to live out her life in quiet contentment.

The scent of roasted venison summoned her to the high table. Pleased she had formed a plan, she even managed a faint smile of greeting as she took her seat next to Edmund.

"Will your son be joining us?"

Her heart lurched. Sweet Jesu, how did he know? Of course—his squire had seen Will. Struggling to keep the tremble from her voice, she replied, "No. Will is a little too young to eat at the dais."

"How old is he? Old enough to hold a spoon, surely, if he's old enough to play with this." He held up a wooden soldier. One of Will's.

She licked dry lips. "Where did you find that?"

"In the undercroft. As I have time to spare, I'll return it to him after the meal if you tell me where to find him."

Her knife slipped as she sliced a piece of venison, splashing sauce down the front of her bliaut. She picked up her napkin and dabbed at the stain, removing every last drop with trembling hands. Blessed Mary, did he suspect the truth? What should she do?

Only one solution occurred to her: distract him.

She flashed him a tight smile. "No need. I'll give it to him myself." She took the soldier, careful not to brush his fingers, and placed it beside her trencher.

Christ give her strength. If she wanted to distract him from Will, she had to confront him now. "Tell me, my lord, why are you so angry with me? Or perhaps it isn't anger. Is it your guilty conscience speaking?" She glanced around to ensure no one was listening and lowered her voice. "You accused me of betraying my vows, but what of your own? Why did you abandon me? Why did you leave when I begged you to take me with you?"

****

The last time Edmund had seen such challenge in another's eyes, he'd had a Saracen's sword at his throat.

Every fiber of his being screamed to press forward. Was it true? Did he have an heir, hiding here in Molbren? But his instincts told him pushing Isobel would only send her fleeing. Besides, she had the answers he'd craved for five years. He mustn't let this chance slip away.

"I did come for you. Although I can't believe you'd call your message 'begging'."

"What do you mean?"

"You said you were betrothed to another, so I should forget you. Which part of that was the begging?"

"I never—" Isobel thumped her goblet upon the table, slopping crimson wine upon the white cloth. She regarded him with narrowed eyes. "You're a bold liar, for someone once so obsessed with honor."

"It's no lie. I remember what the messenger said, word for word. He gave me your ring to prove you'd sent him. The same ring I put on your finger after you vowed to take me as your husband. Then he gave me your message: *Forget me, Edmund. I never loved you, and I'm to marry another.* Tell me, Isobel, how else should I have interpreted that? It doesn't sound like begging to me."

"Merciful saints!" Isobel gazed at the spreading pool of wine for a moment. Even though she pressed her lips together, she couldn't conceal their slight tremble. When she looked up there was a deep sadness in her brown eyes. "That's not what I said. I told my parents about our marriage that night, as we'd agreed. Said I was leaving with you. They locked me up. The message I sent asked you to come and release me. I thought I could trust the servant I sent. Obviously I was wrong."

Her face was open, eyes pleading with him to believe her, but her story still didn't match with his.

"Who sent the message?"

Isobel stared down at her hands. "My mother or father. You were right that they had higher ambitions for me than the third son of an earl." Her voice hardened. "But that doesn't change the fact that you didn't come. You were too quick to believe I'd played you false."

Edmund leaned forward, regardless of the wine soaking his sleeve. "I didn't believe it. I *did* come. I battered your door until my hands bled. The servant who finally opened it wouldn't grant me entrance, but it didn't matter. I saw you, called out to you." He drained his cup, wishing he could erase the memory from his mind. "You didn't answer. Wouldn't even turn and look me in the eye. Then you walked away." The sight had haunted his dreams for months afterward.

Isobel's wide eyes were fixed on his face. God's nails, how could a woman with such a false heart look so innocent? "I don't know who you saw, but it wasn't me. I told you, my parents locked me in my chamber."

Despite himself, his gaze dropped to her mouth, lingered over the plump lower lip, followed its every curve as she spoke.

"They only released me after I agreed to marry Sir Roger. *After* I learned you'd sailed to the Holy Land."

His flare of anger gave him the strength to wrench his gaze back to her eyes. Eyes as cold and hard as her heart. "You lie. I saw you. You were wearing the same green gown you wore the morning we married." The same gown he'd unlaced after they'd clasped hands and exchanged their vows, too impatient to wait until they could find a witness. The same gown he'd eased off her shoulders and flung to the ground before they'd tumbled upon the hay, hungry for the feel of flesh upon flesh. Edmund remembered, too, the triumph of knowing their marriage was consummated: they could never be separated. Even now, with all that had happened since, the memory made his blood sing. He half raised his cup to his lips before thrusting it away from him. He didn't need any more wine; his senses swam enough as it was.

"Are you calling *me* a liar? It might have been my gown, but I wasn't wearing it. But of course that wouldn't have occurred to you—if you'd truly loved me you wouldn't have been so quick to doubt me and cast me aside without even—"

He thumped the table, making the dishes and goblets rattle. "*I* cast *you* aside?" By all the saints in Heaven, he was starting to doubt her sanity. Or his. "You're the one who married another."

Isobel sprang to her feet. A hectic flush painted her cheeks. When she spoke her voice was low, but the tremble in her voice betrayed her. "This is getting us nowhere. I was a fool to think we could reach any kind of understanding. If you'll excuse me, I have work to do, which your visit interrupted. And don't you dare follow me."

He reached out to catch her arm. "Isobel, don't—"

But all his fingers closed on was the trailing end of her sleeve which slid through his grip, and she made her escape.

Hellfire! He took a gulp of wine and slammed the cup back upon the table. She flattered herself if she thought he had any desire to go after her. Why on earth he had ever imagined himself in love with her, he couldn't imagine. Only a madman would want to live with such a harpy. Admittedly the sway of her hips was alluring. He allowed his gaze to linger on her figure as she stormed through the hall. But just because she was as beautiful as he remembered didn't mean he had any intention of pursuing her. Only a fool would choose to reopen old wounds.

Then he noticed the wooden soldier, abandoned beside Isobel's half-eaten meal. He picked it up and studied the crimson and gold chevrons painted upon the shield. No, he wouldn't make the mistake of giving his heart to Isobel again, but they still had unfinished business. If there was any chance he had an heir, he wouldn't rest until he knew the truth. If Isobel thought she could avoid him for the remainder of his stay, she had a nasty shock in store.

"I thought you too old to play with toys."

Edmund glanced up to see Joscelyn hovering at his elbow. He closed his hand around the soldier. "I'm in no mood for jests, Joss. What do you want?"

The smile faded from Joscelyn's lips. "Forgive me, my lord. Ancel and I wondered if you had any duties for us this afternoon."

"Is it still snowing?"

"Yes. I went out a moment ago, and it's coming down as hard as ever."

Edmund grimaced. "In that case there's not a great deal we can do until it stops. We'll have to stay inside. That doesn't mean we stop looking, though. I want you and Ancel to talk with some of the folk here. Don't question them; just engage them in conversation. If anyone does know of Cannington's whereabouts, you might catch them in an unguarded moment."

"What about you?"

"I shall talk to the steward." Edmund glanced at the soldier's head, just poking out above his clenched fingers. "And the Lady Isobel, if she'll deign to speak to me again."

Joss gave a wry smile. "Forgive me for saying so, but when she left, she didn't look like a woman desperate for your company. Perhaps you should let me talk to her."

"No. Leave her to me."

Joss raised his eyebrows. "If you wish, although I doubt you'll have much luck. Everything you say seems to rouse her ire. Anyone would think you had done her some wrong."

"Then they'd be mistaken. It must be guilt making her act this way, because it was she who wronged me."

Light dawned in Joscelyn's eyes. "Ah, so you do have a past with this lady."

Edmund ground his teeth, cursing himself for letting his guard slip. He'd never told Joss about Isobel and wasn't going to tell him the whole truth now. Isobel might have played him false, but she was alone in the world and he wouldn't say anything that might harm her. Or her son.

"I knew her before we left for the Holy Land, and things didn't end well between us." That was a huge understatement. A surge of anger tore through him as he remembered his last sight of her, walking away without a word.

Joss's eyes widened. "I thought you left England in a hurry. Is that—?"

"Keep your thoughts to yourself. Now go and find

Ancel."

Edmund blew out a breath after Joss gave a curt nod and left. Then, still holding the wooden soldier, he went to find Isobel.

****

"My lady doesn't want to be disturbed."

Her guard's voice drifted up to the window above the door, where Isobel stood in the drafty passageway, pressed against the cold stone. So Edmund wasn't giving up. One thought alone hammered though her head: *he suspects!*

Holding her breath, she edged closer to the window. The shutters were open, and this window had no panes, only three iron bars. Her breath misted in the frigid air, and a few snowflakes brushed her face, but she huddled into her cloak and angled her face to get a view of the outer steps.

There was Edmund, on the top step, glaring at the guard, one hand upon his sword hilt. "I have an important matter to discuss with her. Stand aside."

Isobel's heart lurched. She'd placed her staunchest man there, but was he brave enough to face down Edmund?

The guard didn't budge. "I'm sorry, my lord, but my lady is not well and not to be disturbed for the rest of the day. Come back tomorrow."

For a moment Edmund hesitated, as though he contemplated pushing the guard aside. Then his shoulders sagged a fraction. "Inform her I'll return at first light."

He backed down the steps, raising his eyes to the window as he did so. Isobel whipped away into the shadows, her pulse hammering. Had he seen her? She risked another glance across the bailey and saw Edmund striding back to the great hall. She shuddered. Every instinct screamed that he'd seen her. She must keep her wits about her if she was to keep Will safe.

A hand on her shoulder made her spin round with a gasp, but she relaxed when she saw Agnes.

"Are you quite well, my lady? You're as white as the snow." Isobel's maid had become the closest person Isobel had to a confidante here in Molbren. During the black years of her marriage to Sir Roger, Agnes had poulticed too many of her bruises and kept too many of her secrets not to have become highly trusted.

"I'm a little tired, Agnes, that's all. It's these unexpected guests. I have to arrange for the guest chamber to be made up, but once I've done that, I'll rest awhile in the solar." For years she had longed to know the truth, yet now she knew Edmund hadn't left without trying to find her, she felt no peace.

Agnes steered Isobel down the passage to the solar. "Leave the guest chamber to me. I don't mean to speak out of turn, my lady, but I couldn't help noticing one guest in particular has upset you. Just say the word, and I'll add enough soapwort to the earl's wine to keep him abed until the thaw."

Despite her churning stomach, Isobel couldn't suppress a chuckle at the thought of Edmund prostrated by sickness, only to mysteriously recover the moment the snow cleared. "No thank you, Agnes. I don't want to add poisoning to the list of sins he holds against me. He could cause me a lot of trouble with the king if he chose."

"I'd like to help if I can, my lady."

"There isn't much you can do, save ensure his

chamber is comfortable. Make certain he has no call to disturb me here."

"I meant…I meant about the matter of your son."

"Blessed Virgin, is everyone talking about it?" The moment the words were out of her mouth, she could have cursed. Agnes could only suspect, not know. Not until her reaction had confirmed that suspicion. She had trusted Agnes with many things but kept the truth about Will locked away in her heart.

Agnes took her hand and patted it. "Never fear, my lady. I've heard no one else gossiping. I've only noticed because it's my business to take care of you and Master Will. I've long suspected he wasn't Sir Roger's son, and I swear I've held my tongue. There's not been the slightest hint that anyone else has noticed the strong resemblance between the earl and your son. People only see what they expect to see most of the time."

By this time they had reached the solar. Isobel's knees gave way, and she sank upon the settle. "What am I to do, Agnes? I've hardly been able to think since he arrived. I thought he was out of my life for good."

"It's not my place to say, my lady. But you've done right by the folk of Molbren from the moment you first arrived, and I have every faith you'll make the right decision now. Whatever you choose, I'll be there to help you in any way I can."

"Thank you." Some of the gnawing anxiety eased; she wasn't as alone as she'd feared. "I think…what I need now is a quiet space to decide what to do for the best."

Agnes squeezed her hand. "I'll take Will to his chamber, then, and see you're not disturbed." She went to the door, but when she put her hand on the latch, she turned. "I will say one thing, my lady. The moment the earl lays eyes on Master Will, he'll know the truth. How easy will it be to keep them apart?"

It was a good question, and the answer weighed upon her heart: the longer Edmund remained, the more difficult keeping the two apart would become. If Edmund discovered the truth on his own—that she'd kept the existence of his son from him—it could only make matters worse. Increase the risk he'd take Will from her. He might not even see it as a punishment: noble sons were often fostered to connect with other powerful families. As Edmund was only recently returned to England, he might well see the need to increase his influence in that way. Isobel had always known she would have to foster Will out when he was old enough to train for knighthood, but she would have had control over when and where he was sent. If Edmund claimed Will, though, she would lose all say in his upbringing, be dependent on Edmund still granting her access.

Then a thought she'd tried to bury refused to be silenced. Was she justified in keeping them apart? Edmund was Will's father, and contrary to what she had believed, he hadn't deserted her without a thought. According to every law, he was entitled to full control of his son's upbringing. And what about Will? Didn't he have a right to know his father? She had focused on her own fears so much she had forgotten to consider Will's best interests.

Then she remembered Edmund's refusal to believe her explanation, and ice crystallized around her heart. He had abandoned her when she'd needed him, and now his resentment was such it overpowered his reason.

He wanted to believe the worst of her.

She rose from the settle and paced in front of the fire. Edmund could believe what he liked about her; she didn't care. But she didn't want his seething anger and resentment near Will. They were both better off without him.

She would hide Will in the donjon. It was her only choice.

Then she shuddered. If Edmund was angry with her now, that was nothing compared to his fury if he discovered she'd denied him his son.

Chapter Four

The next morning, Isobel rose with a pounding head and sore eyes. Her prayers had alternated between pleas for a miraculous thaw and guidance on keeping Edmund and Will apart. No fresh inspiration struck with the dawn, and when she peered through the window, the whitewashed hills and woods confirmed the Almighty was not on her side.

"Mama, can I play outside today? Please?"

Poor Will. After spending the whole of yesterday indoors, it was cruel to keep him in the donjon today as well, but what else could she do?

She crouched down beside him and unpinned the cloak he'd optimistically flung on before dashing to greet her in the solar. "I'm sorry, my heart." She hesitated. She hated lying, but she could hardly tell him the truth. "I'm going to be busy with the visitors today, and you're too young to go out alone."

"Oh, but—"

"I haven't got time for this, Will. Do as you're told and stay with Agnes."

Will stuck out his bottom lip. "You always say I'm too young for things. I wish I was older. Then I could go out with the soldiers and do whatever I want."

"You'll be older soon enough." Too soon for her liking.

A knock at the door interrupted them, and the

steward entered. "The Earl of Redmarch is outside, asking to see you."

Isobel went cold. "He's here? In the donjon?"

"No, my lady. We followed your orders and wouldn't let him in. He's out in the courtyard."

She pressed her hand to her chest to ease the sudden pounding. He might not be in the donjon now, but this new, cold Edmund wouldn't be turned away a second time. If she didn't agree to see him, he would force his way in, of that she was certain. As much as she wanted to avoid Edmund, she had to ensure he stayed away from the donjon, and she would trust no one but herself to see it done.

"Tell him I'll see him in the great hall. I'll be down in a moment."

She pulled on her cloak and was about to leave when Will tugged her skirt. "What is it, Will? I really don't have the time."

"Can I pretend I'm a soldier?"

"Of course you can," she replied, fighting with the clasp of her cloak pin. "Now be good, and I'll see you later." She ruffled his hair and swept out.

At the first glimpse of Edmund's broad shoulders and tall, upright figure, a thrill shot through her veins. He stood beside the fire, and the sight cast her back to the first time she had seen him. It hadn't been firelight bringing out auburn hints in his raven-dark hair then, but the sun, as he rode up to her father's manor on a warm spring day, bearing a message from his master. From the first she had been struck by his height and strength. Then their eyes had locked, and she'd been lost.

Seeing him again brought back the flutter, the pang

of anticipation. She was sixteen again, swept away by the rush of longing with each whispered exchange, the spark of each accidental brush of their hands, the breathless intoxication of secret meetings throughout that glorious, golden summer.

But of course, all that had stopped when he'd left, abandoning her without a fight. It was vital she remind herself of the pain he'd caused her and forget their infatuation. Because that's all it had been. She'd made a terrible mistake and paid for it, and she'd never allow Edmund to hurt her like that again.

"You wanted to see me?" She forced her face into a calm mask, praying he didn't hear the tremor in her voice.

Edmund's eyes narrowed. "We have unfinished business."

All Isobel wanted to do was run to Will and hide in some dark corner, but that would achieve nothing. She raised her chin. "Then you shouldn't have deserted me. I have nothing to say to you now."

A muscle in Edmund's jaw flinched. "I'm not here to revisit the past. However, I am concerned about the present."

Isobel's ears buzzed, and a wave of dizziness swept over her. She couldn't allow him to ask about Will. The truth would be blazed across her forehead, a burning brand. "Then let's talk about the present," she said, cutting Edmund off before he could draw breath. "You're here to search for the Earl of Cannington. I, as a loyal subject of the king, have no choice but to assist you. And that's the only business we have with each other." A single thought came to her and she grasped at it. "To be honest, I'm surprised you're still here. Were you so weakened by life in the Holy Land that you can't even venture as far as the village in this snow?"

Edmund took a step forward. "Is that where he is?"

Good. She had his attention now, and it wasn't focused on Will.

"How should I know? But think about it: you've searched the entire castle and found nothing. Surely the next place to look is the village and nearby manors? My knights and villagers are loyal to me, but many of them have sons, brothers, and fathers who swore allegiance to Maude."

Please, God, let him forget her son in his desire to succeed in his task.

It seemed her prayer was answered. Edmund beckoned his squires. "Arm yourselves. We're going to search the village." He turned to Isobel. "I require five of your men."

Isobel nodded. She'd have let him empty the castle if it meant he'd leave her to live out her life in peace. "I'll have them meet you at the gates."

She turned to leave, but Edmund called after her. "I'll be back for the noon meal. We can continue our conversation then."

She didn't react but returned to the solar on shaky legs. She had gained some time, but he wasn't giving up.

****

Edmund beckoned Joss to his side. "Round up the men. It's time to go back."

The cold had hours ago worked its way through his layers of clothing and now pierced him to the bone. As much as he wanted to push on to the nearest manor, it would be foolish. The longer they remained out, the

43

greater the risk of falling prey to the cold. They had searched all the likely places in the village and found nothing. It was time to return to the castle. And Isobel.

Climbing back up the steep road to the castle, he had the uncomfortable feeling he was being watched. But each time he looked to where he thought he'd spied movement, he saw nothing. There were strange mounds and ditches up the hillside, forming glistening ripples beneath the snow. Here and there a blackthorn jutted out of the drifts, but nothing large enough to conceal a hound, let alone a grown man. It was his determination to find Cannington that was playing tricks on his eyes. That and the sudden shock of coming face to face with Isobel once again.

He ploughed on through the snow. More clouds had piled up overhead in the time since he had been in the village, and now the first flakes floated down. God's bones, would this winter never end? He buffed his hands beneath his cloak. What he wouldn't give for a tub of steaming water and a goblet of warm spiced wine. His lip curled. Such luxuries were beyond the realm of possibilities when his hostess was Isobel de Brockton. Especially when the lady of the household was expected to assist her guests to bathe.

He tugged at his cloak pin to ease the sudden constriction in his throat. Hellfire! Now he couldn't tear his mind from the thought of Isobel leaning over the tub, her tawny hair loose, the ends trailing in the water, her eyes alight with the promise of pleasure as her hands slid down his chest.

He cursed as the wicket gate swung open to let them in. Snow. Concentrate on that. Freezing snow down the front of his braies. Festering sores on a donkey's scrotum. Not Isobel, and definitely not her—

A stinging slap to the cheek made him stagger. He blinked at his assailant. Isobel. Her eyes blazed, but her mouth worked as though from pain.

"You snake! Where is he?"

He put a hand up to his throbbing face, unable to comprehend what had just happened. "Isobel, what—?"

"Tell me where he is or, king's man or no, I'll have you strung from the highest tower."

"Where who is? Isobel, what are you talking about?"

"My son. Where have you taken him?"

"Your—" Then he noticed the curious glances of the men. Taking Isobel by the arm, he led her inside the gatehouse and ordered the men within to leave. The gatehouse was nothing more than a cramped chamber with a table and two benches beside a lit brazier. He sat Isobel down on the bench closest to the brazier then took a seat opposite her.

"Start from the beginning. What's this about your son? I swear I know nothing about him."

Isobel gazed at him for a long moment, then her shoulders sagged. "You mean you haven't seen him? Oh, God save him, at least if he was with you he would be safe."

A lump of ice lodged in his gut. "Your son's missing?"

She nodded, her chin quivering. "After I'd seen you leave I went to find him. At first I just thought he'd crept out to play in the snow, but I've looked everywhere, turned the castle upside down." Her last words spilt out in a rush. "I...I thought you must have taken him. But if you don't have him..." Tears welled in her eyes, but she wiped them away. "Blessed Mary, where is he?"

"Think carefully. Did he give any clue where he might have gone?" Now was not the time to let bitterness stand between them. Not when a child's life was at stake.

A child old enough to run away. Old enough to be his son?

"I don't think so. Just—" She clapped her hand to her mouth. "Oh, sweet Mother!"

"What is it? What did he say?"

She raised horror-filled eyes to his. "He was going to pretend he was he was a soldier. He said he wished he were older so he could go out whenever he wanted. So he…" Her voice dropped to a choking whisper. "So he could join my soldiers. But I never thought… I thought he meant to play soldiers in his chamber. Not…"

"Not creep out of the castle." Edmund rose, kicking over the bench in his hurry, and shouted for the gate warden. He was already halfway out of the door by the time the man appeared. Edmund grabbed him by the shoulders.

"You! Can you swear you've had your eye on the gate the whole morning?"

The man's eyes slid past Edmund to settle on Isobel, then back again. "I…I might have come back here from time to time, to warm up, but I swear I left the door open and kept an ear out for the gates. No one arrived until you just now, I vouch my life upon it."

Edmund tightened his grip, his thumbs digging beneath the man's collar bone. "But what about a boy? Would you have noticed a small boy slipping through the wicket gate?"

The man's stricken gaze told Edmund all he needed to know. Behind him, Isobel gave a low moan.

"Forgive me, my lady," the man babbled. "I never dreamt the young lord would try and leave."

Tempted as he was to shake the man until his teeth rattled, Edmund released him. He shrugged his cloak back across his shoulders. "There's no time for excuses. Go and round up my men. We'll leave immediately."

"I'm coming too." Isobel strode to the door, but Edmund caught her arm.

"You'll only slow us down. Stay here in case he's still within the castle." And how could he concentrate on the search with this...*awareness* of her burning in his flesh whenever she was around? No, far better she remain.

Isobel simply pulled her cloak more tightly around her shoulders and pushed past him on her way to the gate. "We're wasting time. This is my son!"

Edmund had no choice but to follow. "Stay close and do exactly as I say."

"I will, if you can keep up." She marched down the track, her cloak a crimson swirl against the snow. She turned to the men. "Spread out." She had to raise her voice to be heard over the wind. "We must look for tracks before the new snow covers them."

Joss and Ancel glanced at Edmund in silent question. Edmund nodded, and the group fanned out, eyes down. Edmund did the same, straining his eyes for any sign of a child's footprints. Isobel's defiance rang in his ears: *this is my son!* Was it a last, desperate attempt to deny him his son, or was it her way of telling him Will wasn't his? He did his best to push the question from him mind. Whatever the truth of the matter, a young boy was out, alone in what was fast becoming another blizzard.

Ahead of him, he saw Isobel stagger and plunge into what must have been a ditch concealed by new snow. She sank up to her waist and scrambled to climb out, but she was hampered by her heavy skirts, which by now must surely be drenched by melting snow. Forcing his way against the headwind, he ploughed a path toward her and grasped her by the wrist. "Now will you see sense and return to the castle?" He hauled her out.

He put more force into his action than intended, and Isobel staggered forward into his arms. For the space of a dozen frantic heartbeats, they stood locked together, her body pressed against his as she struggled to regain her breath. The wind had ripped off her veil, and her braids had unraveled. Tawny curls whipped his face, carrying with them the lingering scent of rosemary. For a fleeting instant, he closed his eyes and breathed in the scent that took him back to stolen trysts on summer evenings.

Then she shoved him backward and snarled at him. "Get your hands off me."

But as quickly as the flare of temper arrived, it drained away and her face crumpled. "Oh, God. What if Will's down there, buried?"

Before Edmund could stop her, she slid back into the ditch and scrabbled in the snow, crying out her son's name.

Cursing, he pulled out his knife, cut off a stout branch from the skeleton of a nearby blackthorn, and lowered himself beside her. He flung an arm around her shoulders and pulled her upright. "Wait!" By this time he had to lower his mouth to level with her ear to make himself heard over the keening wind. "There's a quicker way to do this. Stand still."

Surprisingly, she did as he bid and ceased her frantic search. Praying his improvised staff would meet nothing more than rocks and frozen ground, he sank it into the drifts at regular intervals and quickly worked his way along the length of the ditch. He blew out a shaky breath as the last probe failed to meet anything soft. He flashed Isobel a grim smile. "Nothing. He's not here."

"Thank God." She looked ready to collapse, but Edmund realized nothing would induce her to leave the hillside until they had Will. If it was his child, he would feel the same.

If Will was his child.

Forcing himself to focus on nothing but the task at hand, he ignored Isobel's objections and lifted her out of the ditch, then scrambled up beside her. He thrust the staff into her hands. "Here. Use this to probe ahead. It'll save you tumbling into more ditches." And would find any body buried beneath the drifts. He knew better than to put that into words, but from the dawning horror on her face, he saw the same thought had occurred to her.

He broke off another branch and moved a couple of paces to her left to cover more ground, calling Will's name at intervals. But the wind tore the words away; the boy wouldn't hear, even if he was lurking behind the bush right next to him.

Lurking behind a bush…What did that remind him of? Of course—his odd feeling of being watched when he returned from the village. There had been no hiding place large enough to conceal a grown man, but a young boy?

He hurried up to Isobel and took her arm. "This way, hurry!" He guided her around the hillside, sliding on patches of ice, until he came to the place where he had been aware of eyes upon him. Here the snow rose high in a series of glittering waves, frosted bushes growing in the space between. He prodded one of the waves and was surprised to meet solid earth instead of a soft drift. "It's a bank!"

Isobel nodded. "There are tales of a fort on this hill long before the castle was built." Sudden hope blazed in her eyes. "Will likes to play here in the summer."

With a fresh spring in her step, she hurried to the first of the banks and cupped her hands to her mouth. "Will, where are you?"

The wind rose again, and Edmund hurried to the farthest bank also calling out Will's name. A faint noise from beneath a sprawling bramble bush snagged his attention. Was that a cry? Ignoring the bite of cold, he dropped to his knees and shoveled aside the drift of snow piled against the bush. Then he peered into the gap between the thorny branches and the snow to see a neat den of leaves and moss pressed out beneath the bramble. A shock of curly, tawny hair suddenly appeared in the gap, and a pair of slate-blue eyes, framed with thick, dark lashes and brows gazed up at him. It was a sight Edmund knew well; he saw those eyes reflected back at him every time he polished his sword.

All doubt was gone. The boy's age and features proved that he was looking at his own son. His heir.

His throat strangely tight, he reached out a hand to

the lad. "You must be Will."

The boy nodded and took Edmund's hand. Edmund lifted him into his arms and tucked him under his cloak to warm him. "You've given your mother a nasty scare."

Before he could say anything else, Isobel dashed to his side and flung her arms around Will, heedless of the way her embrace necessarily included Edmund. "Thank God you're safe!" she said, her voice muffled by Will's hair. Then she lifted her eyes to Edmund. "Thank you."

Her face was so close to his, he could have lowered his mouth to hers as he had done many times before. But this was different. Now there was a boy between them. His heir. And Isobel had deliberately kept the truth from him. He pulled clear of the embrace, refusing to relinquish Will to Isobel's arms. "He's icy cold. We must get him to the castle."

And once he was assured Will was safe and well, he and Isobel were going to talk. This time he would force her to tell the truth.

Chapter Five

He knows! Isobel dashed after Edmund and Will as fast as the icy conditions would allow. Of all the people who could have found him, why did it have to be Edmund? Even as she fretted over how pale and subdued Will looked, huddled under Edmund's cloak, she tried to force her numbed mind to work out what to do next. There was no denying the truth now, but how did she explain why she had hidden Will from Edmund? A leaden weight settled in her stomach. She had gambled her and Will's future and lost. *Holy Mother, don't let Edmund take Will away.*

Straining her frozen limbs to the limit, she made every effort to catch up with Edmund. Not for one instant did she take her eyes off him or Will. As she watched, Edmund signaled to one of his squires. The lad ran up, and Edmund barked out several orders, although the wind snatched them away before they reached her ears. However, the pause enabled her to gain on him, and she reached his side when they were still a stone's throw from the castle gates.

"How is he?" She stroked Will's cheek and sucked in a breath. Sweet Jesu, his flesh was like ice.

"Chilled to the bone, but shivering, which is a good sign. He should do well enough if we get him into a hot bath straight away. I've sent Joss ahead to warn your servants."

Will gave her a weak smile and turned his face to nuzzle Edmund's chest.

It was as though an invisible cord connecting her very core to Edmund gave a sharp tug. She swayed toward him, dizzy with a sudden yearning to bury herself in his embrace, breathe in his familiar scent of musk and leather. Take the same comfort Will had found, cradled and protected in those strong arms.

Another gust of wind blew snowflakes into her eyes, shocking her out of her daze. By all that was holy, what was she thinking? This was the man who had betrayed her. She would never find comfort in his arms.

Agnes was waiting for them at the solar door. Isobel wished there was some way to exclude Edmund, but despite the significant stare she fixed on her maid, Agnes bundled them all into the chamber and unpinned their cloaks. The fire in the hearth had been stoked to a roaring blaze, and two maids were erecting a screen around a steaming tub.

Once Agnes had flung their cloaks over the screen to dry, she reached up to Will. "I'll take him, my lord. You and my lady should sit by the fire to warm through."

She let Agnes take Will from her arms but found her voice. "I'm sure the earl will be more comfortable in the guest chambers." To the maids who had just finished arranging the screens, she said, "Please provide Lord Edmund with a bath in his chambers." They nodded and closed the door behind them.

By this time Agnes had finished undressing Will and lowered him into the tub.

Will whimpered. "It's too hot."

Isobel dipped a hand into the water and satisfied

herself the water wouldn't scald him. "That's because you're so cold," she said. "I know it's painful, but we have to get you warm. You could have frozen to death out there, Will. What were you thinking, going off into the snow like that?"

"You said I could pretend to be a soldier, so I did. When they went out, I followed." His lip wobbled. "I wasn't alone, because I was with them, but I couldn't keep up and I got lost."

Isobel drew a dismayed breath, remembering how distracted she had been that morning. "Oh Will, I'm sorry. I—" Suddenly her shaking legs couldn't support her, and she clutched the side of the tub for support.

Strong hands caught her arm and guided her into a chair next to the fire. "Now will you do as you're told? Your maid has everything under control."

Edmund. Trust him to stay when he wasn't wanted.

"You must be chilled yourself, my lord. You should return to your chamber."

"I will wait here."

Isobel massaged her temples. She couldn't summon the energy to fight. Especially now the unspoken truth hung in the air between them.

A splash caught her attention, and she glanced over her shoulder to see Will smile and set up waves that threatened to spill out upon the floor rushes.

"Look, Mama, I'm rowing a coracle down the river!" Will's cheeks were pinking up. He was clearly recovering far faster from the experience than she was.

Then a glance at Edmund made her heart stutter. He was watching her with the implacable gaze of a hawk regarding its prey.

She lowered her voice. She didn't mind Agnes

hearing, but she wanted to shield Will for as long as possible. "Please, Edmund, leave us be for today. I need to be sure my son is well."

Fire kindled in his eyes when she said "my son," and if she could have caught back the words, she would.

"As do I." He took a seat in front of the fire and stretched out his long legs to warm his wet boots. Short of summoning several guards to forcibly remove him—creating a scene he no doubt knew she'd hate Will to witness—it was clear he was staying.

"Very well," she said through gritted teeth. "If you insist on staying, don't expect me to nurse you if you take a chill."

"I know better than that."

Isobel turned her back on him and knelt beside the tub. But even as she chatted to Will and felt his hands and feet to reassure herself he was warming up, Edmund's gaze burned a hole between her shoulder blades.

Finally she turned. "As you can see, Will is well. I thank you for finding him, but I must put him to bed now. Anything further you have to say can wait until tomorrow."

It was futile to hope there wouldn't be a reckoning between them, but she prayed that he would recognize the unspoken message: *not in front of Will!* Once they had needed no more than a look, a smile, a shared glance, to express more than a thousand words ever could. But now there were five years of pain and grief between them even the plainest words were going astray.

Deep lines scored Edmund's brow as he appeared

to ponder her statement. Finally he rose. "Very well. But I insist upon a meeting tomorrow morning."

She nodded, not trusting herself to speak.

She kept her composure whilst tucking Will in bed and placing heated bricks, wrapped in linen, at his feet. Even when she and Agnes were alone in her chamber, she managed to smile and reassure Agnes she was well. It was only after Agnes had helped her out of her still damp gown and into a dry shift and left her chamber that she allowed her feelings to show. She sank down upon her bed and pulled her knees to her chest. She fumbled for her paternoster beads, trying to take comfort in the repetition of familiar prayers, but no peace would come. Now there was no need to quell her emotion, violent shivers shook her whole body.

How could she make Edmund understand why she had sent him no word of his son? Most importantly, was there any way she could persuade him not to take Will away?

For it was clear her interlude of peace and independence was over. Whatever happened tomorrow, one way or another, she was about to become dependent upon a man yet again. It had never gone well for her before, and she doubted this time would be any different.

****

At first light, Isobel rose and pulled on a bliaut. She'd have preferred the moss green traveling gown she'd worn yesterday, but Agnes had taken it away to dry. She couldn't help feeling that after Edmund's jibe about widows in crimson gowns, she ought to dress more soberly, especially as she didn't want to provoke him. But her coffers were full of gowns of varying shades of crimson, poppy-red, sapphire, and other bright colors. In the end she opted for a gown of amethyst wool, as the closest color she had to a widow's black. She prayed Edmund would overlook the extravagant gold embroidery, picked out in seed pearls that adorned the neck, sleeves, and girdle.

She summoned Agnes to lace up the side of her bliaut and braid her hair.

"There will be no dismissing the earl today," Agnes said, pinning a single braid into a heavy coil at the back of Isobel's head. "What will you say?"

Isobel fiddled with her enamel-backed mirror. She had thought of nothing else all night. "I can only tell him the truth again and pray he'll listen this time. I tried before, and that didn't end well."

But had she tried hard enough? She turned the mirror over and over in her hands, seeing images of red, green, and blue enameled birds alternating with her haggard face, shadowed with worry. No, she had lost her temper and stormed out, letting her fear and hurt at Edmund's disbelief get the better of her.

Agnes patted her shoulder. "I don't say it will be easy, but the sooner it's done the better. He seems to have a genuine concern for Will. Not like Sir Roger, who had the poor child cowering in the corner the moment he heard his voice."

Isobel's heart clenched. "I never want to put Will in that position again. After Sir Roger died, I hoped…" Her voice shook, and she set the mirror on the table with a sigh. "Well, it's pointless to wish for what I can't have." She rose to her feet. "You're right. I need to face Edmund and get this over with."

She only paused long enough to look in on Will

and satisfy herself he was peacefully asleep. Then she went to find Edmund, a knot in her stomach tightening with each step.

It was a good thing she'd decided to go to Edmund at the earliest hour; she met him at the doorway to the great hall, clearly on his way to find her. If she'd left it any longer, he would have confronted her in the solar, within earshot of Will. At least this way she could choose a private chamber. She led him into one of the offices adjoining the great hall. It was a stark, cheerless room, with no decoration on the lime-washed walls and only a large oak table and two benches for furniture. A brazier stood in the corner, but it was unlit. The chamber was so cold their breath formed puffs of mist in the air, but this was the most secluded chamber available, and Isobel wanted no witnesses for this talk.

The moment the latch clattered into place behind them, Edmund glared at her. "How long have you known he was mine?"

No concern over Will's health this morning. No sign he had any desire to learn anything about his son other than his right to own him. Edmund's lack of concern helped harden her heart. "I knew from the first."

"You knowingly foisted a bastard on Sir Roger."

Isobel pulled herself up to her full height. "What was I supposed to do? You were gone."

Edmund threw up his arms. "There you go again, accusing me of abandoning you. Yet when I came, you ignored me."

The sharp retort died on Isobel's lips. Her shock and fear for Will had driven Edmund's earlier explanation from her mind. "I don't understand," she said. "You said that before. I thought you were lying. Making excuses."

His eyes flashed. "I don't make excuses. I know what I saw."

"Tell me." As painful as it was to recall the wrenching grief she had experienced when she'd finally accepted her husband of only a few days had abandoned her, she couldn't turn her back on the answers, even if they were five years too late.

Edmund focused on a point above Isobel's left shoulder. "As I said, I came to your father's manor. When a servant opened the door I saw you there, in the great hall."

"But it couldn't have been me. My parents locked me in my room the same evening I told them we had married. They didn't let me out until the day of my marriage to Sir Roger." Her father had been determined to make a powerful alliance by marrying her to a Marcher Lord; her mother, as ever, had refused to take her side.

"It looked exactly like you. It wasn't just the gown, or even the figure, but your hair was loose beneath your veil. Maybe another woman could have worn your gown, but no other has hair like yours."

Isobel felt as though she'd been staring at a chess board for hours before seeing the one move that would get her out of trouble. How had she not seen it before?

****

"My hair! So that's why she did it."

"Did what?" What excuse had this infuriating woman concocted this time?

"My mother cut off my hair. She must have pinned it onto the head of one of the serving girls. There was one with a similar height and figure. It would have been easy to dress her in one of my gowns and veils and have her ready in case you arrived."

Edmund thought back to the moment he had called out to Isobel, and she'd walked away without turning. Could Isobel be telling the truth? Had she been locked in her chamber while an impostor convinced him she cared nothing for him?

If that was the case, everything he had believed for the past five years was a lie. It would mean Isobel wasn't the heartless doxy who had cast him off at the promise of marriage to a man of far greater wealth and position, and he had been duped by her parents.

It would mean he had abandoned his pregnant wife, and he wasn't as blameless as he'd believed.

"You were still too quick to give in." He wasn't going to give up the moral high ground that easily. "You could have waited, made another attempt to contact me. You didn't have to marry straight away. No one can force you to marry without your consent. Besides which, you knew perfectly well your marriage would be invalid."

"I didn't see you come forward to assert your prior claim. You could have tried again. You *should* have tried again, fought for me. But you let me go and left for the Holy Land." She pressed her fingers to her temples. "And I did wait. I held out against my parents until I knew beyond a shadow of a doubt that I was with child and still you didn't come. Did it never occur to you that you'd left not only me, but your child? Did you think of that while sailing off on your righteous quest?"

The blow struck sharper than a knife between the ribs. He should have considered it but hadn't. What kind of man did that make him? He had been too full of anger and grief over her betrayal to consider he might be betraying his own son.

His own son! The words whirled through his mind. He should be feeling something—joy? Pride? Fatherly love? Instead he felt nothing but cloying shame. He'd been taken in by Isobel's parents, leaving Isobel to suffer the consequences alone.

Isobel drew a deep breath and smoothed the front of her gown with shaking hands. "When it was clear you weren't coming back, I knew I had no choice. If I didn't marry Sir Roger, my child would be labeled a bastard. Tainted for life. I could have coped with the scandal but would never force my child to live through such shame."

His throat ached. How had it never occurred to him what he had left her to endure alone? "Did Sir Roger know?"

"He never said anything, but I'm certain he guessed. He…he made that quite clear." She swallowed and raised her hand to her upper arm as though rubbing at a bruise. "Maybe if he'd been able to…" She grimaced. "If he'd got an heir on me, he would have disowned Will. I think his pride stopped him from admitting he'd been unable to get me with child."

Edmund stepped closer and reached out to touch her arm but jerked his hand back at the last moment. He'd lost the right to comfort her. "What about Will?"

"He thinks Sir Roger was his father. He's too young to understand. Please say nothing to him."

"He's my heir. A four-year-old should be able to understand that." He couldn't remember a time when he'd not understood how his own parents felt about him. He'd always known they'd regarded him as an unnecessary encumbrance. He hadn't been that much older than Will when their lack of affection had been demonstrated to terrifying effect. More and more he couldn't imagine how anyone could treat a child in that way. He'd only known he had a son for a short time, but already he wanted to ensure Will never suffered the same fate. To be fair to Isobel, whatever her shortcomings, all her actions toward Will had demonstrated her love and desire to protect. But a boy needed a father, too, and clearly Sir Roger had not been a good father to Will.

"What do you mean to do?" Isobel clutched the pendant at her throat. He followed the movement, couldn't resist running his gaze over the slender column of her throat. He could almost smell her rosewater scent, feel the beat of her frantic pulse beneath his lips…

Concentrate! He dug his nails into his palms, willing the fog of lust to clear.

He drew a deep breath. "There's only one thing I can do." Maybe he didn't know how he felt about having a son, but Will was his heir and needed a father. As much as he rebelled at the thought of allowing Isobel to get close to him again, he had to act with honor.

"Will deserves to know his father, and there's only one way that can happen. I mean to marry you. Again."

He would claim his heir and be a father to Will, but he would have to guard his heart. He couldn't allow himself to fall in love with her again. Love made you weak. He would never hand Isobel the weapons to hurt him again.

Chapter Six

Isobel sank upon a bench. It felt as though the walls of the stark chamber were closing in on her. Marriage. It was impossible to ignore the contrast between Edmund's toneless statement with the joyful eagerness bubbling out of him when he'd asked her to be his wife the first time. He'd burst into the ramshackle hut, seized her by the waist, and swung her around until they'd both collapsed, giddy with laughter upon the hay. Then, after pulling a strand of straw from her hair, he'd told her of his plan to keep them together: a clandestine marriage. Every bit as binding as one that took place in front of witnesses.

As long as neither spouse could be talked into denying their vows.

Isobel had been innocent of the world then. She'd never doubted their determination to stay together, no matter what her parents tried to do to dissuade her. She had taken Edmund's hand, and they'd plighted their troth without hesitation.

But that was five years ago. They were different people now. There was no eagerness in Edmund's expression, only the stern face of a man honor-bound to do his duty.

Her fingers groped for the cross at her throat. "Why are you doing this? I know you don't wish to marry me any more than I want to marry you. Or any man."

"We are *already* married. You might not like it—by all the saints, I know I don't—but there's no escaping the fact." Edmund dropped onto the opposite bench and leaned forward.

Isobel, unable to meet his gaze, focused on the wolf's head brooch pinning his cloak at the shoulder. If she studied the sharp silver teeth snarling at its prey, she could ignore the stab of pain.

He didn't want to marry her. Although why that should matter when she had no wish to disrupt her peaceful life, she couldn't say. "Then why? If it's to do with Will, I promise not to keep you apart; you may see him as often as you like."

"Will is my heir. My legitimate heir. If I visit frequently, how long, do you think, before people see Will's resemblance to me? How long before tongues start to wag?"

"Then we'll go to one of my other manors. It's remote…right on the edge of Welsh territory. My people are loyal; they'd never—"

"No!" Edmund's fist crashed onto the table so hard she was surprised he didn't dent it. "This isn't open to negotiation. I mean to claim Will as my heir and to do so, we must be married. I'm an earl now. King Stephen expects me to marry to secure the succession. When I thought you were married, I held my peace, not wanting to bring you shame or dispossess any children you'd had by your husband. But you're widowed and your only child is mine. I *will* claim him."

"But you don't know Will, nor he you. You could marry another, and none would be the wiser."

"*I* would know. Would you have me break my

wedding vows as you did?"

She jerked back her head and took in the deep furrow between his brows and the bitter twist to his mouth. He might have understood why she had married Sir Roger, but there was no forgiveness there. Not that she blamed him. After all, she hadn't forgiven him for giving her up so easily. Hardly a sound basis for a marriage.

She drew a breath. "I don't want a husband. It's taken years, but I've finally got a life that I like. An independent life. I don't need a husband." And more than that, although she could never tell Edmund, being married meant sharing a bed. She didn't know if she could ever bear a man's touch again. Not even Edmund's.

"Whether you want or need one is beside the point. I *am* your husband. We're already married, Isobel, you can't deny it." Edmund leaned forward until his face filled her vision. "I'm offering to give you a public wedding to save you the disgrace of admitting you were in a bigamous marriage with Sir Roger, but we don't need a wedding to be married."

An icy chill crept down Isobel's spine. "Are you threatening to make our marriage public if I refuse you?"

Edmund cursed. "We may be estranged, but I thought you knew me better than that. You're my wife. I would never shame you."

Not because he cared for her, but because he saw her as his property. "Is there truly no other way?"

"I'm not just thinking of myself; I'm thinking of you and Will. You're not as overlooked here as you seem to think. When I was at King Stephen's court, I heard mutterings about you. I didn't pay them much heed at the time, because I didn't know when men spoke of Sir Roger de Stanton's widow, they spoke of you."

Isobel licked dry lips. "What did they say?"

"That Molbren shouldn't be allowed to remain under the rule of a woman. There's more than one lord whispering those thoughts into the king's ear. And although you can never be forced to marry against your will…"

"…To deny the king would be foolish indeed," she finished for him with a sigh. The king could strip her of her lands, leave her destitute. Worse, he could take Will from her to foster with another lord.

"I won't see you married to another," Edmund said. "I won't allow another man to be father to my heir."

That was all there was to it, of course. He didn't want to be married to her. She swallowed against the sudden tightness in her throat. "Yet you say you won't make our first marriage public. How can you claim Will as your heir unless you do?"

"I'll apply to the archbishop to have our former marriage recognized later on. If we do it quietly, I doubt it will attract much gossip. Not when everyone's attention is diverted by the feud between Stephen and Maude."

"I see you have an answer for everything." It was clear she didn't have a choice, but she could at least attempt to set the terms. "If I agree, it's on two conditions."

"Name them."

"First, I won't deny you access to Will…to your

son. But as Earl of Redmarch you will be spending most of your time in your own lands. When you go, I will stay here. With Will."

Edmund frowned. "He'll be Earl of Redmarch himself one day. He has much to learn."

"But not yet—he's only four." The heavy weight in her chest was due to her fear of losing control of Will. Nothing at all to do with disappointment that Edmund wasn't fighting to keep her with him as well. "When he's seven he'll be old enough. Not before."

Edmund gave her a long look, then nodded. "Very well. Until then he may stay with you. What's your second condition?"

"We delay the wedding until Will's ready to accept you as his father. Until *I* say he's ready."

Edmund frowned. "And how long will that be?"

As long as she could stretch it. That way there was still the hope she could find a way out of this mess, that she could assure the king of her loyalty and strength. "It's hard to say. Will's just a child, and his experience of fathers hasn't been a happy one."

"I suppose that's reasonable. Very well, you have your delay, but it can't be for long. I want Will as my legitimate heir before I leave."

A stay of execution, but not a lengthy one. Still, considering she had been bargaining with an empty hand, she had fared better than expected. Probably because Edmund had no greater desire to be tied to her than she to him.

Edmund rose. "Then the sooner I meet Will, the better."

"But he might still—"

"Now."

****

They walked to the solar in silence; once there, Isobel went to fetch Will. Edmund wandered around the chamber, taking in what he'd been too exhausted to notice the day before. It was a pleasant room with whitewashed walls, hung with tapestries depicting a woodland scene through all the seasons. A canopied fireplace dominated one wall, the fierce flames casting a warm glow. Three wooden chairs and a table holding a chessboard stood beside the fireplace, and a long settle occupied the opposite wall, scattered with jewel-colored cushions. Soft lamplight shone from wall niches. The whole chamber reflected Isobel's love of nature and bright hues. A peaceful haven, despite the whistle of the wind through the gaps in the window panes.

As soon as Isobel led Will from his room and into the solar, Will shrank against his mother's side, as though trying to bury himself in her skirts as thoroughly as he'd concealed himself in the brambles.

"This is the Earl of Redmarch," Isobel said to Will. "He wanted to see for himself that you're recovered from yesterday." Her voice cut like steel, defying Edmund to declare his true relationship to the boy. "I think you have something to say to him, don't you, Will?"

The slate blue eyes peered out from the folds of Isobel's gown. "Thank you for finding me," he said. "And for bringing me back home."

Annoyingly, it was clear Isobel was right about Will. There was a wariness to him that spoke of past maltreatment. If he strode up to Will now and told him he was his father, the poor boy would probably shrink from him. This required patience. A pity he didn't have much.

Right now, Will needed reassurance. But how? Usually Edmund would rather eat camel dung than talk to a child. Then he remembered the wooden soldier. He'd stowed it in his leather pouch for safekeeping and forgotten all about it in the worry of the search. Now he pulled it out and handed it to Will.

"I found this the other day. I think it must be yours."

Will's eyes lit up. "My soldier!" he cried. "I thought I'd lost it." He darted out from Isobel's protective hold and took the toy.

Isobel raised her eyebrows. "What do you say, Will?"

"Thank you."

"You're welcome." But it was going to take more than the return of a favorite toy to put Will at ease. If he was being honest, Edmund had to admit he wasn't at all comfortable with Will, either. He had no experience with children. He'd had some mad idea that there would be a connection between them because Will was his son, but try as he might, he couldn't sense any kinship, any bond. He had no idea what to say.

"You'd be better off playing with toy soldiers than leading real ones a merry dance out in the snow." In his head, the words had sounded lighthearted, meant to make Will laugh. But they came out as stern and disapproving as though spoken by his own father.

Will's brows drew together, and he shot a glance at Isobel before scurrying to the window seat at the other side of the room. Edmund couldn't blame him. If he'd been trying to prove to Isobel he could be trusted as a father, he'd failed dismally.

No doubt Isobel would make the most of it. She was probably planning to turn Will against him, make it impossible for him to claim his heir. Well, she'd pitted herself against the wrong enemy. He'd never been overcome by an enemy before, and he wasn't going to lose now. All he needed was careful planning. Whether she liked it or not, Will was his heir, and he wouldn't be denied.

Seeing the wooden horses lined up beside Will's seat gave him an idea.

"I see you like horses, Will." Edmund forced a smile. It felt like a constipated grimace. He could only pray it looked more reassuring.

A half smile lit the boy's face. "Horses are my favorite thing in the world," he said. "When I grow up, I'm going to be a knight and ride a horse just like this." He held up a horse that had been painted a dappled gray.

"My horse looks a bit like that."

Will nodded, his hair falling into his eyes. "I know. I watched you ride in. Your horse is the finest in the stables."

"Would you like to see him?"

Although his eyes were on Will, he was acutely aware of Isobel, who stood at his elbow. He didn't miss her rigid stance, the way her hands balled into fists when Will leapt down from the window seat.

"Can we go now, Mama? Please?"

Yes. If Isobel planned to keep him from his heir, she'd made a grave mistake.

"It's too cold for you to go out, Will." Isobel put her hands on her hips and glared at Edmund. "I think you should stay inside after the fright you gave us yesterday."

In Edmund's opinion, Will looked none the worse for his ordeal. In fact he glowed with health and if he was anything like Edmund, would chafe at being penned indoors. "It is cold out, but you'll be plenty warm if you put on some warmer clothes. Go and ask your nurse to find some for you and then we'll go and meet my horse."

Will scampered off, calling for Agnes.

"How dare you overrule me in front of my son?" Isobel stalked toward him, fists clenched, the tendons on her neck as taut as bowstrings.

"He is also *my* son. Never forget that. You wanted Will to become accustomed to me. How is he to do that if you don't let us spend time together?" He began to understand her anger. "Admit it: you're afraid Will might actually come to like me."

"Don't be ridiculous." Isobel stalked to the window and sat on a stool in front of a large tapestry frame, her skirts swirling upon the rushes. He read disdain in every gesture, from the way she turned her face away to the vicious stab of the needle into the canvas. The unspoken message being: *Will could never like a man like you.*

Edmund paced to the fireplace. Needing something to occupy his hands to stop himself from punching the stone canopy, he picked up a chess piece from the board beside him. Of course, fate must have been laughing at him: the piece he'd blindly grasped turned out to be the red queen. He turned it over and over in his hands studying a white patch on a fold of the queen's robe, where the red stain had worn away to reveal the ivory beneath.

Whoever had created this game must have had a woman like Isobel in mind when he decided to endow the queen with so much power. Women had much more strength than they were given credit for. Or Isobel did, certainly. But if she wanted a battle, she had picked the wrong man to defy. Will was his heir, and no one was going to stop him claiming Will as his own. Not even Isobel.

If only they could be civil to one another. If only every interaction between them didn't make the air crackle with unspent lightning. Try as he might, he couldn't forget that Isobel had once been the one who had spurred him to excel, his very reason for living. Seeing the angry, bitter woman who had taken her place was all too harsh a reminder of what he had lost. What they had both lost.

Isobel was right about one thing; it would be best not to be faced with a daily reminder of the mistakes of his youth. For the sake of his sanity he needed to stay away from Molbren, away from her, as much as possible.

Will's arrival, trailed by a protesting woman— Agnes, he presumed—shook him out of his musings. He replaced the queen on the chess board and pulled his cloak around him. He might find the boy difficult to talk to, but at least a visit to the stables would get him away from Isobel.

Will stopped by his mother. "Why aren't you dressed to go out, Mama?"

****

Isobel opened her mouth, an excuse on her lips, but Edmund answered first.

"Your mother is busy with her tapestry. We'll go without her."

How dare he speak for her? She jammed her needle into the edge of the canvas and rose. No matter that a smelly, freezing cold stable was the last place she wanted to be, she wouldn't let him get away with that. "One moment, Will. I'll fetch my cloak." Edmund had got his own way with the marriage, but she would show him it didn't mean he could rule over her the same way Sir Roger had. The way her father had ruled over her mother. If she was to survive this marriage, she must assert her authority from the start.

Edmund followed her out of the solar. "There's no need for you to come," he said. "I'll take good care of him." His reluctance to be with her was obvious.

The sting drove out her own reluctance to be near him. "You forget that Will is only four, and he's never so much as laid eyes on you until now. He's bound to be nervous around you—you're nothing but a stranger to him."

She marched to her chamber to collect her mantle.

When she returned, her vair-lined cloak bundled around her, she found Will eagerly asking Edmund what his horse ate, how old it was, and how fast it could gallop, not leaving Edmund space to answer. Amid a surge of resentment, she crouched in front of Will to fasten his cloak. The circular silver brooch flashed in the lamplight and for an instant, Isobel caught a glimpse of her face, reflected in its gleaming surface. Her mouth was turned down, and her eyes hard and angry.

She straightened Will's cloak with painstaking care, then smiled at them both, her face aching with the effort. "There. Shall we go?"

But even when they reached the stable, she couldn't focus on Will's excited chatter. All she could see was her angry, bitter face. She fingered her garnet cross. Blessed saints, what had she become?

What was Edmund turning her into?

Chapter Seven

"Look at me, Mama!"

God save her, there was Will, eyes shining, perched on the back of Edmund's magnificent gray palfrey. Edmund stood beside him, one arm steadying Will, to stop him sliding off the horse's back. How long had he been up there?

"Be careful, my heart. Don't tug his mane; he might not like it."

Will unclenched his fingers, releasing a handful of snowy mane. "I think he likes me."

The horse whickered and nodded its head, causing Will to squeal with laughter. "See—he agrees."

"Al-Ashab won't hurt you. He's a gentle soul." Edmund patted the horse's neck with his free hand. He seemed much more comfortable with the horse than with Will, and Isobel felt a spark of satisfaction that Will completely ignored Edmund in favor of the horse.

Then burning shame flooded her body. What was she thinking? Wasn't the sight of her reflection warning enough? This bitterness would do neither her nor Will any good. Edmund was in Will's life now, whether she liked it or not, and she knew all too well what bitterness could do to a person. It was time she forgot about her feelings toward Edmund and did all she could to bring Will and Edmund closer. Otherwise she stood to alienate her son as well as Edmund.

Once they were back in the solar, Isobel seized the opportunity when Agnes took Will to his chamber.

She clutched Edmund's arm to stop him leaving. "Are you—" Oh, blessed saints, touching him had been a mistake. As if acting of their own accord, her fingers stroked the solid muscle of his upper arm through his sleeve. She snatched back her hand and took a hasty step back, clasping her hands behind her back. She cleared her throat and tried again. "Do you truly mean to claim Will?"

"Why? Do you still plan to stop me?" His eyes narrowed as though facing down a foe on the battlefield.

She drew a breath. Thank goodness he didn't seem to have noticed her inadvertent caress. "Believe it or not, all I want is what's best for Will. And that's not being caught between two bickering parents."

"What do you suggest?"

"Nothing to put too much strain on our acting abilities. But we should keep any disagreements private. After all, at some point we have to tell Will we're to be married and work out how best to explain you're his real father. It's going to be a big enough disruption to his life without him seeing how much his parents despise each other."

"Isobel, I never—"

"Oh, save your breath. You've made it perfectly clear how you feel." Her lips trembled; she bit the inside of her cheek until she regained control. "I'm merely telling you that I expect you to treat me with respect in front of others, especially Will."

The corners of Edmund's mouth pulled down, but he inclined his head. "I assure you, I'll treat you with respect at *all* times. I'm no hypocrite to treat my wife with deference in front of others, only to brutalize her in private."

Isobel shuddered and stepped closer to the fire to disguise the involuntary reaction as a shiver of cold.

"I expect the same treatment in return." Edmund's voice was harsh. It was hard to believe it belonged to the same man who'd once murmured impassioned troths into her ear.

She swallowed to relieve the thickness in her throat. "Of course." Edmund had changed, but she knew in her heart he could never be cruel. She should be grateful. There were far worse fates than being the wife of a man like Edmund Granville. She should remember that, not mourn the lost love of a foolish, naïve girl who'd thought love could overcome all obstacles.

"Good." Edmund pressed the latch, then paused before stepping out into the draughty passageway. "I'm glad you've put the past behind you."

The moment the door closed behind him, Isobel sank upon a chair and picked up a flagon of mead. Resisting the urge to fling it into the fire, instead she poured a brimming cupful and gulped it down. She closed her eyes, feeling the burn of the strong drink all the way down her throat. How dare Edmund assume she could put the events of the past five years behind her so easily? She wanted to run after him, scream the truth, make him face up to what his desertion had cost her.

A mad urge to giggle nearly overcame her. Hardly the best way to begin their truce, and it wouldn't do for Will and Agnes to witness her yelling obscenities at the king's man. She took another swallow of mead to quell her rising hysteria, but she couldn't suppress a chuckle.

"What's so funny, Mama?" Will ran into the solar and leaned against her knees.

"Nothing at all, Will. I'm in a strange mood, that's all. Come here and tell me how you liked meeting the earl's horse." She lifted Will onto her lap and hugged him close. And while Will prattled away about Al-Ashab, she dwelt on Edmund's parting words. Put the past years behind her? Impossible. They had destroyed the girl who'd bound herself to Edmund. Just as Edmund wasn't the man she'd once known, so she was irrevocably changed. They could never reclaim the love they'd known. The best they could hope for was this uneasy truce. It would be foolish to hope for more. The girl she'd been was dead.

****

There was more snow in the air, but Edmund couldn't face returning to his guest chamber. Not yet. He paced across the packed snow to the far side of the courtyard. As far from the donjon and that infuriating woman as it was possible to be. With his frustration and anger still seething through his veins, he couldn't bear the thought of being confined in the guest chamber, no matter how comfortable. What he needed was a walk in the fresh air to burn off this excess energy.

On the far side of the bailey, he discovered a narrow stone staircase leading up onto the walls. He ascended and walked around the perimeter until he found a niche sheltered from the biting wind. Propping his elbows upon the breastwork, he looked out at the western hills. They ranged in never ending ranks like a besieging army, the farther ranks fading into the horizon until he wasn't sure if he was seeing snow-covered mountains or cloud.

For the first time in years, he wished he had someone he could confide in. So much had happened it was hard to sort out the myriad thoughts and emotions surging through him. His relationship with Joss was strengthening, since he had taken on the lad as a squire in the turbulent days between his knighting and leaving for the Holy Land. It was really only in the past few months, now Joss was older and approaching his own knighthood, that Edmund had started to appreciate Joss as his cousin and friend rather than simply his squire. Although the support Joss had given him since becoming Earl of Redmarch had been invaluable, this new turn in their relationship was still too new to confide such momentous changes in his life.

It struck him then that the last time he'd had a person like that in his life was when he was with Isobel. The day he had lost her, he had lost not only his wife and lover, but his most trusted friend.

Well, the day he confided in her again would be the day King Stephen announced his support for the Empress Maude. He gritted his teeth. He'd never encountered such bare-faced audacity, the way she acted as though she were the only one wronged. As though his heart hadn't been torn from top to bottom the day he'd believed she had cast him off.

It was a wound that would never truly heal, yet here she was, acting like Edmund was the only one at fault and she was purer than a saint. Yet all these years she had hidden his son—his heir—and lived a life of luxury in this safe castle while he faced deprivation, injury, and illness in a harsh land. If she'd given even the slightest sign of acknowledging his hurt as well as hers, he might feel more forgiving.

He glanced back at the donjon. He had half a mind to return and demand she face up to her responsibility for the end of their marriage. They were going to have to spend time together after all. Being with her wouldn't stick in his craw quite so much if she admitted some of the fault.

However, as the chill of the snow and wind seeped into his flesh, his temper cooled. He didn't want to confront Isobel. What was the point? All love for her had died. Their marriage was purely an alliance, enabling him to claim his heir. Isobel had already proved herself as stubborn as a mule, so why waste any more energy on her? He should be satisfied with their truce and forget about her.

Of course, it would be easier to forget if her every touch didn't inflame him. Blessed saints, when she'd taken his arm, every inch of his flesh had cried out to feel her body flush against his. He'd needed all his strength to keep from pulling her close. Even now, his arm burned from the feel of her fingers.

He tilted his head back, letting the wind cool his face. Although diving into a snowdrift might be more effective. No, he mustn't forget King Stephen had sent him here for a reason. The best way to get Isobel out of his mind was to concentrate on his task.

With immaculate timing, Joss stepped into the niche, his cheeks rosy from the chill. "There you are, my lord. I've been looking for you. I wondered if we were going to continue our search. We—"

A howl echoed around the castle walls, chilling Edmund to the marrow.

"God's bones!" Joss had turned pale. "Was that a wolf?"

Another howl rang out, and Edmund leaned over the parapet, scanning the landscape. "That's the last thing we need." The sound echoed from the walls, making it hard to pinpoint the wolf's location, but he guessed it must be in the woods to the east. "If I'd had any thoughts of leaving the castle yet, that would have changed my mind." He gestured out at the icy wilderness. Already the horizon had disappeared behind a gray mist. "There's more snow on the way, and I won't risk getting stranded outside the walls when there's a wolf on the prowl."

Joss squinted at the vanishing hills. "I suppose if we can't travel, neither can Cannington."

"True enough. I hope for his sake he's found shelter."

"I'd almost think you felt sorry for the man."

Edmund shrugged. "As far as I know, his only fault is to back the wrong side. He's never harmed or threatened me. If the king hadn't offered such a rich prize for his capture, I wouldn't be concerned either way. Besides, if he freezes to death or is mauled by a wolf, Stephen might not think I've earned my reward."

And his prize—Cannington's lands and palatinate status for Redmarch—was a prize worth fighting for. He mustn't let Isobel distract him anymore. He had to find Cannington.

He clapped Joss on the shoulder. "Come on. What are you waiting for?" He ran off down the steps.

Joss chased after him. "What do you mean? I thought you said it was too dangerous to go out."

"It is, but that's no reason to waste our time while

we're stuck in the castle. We need to talk to the steward and find out all we can about the lands hereabouts."

The steward would have all the information on the nearby settlements and manors, and the men still loyal to the empress. Of course, Isobel would know these things too, but Edmund had no intention of spending more time with her than necessary.

****

It was all very well deciding to avoid Isobel, Edmund reflected the next day, but when another heavy snowfall had forced the castle's inhabitants to stay inside, the solar was the only place quiet enough to study his maps. Isobel had pursed her lips when he'd entered the solar, but she could hardly deny him entry when she'd insisted he spend more time with Will before the wedding could go ahead.

He pulled a heavy oak table into the light of the largest window and spread out the documents. Will sat in the cushioned window seat beside him. Isobel, her back to him, bent over her tapestry, working on a winter scene. Neither of them spoke, and aside from Will's occasional comments as he played, there was no sound in the solar apart from the pop and crack of logs on the fire and the whine of the wind through gaps in the window panes. Despite all that stood between them, there was something so peaceful about working in silence with his unacknowledged family beside him. He'd never known anything like it, having been torn from his parents at a young age.

A twist of regret tugged deep inside. If he and Isobel hadn't been separated, this scene would have been played out many times over the years. It shouldn't be a novelty.

Did Isobel feel the loss as well? He studied her, safe in the knowledge she would be unaware of his scrutiny. The soft light from the window cast a nimbus around her. She was wearing her crimson gown again, and it glowed like a ruby. He wished she would remove her head rail; he'd always been fascinated by the way sunlight picked out tones of amber, bronze, and gold in her hair. It was a crime to keep such a glory braided and hidden beneath a veil.

He dropped his gaze to her slender waist, the flare of her hips accentuated by the twice-wound girdle. His hands ached as he remembered all too well how it felt to span that supple waist, slide from hip to thigh…

He clenched his fist and forced his attention back to his maps, his nails digging into his palms. Isobel showed no sign of being disturbed by his presence. He'd seen stone carvings display more emotion. It was vital he turn his mind to other matters because no good could come of rekindling his desire.

His reward—that's what he should be focusing on. Cannington's lands and, best of all, Redmarch elevated to a palatinate. Something his father had never achieved. He studied the list of manors the steward had given him yesterday and looked for them on the map. Cannington could be in any of them. It was imperative he worked out the fastest route around them so he could search them before Cannington had a chance to reach Welsh territory.

Then the scent of rosemary teased his nostrils. Blessed saints, anything but that! He shut his eyes against memories of lying with Isobel, limbs entwined, strands of her hair tickling his bare flesh. The same scent clung to it as it did now.

God's blood, he must fight this. Forget. That golden time was over, lost for ever, and endlessly dwelling on it could only lead to madness.

But no matter how he tried to concentrate on the parchment in front of him, the words dissolved beneath glimpses of her smile, eyes dark with passion, lips swollen from his kisses.

He stumbled to his feet, knocking over his chair in his haste, and strode to the door.

Isobel glanced up, the needle poised in her hand. "Where are you going?"

Without a moment to consider his reply, he blurted the first thing that came into his head. "To see your steward."

Isobel frowned. "He won't be there. I gave him leave to visit his sister yesterday afternoon. He'll be stuck there in this snow."

"I'm going to check the accounts and inventories. If anyone's been pilfering food and supplies for Cannington or any other runaway, I might be able to trace it through the steward's records." Hellfire, now he had to spend the day poring over interminable lists. Why couldn't he have thought of a more interesting activity? Still, even though he'd made up his reason on the spur of the moment, it actually made sense. It was certainly an avenue worth investigating.

Isobel's eyes narrowed. "I've given you my word no one's helping him. Do you doubt me?"

Of course he did. Isobel had fought him every step of the way. When he'd found out about Will, he'd thought that was the reason. But what if Will wasn't the only secret she'd been hiding?

"You have a huge household, not to mention the

comings and goings between here and the village. Can you truly vouch for the honesty of each and every one of them?"

Isobel stabbed her needle into the canvas and stood. "They are loyal to *me*."

"I don't doubt that, but until recently Molbren held for the empress. Folk might not consider it disloyal to give aid to one of her supporters."

"Molbren is my concern, not yours. I won't have you poke your nose in my affairs."

"That's not completely true now, is it? In a short time, Molbren will be—"

He broke off as Isobel made a slicing gesture and jerked her head toward Will.

Edmund gave a slight nod. Whatever his problems with Isobel, this wasn't the way he wanted to break the news to Will. Who had paused in his play and watched them, his brow furrowed.

"I'm sorry, Will," he said. I didn't mean to disturb you." He shot a glance at Isobel. "Carry on with what you were doing. Your mother and I will talk outside."

The moment the door closed behind them, Isobel rounded on him. "We agreed Molbren would be my concern alone."

"True, but Cannington is my concern by command of the king. If one of your people is helping Cannington, and he makes his escape, that will be my responsibility, not yours. If I lose my reward, it will be Will who suffers as well as me, once he's my acknowledged heir."

Isobel grimaced and turned away. "I can't stop you. But if you find anything and act without consulting me first, I swear I'll do all in my power to keep Will away from you."

Coming from anyone else, Edmund would have dismissed it as an empty threat, but with Isobel he wasn't so sure. He wouldn't put it past her to take Will and seek refuge deeper in Wales, leaving him helpless to reclaim them.

He gave a curt nod. "You have my word."

"For what it's worth." Isobel's parting shot followed him down the stairs.

Several hours later, Edmund's rumbling stomach told him it must be past time for the noon meal, but he needed to check one final thing. He rummaged through the scroll boxes until he found what he was looking for. By this time his fingers were so numbed with cold that he fumbled to unroll it, but eventually he managed to place weights at every corner, and he ran his blue finger along the list of recent purchases. Halfway down, he stabbed the scroll with a triumphant cry and sprang to his feet. He snatched up the scroll, together with the steward's accounts and sprang up the stairs, two at a time.

He burst into the solar and flung the documents upon the table beside Isobel.

"Your steward's betrayed you."

Chapter Eight

Isobel sat back, eyes wide. "There must be a mistake. Simon's a good man. He has my complete confidence." How dare Edmund think he could come between her and one of her most trusted men? Thank goodness Agnes had taken Will away for his meal: she could give Edmund a piece of her mind without Will as a witness.

"Then he's taken advantage of you. It's all here." Edmund jabbed a finger at the scrolls. Isobel glanced at them, wishing, not for the first time, that her parents had taught her more than the basic letters. The flowing lines of ink meant nothing to her.

It made her vulnerable. Dependent. She stared at the script, willing it to form words she understood.

She pressed damp palms upon her skirts, burying them in the folds of wool to hide their trembling. She'd never had reason to doubt Simon before; he had always seemed unswervingly loyal. And now the man telling her he had evidence to the contrary was the last man on Earth she wanted to trust.

Facts. She needed facts. She might not be able to read, but she had an excellent memory. "Tell me exactly what proof you've found." Simon was away from the castle, but she would take the documents to her scribe and have him read them to her. If Edmund was lying, she would catch him out.

"It starts here." Edmund stabbed at a line on one of the lists. "And can you guess the date?"

"Just tell me what you've found without turning it into a mummers' play."

"It starts two days after Cannington escaped from the siege. And it gets more interesting."

Cold apprehension snaked down her back. "What do you mean?" She was curious, despite herself. She couldn't sense any falsehood from Edmund, and she couldn't see why he would have any reason to lie to her. At the same time, she hated to think Simon was dishonest. She needed him on her side if she was to cling on to any semblance of independence. Edmund wouldn't let her keep control of Molbren if she couldn't rely on her steward.

"Your steward lists the purchases of food and drink, but the inventory records fewer items than purchased being added to the castle's supplies. Enough to feed a man for a week. More than that, a quantity of linen and woolen cloth has also gone missing. At first I thought the steward was recording more purchases than had actually been made so he could keep the unused money for himself, but when I saw how close this was to Cannington's escape, I saw the supplies were enough to feed and clothe a man and tend his injuries while he's in hiding."

"You think Simon is concealing Cannington?" Her lips suddenly dry, she could scarcely force out the words. Then she shook her head. "No. I've known Simon for years. He's as true as a plumb line. I don't believe it."

Edmund picked up a scroll and waved it in her face. "It's all here."

She snatched it from his hand. "Even if it is, there has to be a good reason. The dates are just coincidence. It's your obsession with Cannington that's leading you to accuse a man falsely."

"Cannington was seen heading in this direction. He must be on his way to kin in Wales, and he'll have to pass directly through these lands to reach Welsh territory. It's more than coincidence."

"I won't have him accused unjustly. Him or anyone under my protection."

She sprang to her feet, meaning to order him from the solar, but when she saw his expression, her breath hitched. For the first time since he'd stormed back into her life, his face was unguarded, open. This was the Edmund she remembered: passionate, strong in his beliefs.

Unbidden, her feet took a step closer, a needle drawn to a lodestone.

Memories of lying by his side consumed her. It hadn't all been about desire; they'd held one another and spoken of their plans for the future. Edmund had looked forward to becoming a knight, spun dreams of helping the oppressed, fighting injustice.

She'd been alone for so long. *You don't have to be alone any more.* The treacherous voice whispered in her ear, wove dreams of being in his arms, languid from their loving, sharing their hopes and fears. She could almost feel his hand caressing the small of her back.

"You have to admit the circumstances are highly suspicious, Isobel."

The spell was broken. She gasped and stepped back. This wasn't the man she'd loved. Not the man who'd called her *ma belle* and promised to guard her from every hurt. It was important she remember that. Remember he had left her to face pain and humiliation. He was manipulating her, using circumstance to separate her from someone she trusted. Depended on.

"I won't see a man hanged merely on suspicion." She gathered up the rest of the documents from the table. "I'll examine these, and if they show what you claim, I'll speak to Simon when he returns."

"You will not. It could be dangerous. And I can't wait for him to return. For all I know, he's arranging Cannington's escape as we speak. His sister's husband has a manor only an hour's walk away. That's where he'll be hiding Cannington, and that's where I'm going."

"There you go again—accusing him with no proof. He is my steward in my castle. He's Molbren's business, not yours. I'm the Lady of Molbren. I deal with my people, not you." She gestured toward the window where the shadow of heaps of snow could be seen piling up on the stone sill outside. "No one is going anywhere in this. If it's possible to leave the castle tomorrow, we'll leave at first light. Together."

Her heart gave a treacherous thud at the prospect of more time in Edmund's company, but she ignored it. She was accompanying Edmund to ensure Simon got a fair chance to explain himself. That was all. With luck Edmund's suspicion would prove to be unfounded, and they could return to ignoring one another again.

****

True to her word, Isobel was ready to leave at first light. Bundled in her warmest riding gown, sturdy boots, and a thick cloak, she was prepared for the walk through the snow to the manor at Ffynnon Wen.

However, Edmund, when he arrived with his squires, shook his head.

"I've had a word with your stable master. He says it's good road all the way to the manor, so it will be easier to ride."

"Are you sure it's safe?"

"Of course it's not safe. Where there isn't deep snow, there will be treacherous ice. If you're afraid of a fall, you should stay behind."

She would much rather be in the warm solar than risk broken bones in the ice and snow, but she refused to let Edmund scare her. "I know what you're trying to do, but you can't make me change my mind."

Edmund narrowed his eyes, and Isobel could almost hear the retort he longed to make. *You changed your mind about our marriage.* She ignored him and beckoned to the stable hand who approached with her mare. If Edmund chose to believe the worst of her, it hardly mattered any more. They were only marrying for Will's sake.

"It's not just the snow I'm worried about," he said. "Don't forget there's a wolf somewhere out there."

Isobel shivered. She had heard the wolf again last night, its mournful howl keeping her awake. Her misgivings must have shown in her face because Edmund gave a satisfied smile.

She squared her shoulders. "You have a sword. I doubt a wolf would be foolish enough to attack, but if it does, it's your chance to show what you learned in the Holy Land."

She moved to her horse, and one of the grooms helped her into the saddle. Edmund turned away without a word and mounted Al-Ashab.

Much to her chagrin, when they set out, she found herself riding level with Edmund. A groom led the way; he knew all the tracks well enough to keep them from straying, even though the way was buried beneath a sheet of untouched snow. Isobel, determined not to be left behind, urged her mare to follow close behind, but Edmund seemed equally determined not to let her pull ahead and quickly caught her up. The two squires brought up the rear. From the jovial conversation that drifted up the trail, they were enjoying the chance to ride out after being cooped up in the castle.

Despite the company, Isobel had to admit she was glad to be out as well. The air was sharp and clear. The storm had swept away all the gloom, and now the sun glinted in every grain of snow and every puff of breath. Their road took them away from the village, across a forested hillside. Gnarled oaks, creaking beneath their burden of snow, arched over the track, forming a glistening tunnel. The manor lay on the other side of the hill, and Isobel shivered as she peered beneath the ice-covered boughs into the shadows beyond. Had the wolf they'd heard taken shelter in there? No, surely not. It was just the snow that had carried the sound, making it sound as though the wolf was closer than it really was. No wolf would choose to live so close to a village. Nevertheless, she was glad when the trail emerged from the tunnel and out onto bare hillside.

When the party arrived at Ffynnon Wen and were shown into the great hall, Simon came to greet them, his face wreathed in frown lines. "Has something happened, my lady?" Then Edmund moved to stand in front of Isobel, his hand on the hilt of his sword, and Simon's eyes grew wide. He moistened his lips. "My lady?"

Isobel refused to stand back while Edmund intimidated her loyal steward. She gestured to the table. "Nothing's wrong. However, I have some questions for you. Perhaps we could sit and have a drink to warm us after our ride?"

"Of course, my lady." Simon gestured to a servant, and soon they were sitting around the table with goblets beside them, enveloped by the comforting scents of woodsmoke, candle wax, and spiced wine. For a while, as Isobel sipped her drink, relishing the burn spreading though her chest, there was no sound but the snap and fizz of blazing logs in the hearth.

As soon as the servant cleared the empty cups, Isobel, sensing Edmund's impatience, knew she had to speak before Edmund tried to take control of the conversation. She clasped the arms of her chair and leaned forward. "Simon, you have been invaluable since I appointed you as steward, so I hope you can explain something to my satisfaction."

"Certainly, my lady. What do you wish to know?"

"There seems to be a discrepancy between the number of certain items of food and cloth purchased and what is in our stores." She listed each item from memory.

Simon licked his lips. "Are you accusing me of theft?"

"I'm not accusing you of anything." Not like Edmund, who would tear this manor apart looking for Cannington given half the chance. She had to admit, her arrival through the snow, accompanied by three armed men, must make it look as though she had already judged and condemned her steward. "However, I would like you to account for the differences."

Simon's fingers worried at a loose thread on his sleeve. "I'm sorry, my lady, but I can explain."

A chill crept down her back. Was Simon admitting his guilt? She'd been expecting to find he'd made a mistake in the accounts. Not this.

Edmund stirred. "And can you also explain why the goods you stole are precisely what someone harboring an injured fugitive would need?" His tone was conversational, but every word dripped with deadly intent.

Simon's face drained of color. "I know nothing about the fugitive, I swear." He turned to Isobel, face pleading. "You have to believe me, my lady. I did take those things, I don't deny it. But it was for my sister, and I was going to replace them as soon as I could."

His shock was unfeigned, she was sure of it. "I need a full explanation. Why would your sister need you to steal for her? Surely her husband provides for her." She looked around the hall. "Where is Sir Henry, anyway? I'd have expected him to greet us." Sir Henry wasn't the richest of her knights by any means, but he should have enough to provide his wife with all the necessities of life.

Simon looked between Isobel and Edmund, then his shoulders drooped. "You'd better come with me."

He led then into a small chamber behind the hall. The shutters were closed; the only light came from a few feeble rush lights set in their niches.

"Emmeline, we have guests," Simon said.

It took a moment for her eyes to adjust to the dim light, but when they did, she saw most of the chamber was occupied by a large bed. A woman whom she recognized as Emmeline, Simon's sister, rose from her chair beside the bed.

"I'm sorry you had to come all this way, my lady." Emmeline's voice was hoarse and deep lines around her mouth and eyes made her look far older than her five-and-twenty years. It was the face of a woman exhausted beyond measure.

Then the bed creaked and Isobel studied the figure in the bed. It was no outlaw, but Emmeline's husband, Sir Henry, his leg wrapped in a splint, his face gaunt from long illness. His eyes were closed and from the looks of him, he was drifting in a fever she doubted he'd recover from.

"What happened?" she breathed.

Simon answered for his sister. "He took a bad fall from his horse, while out hunting before Christmas. He broke his leg, and it festered. Emmeline used up all the spare linens in the house and without money for more or the means to make any…"

"You took from my stores."

Simon nodded. "And food when Emmeline's grew low. She needed it in a hurry, or I'd have bought it myself. I meant to replace what I took, but there hasn't been time."

The man on the bed stirred and cried out. Isobel put a hand on Simon's arm. "Let's go back to the hall to talk about it."

Isobel was relieved to get away from the depressing atmosphere of the sickroom. They sat back around the table and listened while Simon explained how he'd used up all his money providing for his sister and been forced to steal when they needed more supplies.

"You have to believe I always intended to replace what I took, but I was desperate. I couldn't think of another way to get what we needed."

Edmund, she was sure, would punish the man. Theft was theft. However, she couldn't dismiss his years of loyalty so lightly. She could sense nothing but the truth—his worry for his sister and shame over his actions were genuine, she was sure of it. Certainly the timing of the theft, and the fact it hadn't happened since, tallied with what Simon said.

"Why didn't you come to me about it? You must know I'd never turn my back on someone who needed help."

"I beg your pardon, my lady, but you were recently widowed yourself. I didn't want to burden you with my problems when you were struggling to make terms with the king with no man to help you."

Why did everyone assume she needed a man to take care of her? "You should have come to me, Simon. It's up to me to decide whether a problem is too much for me."

She gazed at the fire, seeking answers in the glowing embers. She didn't want to give Edmund grounds for believing she was too weak to handle her lands. She wanted him to have confidence in her abilities, to leave her here in peace as soon as he was able. But she couldn't in all conscience punish Simon too severely for doing the honorable thing by his sister.

"I expect you to pay back the value of the goods as soon as you're able," she said finally. "And it goes without saying that if anything similar happens in the future, you are to come to me. The people of Molbren are my responsibility. If any of them are in trouble, I expect to be told so I can give all possible support."

Simon straightened up, his eyes widening. "Of course, my lady. Thank you."

"Upon my return, I'll go through my stores and send enough food to last your sister through the winter. That will be a gift. I don't expect any repayment. Agnes can recommend a maid who is knowledgeable about healing; I'll send her to help."

A broad smile lit Simon's face. "Thank you, my lady. You have my word I'll never steal from you again."

"This is your final warning, understand. I'll be keeping a close eye on you, and at the first sign of wrongdoing, I'll cast you out. I won't be taken advantage of."

Simon's effusive thanks were still sounded in her ears as they made the return journey. The chiming of the horses' harnesses accompanied her like victory bells.

"You'll have to look elsewhere for your fugitive," she said to Edmund, unable to resist the temptation to point out how he'd be set to condemn an innocent man.

"I'll admit I jumped to the wrong conclusion if you'll acknowledge I was right to accuse your steward of theft. Whatever his reasons, he did steal from you, Isobel."

They had now reached the tunnel of oak boughs that had so unsettled her on the outward journey, but this time Isobel couldn't believe she'd let her fears get the better of her. It was a clear, sunny day; she'd proved to Edmund she was capable of dealing with a difficult situation. As long as things continued in the same vein, Edmund could have no possible reason to demand he take control of Molbren. She'd shown she could look after herself. She guided her mare beneath the boughs with a light heart.

"I know you think I've been too easy on him," she said, "but I couldn't in all conscience punish him for helping his sister."

"I'm not saying you were wrong."

Isobel's surprise must have carried through to her mare, because the horse lifted her head and swiveled her ears. She patted the mare's neck to calm her and simply said, "Was there a comet in the sky today, and I missed it?"

Edmund shook his head. "What do you mean?"

"To hear you agree with me is nothing short of a miracle. Surely great portent must have heralded such an event. If not a comet, then at least a plague of frogs."

Edmund's lips twitched. "I'm not agreeing with you either. It was a risk, but if he truly means not to repeat his crime, you've earned yourself a devoted servant for life. Although answer me one thing."

"What's that?"

"How do you intend to check if he's cheating you again?"

"I—"

But she paused when a sudden rustle in the undergrowth caused her mare to toss her head, showing the whites of her eyes. She patted the horse's neck again, surprised her usually placid mare was so skittish. "What's wrong with you today, girl?"

Then a blur of gray leapt out of the woods straight in front of her: a huge wolf, its mouth stretched in a dagger-sharp snarl.

Chapter Nine

Edmund was only aware of a single thought: *save Isobel!* He vaulted from the saddle and flung himself in front of Isobel's mare, drawing his sword in one flowing movement. The mare reared, and Edmund ducked to avoid the flailing hooves, then dropped into a crouch, holding his sword in front of him, grounding the hilt. Before Edmund could do any more to brace himself, the wolf landed on his sword, and it took all his strength to keep from being knocked onto his back. The world narrowed to yellow fangs and ice-gray eyes. Blood roared in his ears, battling with the scream of horses and the choking snarls of the wolf. He clung to the hilt of his sword as the wolf writhed in its death throes, inches from his face. A ribbon of drool landed on his cheek. Merciful God, why wouldn't it die? His palms burned; his sword hilt ripped into his flesh, slick from mingled sweat and blood. Sweet Jesu, the beast was going to wrench his shoulders from their sockets. He couldn't hold on much longer. And when he let go, those razor-like fangs would sink into his throat. He was going to die with the stench of rotting meat and coppery blood filling his nostrils.

And who would take care of Isobel?

Then the weight dropped away and Edmund swayed, nearly toppling forward onto the wolf's motionless corpse. He staggered to his feet and pulled the sword from the wolf's chest, breathing a prayer of thanks to all the saints he could think of for guiding his sword to strike a killing blow. He thrust the blade into a snowdrift to clean it, then returned it to its sheath. It took several moments for his fingers to relax their grip.

Only when the roar in his ears died did he hear a shrill whinny. He spun round to see Isobel clutching her mare's neck, struggling to control its terrified rearing. From the corner of his eye, he saw Isobel's groom picking himself up from the drifting snow at the verge; the man must have been knocked there by the panicked mare. Joss and Ancel were too far down the trail to be of help. Forcing his aching muscles to move, he sprang to the horse's side and managed to grasp the bridle. The mare flung up its head, but Edmund hung on with a death-like grip, wincing at the fresh pain in his torn palms, and spoke to the animal in soothing tones until it calmed.

Breathing heavily, he turned to see how Isobel fared. She clung, white-faced, to the saddle, the reins tangled around her wrist.

"Are you hurt?" he demanded.

She shook her head, biting her lip.

"Here, you'll feel better with ground under your feet." He lifted her down from the saddle. Feeling her tremble in his arms, he spoke to her in the same tones he'd used to calm the horse, repeating the words over and over. "You're safe now. It's all over."

She staggered and clung to him; her rapid heartbeat thundered against his chest, matching his own pulse. Her breath came in gasping sobs. While the groom took care of her horse, and Joss and Ancel dealt with the wolf's carcass, Edmund held Isobel close and rested his cheek against her head as he waited for her breathing to ease. Just for this one moment he could forget the battle they waged and enjoy the feel of her, the scent of her hair.

Remember how right she felt in his arms. Remember he cared for her.

Finally, Isobel stepped back, leaving a chill space against his heart. She straightened her head rail with trembling fingers.

"Are you sure you're not hurt?" Edmund asked.

"No, I—oh, your hand!"

Edmund looked down and saw blood dripping from his right hand. A trail of crimson blooms marked his path through the snow.

"Did the wolf bite you?" Isobel snapped, her voice urgent.

"No, I don't think so." Edmund struggled to make sense of his blurred recollections.

Isobel took his hand and turned it palm up to inspect the tear across his palm. It was only the lightest of touches, but jagged sparks shot up his arm and down his spine. He clenched his teeth, struggling to control the surge of heat.

"It doesn't look like a bite." Isobel was still inspecting the wound, oblivious to the turmoil she caused him.

He dragged his thoughts away from the touch of her fingers and shook his head. "It was the sword hilt. That damned beast nearly tore it from my hands."

Isobel gave a tremulous smile. "That's a relief. If it had bitten you…"

Edmund nodded. She didn't need to say anything more. He'd seen men die from fever following even the smallest of animal bites.

Isobel removed her head rail and veil and folded the strip of linen into a makeshift bandage. "Here," she said, binding his hand with it. "This will do for now. I'll tend to it properly when we get back."

They returned to their horses, but her groom straightened up from his examination of Isobel's mare and shook his head. "I'm afraid you can't ride her, my lady. She's gone lame in her left hind leg. She should be able to keep up with the group without a rider. You can take my horse, and I'll walk."

"No. We all need to ride. We can't risk the group getting too spread out, in case there's another wolf on the prowl." In fact, Edmund was confident the wolf had been alone: he'd noticed a gash in the beast's flank that looked like an old, unhealed injury. Unable to hunt with the pack, it must have been driven close to dwellings by sheer desperation. Still, one shock was enough for one day. He wouldn't relax his vigilance until they were safe within the castle walls.

"You will ride with me," he said to Isobel. "Al-Ashab can easily bear two riders."

It was the rational thing to do. He tried to shut out the nagging voice pointing out that all the horses could easily carry two.

It was impossible to ignore the effect supporting Isobel in the crook of his arm had on him once they resumed their journey. She clung to the pommel of the saddle, clearly trying to ease her weight forward so she wasn't leaning against his chest, but even so, sitting crosswise on the saddle meant her backside was pressed against his thigh. Her hair, free of her veil, was working free from her braid, and silken tendrils stroked his cheeks, teasing him with the scent of rosemary. He was forced to picture piles of fly-blown camel dung to keep his body under some semblance of control.

Nevertheless, this was preferable to see her in such a position with one of his squires. The brush with disaster had forced him to confront an uncomfortable truth: he still had feelings for Isobel. Oh, not love. He would make sure he never allowed himself to be so weak again. But aside from the desire he'd struggled to keep in check since he'd arrived in Molbren, he now acknowledged his feelings ran deeper than that. When the wolf had pounced at her, he'd known if anything had happened to her it would have been his responsibility. She was still his wife—nothing would ever change that. And he wanted to protect her and provide for her as was his duty.

That was it, of course. It was only his need to do the honorable thing, do his duty, that stirred these feelings in him. Nothing more. Still, it brought to mind the question the wolf had interrupted. It was odd how only earlier, he'd meant to goad her by pointing out she didn't have the means to check the accounts herself. Now he wanted to support her. She would never ask for help, not from him, anyway. But now he could see a way to help her.

It would mean spending more time in her company, but that didn't matter. If this was how he could provide for her, then it was what he would do.

****

Isobel gripped the saddle and pulled herself forward yet again. It would be too easy to relax into Edmund's hold and rest her head against his shoulder, taking comfort in his strength. It dismayed her how natural it had felt to surrender to his embrace, and the yearning ache that had pierced her heart truly terrified her, even more than the wolf attack. The events of the attack had passed by in a blur, over before she'd grasped what was happening. However, the effects of the embrace still lingered, to the point she doubted things could carry on as before.

Up until the attack, she'd thought they would continue to blame one another for giving up on their marriage, but now it seemed they might be able to move past it. Yes, Edmund had given up on her too soon, been too quick to believe she'd played him false, yet he hadn't hesitated to put himself between her and the wolf. When she'd needed him, he'd been there. Wasn't that what husbands were supposed to do?

More than that, though, was how he had comforted her while she recovered from the shock. The way he'd held her, nestled in the crook of his shoulder…she'd forgotten how it felt to be cared for, cherished. A long-dormant longing awoke in her, wishing it could be like that always. It couldn't, of course. They had both suffered too much to be able to return to the past.

Still, she would make more of an effort to get along with him. No more sharp-tongued retorts. His actions today proved that whatever their past, he deserved better from her. If only she could return to the person she'd been five years ago, maybe they could even find contentment in an amicable marriage. But when a jolt sent her sliding back to press against his chest, she flinched.

She both craved and dreaded his touch.

****

True to her new resolution, as soon as they were

safely back inside the castle and the grooms were leading their horses away, Isobel turned to Edmund. "Come and warm yourself in the solar. Will would like to see you, I'm sure."

The flash of surprise in Edmund's eyes told her how accustomed he must have become to her barbed comments. Of course, he'd given as good as he'd got up until now, so she braced herself for a goading remark. Instead she was pleasantly surprised when he gave a half smile. "Thank you, I will. I have a proposition for you."

Her curiosity was aroused, but finding out more would have to wait. As soon as they entered the solar, Will ran up to Isobel and flung his arms around her legs, demanding a story.

"Come and sit on my lap, then," she said. In a way, it was a relief to have Will to divert Edmund's attention from her. Even when she wasn't looking at him, her spine tingled with the awareness of his presence. His actions today and being held by him on the ride home seemed to have broken down a barrier, leaving her feeling raw and vulnerable in his presence. It was a comfort to have Will there.

When she tried to think of a story to entertain Will, the only idea that came to her was the wolf. She edited the tale to play down the danger, but Will's eyes grew round as she described what Edmund had done. When she finished, he turned to Edmund with shining eyes. "Did you bring it back? Can I see it?"

Edmund shook his head. "We had nothing to carry it with, but I've sent some men to fetch it." Edmund addressed Isobel. "I thought Emmeline and her husband might find a use for the pelt."

By rights, Edmund could claim the pelt for his own. "That's very kind of you," she said. Maybe he was trying to make amends for suspecting her steward of harboring Cannington.

"Did the wolf bite you? Is that why you have a bandage on your hand?" Will asked. The story had obviously captured his imagination, taking away his shyness around Edmund.

"Not a bite, just a cut from my sword hilt."

"That reminds me, I should bathe it for you." She squeezed Will's arm. "Run to Agnes and ask her to fetch some water, linen, and yarrow leaves."

When the items arrived, Isobel drew up a table to catch the warmth from the hearth and placed a lamp on the table so she could examine the cut. She sat beside him and bathed away the blood.

There was something intimate about touching him like this. Coming so close to being held by him on their shared ride, it brought the memories flooding back. She had always loved his hands, his long, square-tipped fingers strong yet gentle. At least, they had always been gentle with her. His palms and fingers were callused now. Through wielding a sword, she guessed. How would they feel against her skin now?

She blinked away the pictures that came to her. It wasn't wise to think of him in that way. He might bear the outward scars of the recent years, but her scars were no less real even though invisible. She wasn't sure if she could endure another man's touch. Even if it was Edmund's.

Grappling for a distraction, she remembered what Edmund had said earlier. "Did you say you had a proposition for me?"

"More an offer of help."

"What do you mean?" She didn't want help. She didn't *need* help. Help was just another word for interference. She thought she'd already made it clear that she intended to run Molbren without interference from him or anyone else.

"As I tried to point out before the wolf attacked, you're going to have a problem overseeing your steward's accounts if you can't read or do arithmetic."

"I…" The heat of a flush rose to her cheeks, and she lowered her head, as though studying every line and crease on his palm, praying he wouldn't notice. "I suppose I could ask the scribe to read them for me. He read them for me this morning."

"But you were only checking to see if they said the same that I'd told you. He didn't have to interpret them for you. If you're to check Simon's accounts, you need to be able to study them for yourself."

"I'll find a way," Isobel replied. She'd been right: he did mean to interfere. He would take over, and before she knew it, Edmund would be the master of Molbren, and she would have to defer to him over even the most minor of decisions.

"Yes, you will. That's what I'm offering."

Isobel paused in patting the cut dry and looked up, startled. "You're not going to take over yourself?"

"No. It will involve hard work at first, though."

"I don't mind hard work. Just tell me your plan."

"I'll teach you to read, write, and do arithmetic."

"Do you think I can learn?" Isobel could hardly believe what she was hearing. Her mother had taught her the alphabet, but her father had put a stop to any further learning, saying she was going to be a wife, not a nun. As usual, her mother had deferred to his decision, despite Isobel begging her to try and change his mind. It had left her unable to even read or write a letter without being dependent on first her father's servants and then Sir Roger's.

What would her life be like now, if she'd been able to write a letter to Edmund instead of having to send a verbal message?

"Of course you can. You're an intelligent woman. What do you say? You might struggle at first, but think of the advantages."

Edmund clearly didn't understand how important this was to her if he thought he had to persuade her. She lowered her head to hide the welling tears. Independence. He would give her the means for true independence.

Yet, strangely, this offer of independence gave her hope for their marriage. Maybe being married to Edmund wouldn't be so terrible.

Chapter Ten

Edmund wrote a phrase and passed the parchment to Isobel. "Read this."

She ran her finger under the words as she read them out. "Six bushels of barley." She was a fast learner; aside from "bushel," she had recognized the other words on sight.

"Good. Now copy it out."

For a while the only sound in the solar was the scratch of Isobel's quill and the hiss of snow upon the window panes. Five days of snow. Five days of being unable to continue his search for Cannington. Five days of confinement in this chamber with Isobel, unable to avoid her until they parted for the night. Even then, lying alone in his chamber, he couldn't escape: the slant of her brown eyes, the curve of her lips was branded on his mind and followed him into his dreams.

On this particular day they were alone, so Edmund didn't even have Will's chatter to distract him from Isobel. In order for them both to fit between the table legs, it was necessary to sit close together. Isobel's thigh pressed his, and their arms brushed each time one of them wrote something on the page. Did each touch crackle like lightning upon her flesh as it did with his? He studied her face as she bent over the page, lips pursed, her brow furrowed in concentration, seemingly oblivious to all but the work she was absorbed in.

He should be pleased she didn't feel the same desire. Her lack of response would make it easier to subdue his own urges. Eventually.

"I'm getting better at reading and writing short phrases," Isobel said, scratching out the final "y," adding a curling flourish to its tail. "But when I look at words on a page they are all run together, I can't work them out."

Edmund rose, glad of the excuse to move. "It's time we looked at a book. Do you have one?"

Isobel nodded. "I'll fetch it."

She left the chamber and returned, carrying a large wooden box, decorated with carved flowers and birds. "It's a bestiary."

She drew out a leather-wrapped bundle and placed it on the table as gently as though it were a newborn infant. She untied the cord and peeled away the covering, revealing embossed leather, glossy from years of handling. The spine creaked as she opened the book and revealed page after page of jewel-bright pictures upon translucent vellum.

"I've seen bestiaries before, but never as magnificent as this," said Edmund, awed by the exquisite detail of the feathers in a peacock's tail.

"It was my mother's. She used to let me look through it until my father—" She clamped her mouth shut.

Edmund looked at her, surprised by her closed expression. "What did your father do?" Isobel had never told him much about her parents, except to say they were opposed to their marriage. He had never pressed her, only too aware of his own reluctance to speak of his childhood.

"Nothing. He just...he didn't like me wasting time on foolishness like looking at a bestiary when I could be learning how to be a dutiful wife. My mother, as usual, gave in without a fight."

She turned the page, and Edmund forgot the mystery of Isobel's parents, caught up in the beauty of the illustrations. Each new page brought a fresh wonder: a dolphin leaping through aquamarine waves; a crouched lion, its mane all the colors of Isobel's hair; a pale gray dove perched in the skeleton of a tree.

He glanced at the text, and his heart seized. He reached out to turn to the next page, but Isobel stopped him. "You see, the title is written in large, clear letters and I can read that: 'Turtle Dove.' But the rest of the writing is so close it's hard to pick out the individual letters. And I've longed to find out what it says. I've always thought the turtle dove looks lonely, sitting in that bare tree."

He was being foolish, taking words about a mere bird and applying them to himself. She would never know their significance. Swallowing against the thickness in his throat, he said, "We'll read it together."

With his help, Isobel formed the sounds of each word, one syllable at a time. Every now and again she would hesitate, but her confidence increased as she grew accustomed to deciphering the close letters.

"The turtle dove mates only once and remains faithful even should its mate die. When widowed, it will never more perch upon greenery but will fly to the desert." Isobel looked up. "How sad. Did you see widowed turtle doves in the desert?"

"I saw many doves, but I never paid them heed." Edmund's fingers drummed out a rhythm upon the table top. "If this page makes you sad, let's read another." Again, he tried to turn the page, but Isobel stopped him.

"Don't. I want to see what the rest of it says."

Edmund clenched his fists to stop his fidgeting. "Try reading the next line without my help." He had picked up the quill—when had that happened?—and twisted it between his fingers while Isobel bent over the page again.

The whole length of her thigh pressed against his leg. How could she concentrate with this burning heat between them? As they were alone in the solar, she had set aside her veil. Her hair, braided into a thick plait, swung over her shoulder. He only had to tilt his head a little, and he would feel its softness against his cheek. She must have washed it last night, because its sweet scent teased his nostrils. He was mere heartbeats from burying his nose in her tresses and breathing deep, savoring it in the same way he'd once seen her close her eyes in ecstasy over the taste of marchpane.

"Let that be a lesson to all who are wed," Isobel read out, oblivious to his turmoil. "God joins them into one flesh, and nothing can part them."

This was too much. Edmund sprang to his feet and paced to the table holding the wine flagon. He poured out a brimming goblet-full, slopping crimson wine into the rushes on the way back to Isobel.

Isobel was running her index finger under the words she had just read, the corners of her mouth pulled down. "Is the writer saying widows should never remarry? If so, he should blame the men who pressure them into remarriage, not the poor women who are forced into it against their will."

"I think it's more an exhortation for fidelity within

marriage."

"Then it's addressed to women alone, for it's always the woman who is expected to remain chaste, while having to turn a blind eye to her husband's philandering."

"You should take care to remove the log from your own eye before pointing your finger. Remember you were still married to me when you wed Sir Roger." The words poured out before he could stop them. A flood of bitterness and bile pent up within his heart that he'd scarcely been aware of.

Isobel sprang to her feet, fire in her eyes. "How dare you blame me for that? You know I was forced. Would you have your own son branded a bastard? Besides, you can't expect me to believe *you* remained chaste for five whole years."

"If I make a promise, I keep it. And I promised to remain faithful."

The shock on Isobel's face must surely be mirrored on his own. God's bones, how had that slipped out? He'd never meant Isobel to know. Not when the knowledge would tip the balance of power in her favor.

Isobel opened her mouth, then closed it. There was silence in the room, save for their ragged breaths and the blood pounding in Edmund's ears. Isobel's eyes searched his face, then after a pause that stretched out for eternity, her face cleared. "Oh," she said, and sank down upon the chair as though her legs would no longer support her.

****

He had remained faithful! Throughout all those years he had never strayed. Her heart swelled. He still saw her as his wife.

113

He was still hers alone.

Edmund held his hands to the flames, turning his face away from her, but not before she caught the dismay in his eyes. Of course he wouldn't have wanted her to know. Especially as…

The warmth leached out of the room. Especially as she had obviously not been faithful. She opened her mouth, longing to tell him what Sir Roger had done to her. How he had forced her when all along her heart had bled for Edmund. Her throat ached with the words she longed to say, but it was as though her voice was paralyzed. There were no words that could adequately describe what she had endured. Even if it meant Edmund despised her forever, she didn't possess the courage to give voice to her experience.

In the end all she could say was, "It must have taken great strength to hold to your vows." Whatever else stood between them, she didn't want him to think she saw his fidelity as a weakness. No, she was the weak one, unable even to put her fear into words.

It was like being locked in her room all over again, unable to communicate. If she could only reach him, explain, there was a chance she could regain his trust. But she couldn't have been more helpless if she truly was behind a barred door.

Then Edmund returned to the table, his face a mask. "It's futile to dwell on such things." He pulled the bestiary toward him and turned the page. "Your reading is improving every day. Now read the next page."

The black slash of his brows sent his message as clearly as words: *We will never speak of this again.* She turned to the book with the burden of fear still heavy on her heart. It was too late; the opportunity for confidences was gone.

****

Gratitude. On the day Edmund had arrived in Molbren, if someone had told Isobel that before long her anger toward him would be replaced by gratitude, she'd have accused them of insanity. But now she had to admit Edmund had done her a great favor. Under his tutelage her reading and writing was vastly improved, and soon she would be able to interpret her steward's accounts. More than that, she now had the wherewithal to write and read letters, to communicate with people beyond the bounds of Molbren without the help of a scribe.

Instead of chaining her down, Edmund had set her free. Above everything else, she now knew he'd remained faithful to her all this time.

However, she wasn't altogether comfortable with this new feeling. Edmund had given her this great gift and what had she given him in return? She hated to be indebted to anyone, least of all him.

It was only the morning after their lesson with the bestiary that the answer dawned on her. Will. She had given him Will. Yet so far, aside from allowing Edmund to see him, she'd done nothing to promote their relationship. Edmund was still awkward with Will, and Will was shy around Edmund. What she could do for Edmund in return was help him get close to his son. What might bring them together? At any other time, the obvious answer would be to take him riding, but even though the sun had finally returned, the snow was still far too deep.

A delighted smile curved her lips. Of course! The

snow. And not only would it give them a chance to get closer, she hoped it would bring back Edmund's playful side.

****

Isobel lagged behind as they crossed the bailey. She wanted to observe Edmund with Will. Will jumped from one unmarked patch of snow to the next in his quest to make a clear trail of footprints. Thankfully the snow was packed hard; otherwise he would have sunk up to his knees with all that had fallen over the past days.

They picked their way to the postern gate on the south wall and waited while Edmund wrenched open the frozen bolt. The gate opened onto the orchard: a wide area between the outer wall of the castle and the river cliff. A red sandstone wall marked its outer limits. It was usually a green space, the grass cropped short by a handful of goats allowed to roam freely. However, the goats had been moved to stalls for the winter while a thick, white blanket smothered the grass. Now the orchard was a sparkling cathedral, pillared with apple, pear, and damson trees, its vaulting a latticework of frost-rimed branches. Even the thatched hut beside the outer wall had been transformed into a glittering fairy howe by the snow.

"What shall we do first?" Will clung to Isobel's skirts, casting sideways glances at Edmund. She'd hoped Will's naturally playful nature would overcome his wariness once he was in such a magical location, but it seemed he would need to be helped along.

"What games did you play in the snow when you were a boy?" she asked Edmund.

"I never played in the snow."

Isobel looked at him in disbelief. "Surely everyone played in the snow as a child? Even my mother played with me and helped me build snowmen." Until her father had put a stop to it.

"Not mine."

His face was closed. Isobel started to wonder if this outing was doomed from the outset. She wished now she had made more of an effort to find out about his childhood when they had been lovers all those years ago. At the time, the present had seemed so sweet; she had believed the past powerless to touch them, but now she wondered if it would have eventually reached out to destroy them, even then, when their love had felt strong enough to take on the world. What terrible deed had his parents done, that even now he refused to talk about it?

A glance at Will's face showed it crumpled in disappointment. For his sake she had to try, even if Edmund could never care for her in the same way again.

She forced a smile. "I know—we can build a snow castle." She bent down and scooped up a handful of snow, grateful for her sheepskin gloves. She piled on more snow, forming it into a high mound. "Look. This will be the donjon."

Will dashed to the pile, giggling, and plunged his hands into the snow. "Yes, we can build our own ice castle! I'll make the great hall."

Isobel smiled at him. "What a good idea." She cast a glance at Edmund. He was hovering a few paces away, studying the overhanging branch of a pear tree, looking as though he would rather be fighting off a horde of Saracens with naught but an eating knife. "You've been to more castles than I, Edmund. What else do you think we need to keep it safe from enemies?"

Edmund watched them for a while. "You need firm foundations," he said finally. "Your tower is already starting to lean." He paced out a circle beside them, compressing the snow into a firm pack, each step making a pleasing crunch. "Build your castle here, and it will be much stronger."

Isobel eyed the area, her eyebrows raising when it dawned on her how large a space Edmund had firmed up. "This will be a castle fit for a king if we're to fill an area that size."

The corner of Edmund's mouth quirked. "I don't believe in doing things by halves. If we're going to build a snow castle, I want it to be the finest in the kingdom."

"Me too!" Will flung himself upon his knees and scooped up more snow. "I want to make the biggest castle in the whole world!"

Soon Will forgot his shyness and worked side by side with Edmund, asking him about castles in the Holy Land. The cold was forgotten as the castle rose toward the snow-laden branches overhead. It warmed Isobel's heart to see Will's eager smile as Edmund showed him how to carve out crenellations into the top of each tower.

Although she hadn't been aware of her tense vigilance whenever Edmund was with Will, its relaxation lightened her heart. If Edmund didn't do anything to destroy Will's trust, she would hold to her decision and tell Will Edmund was his true father. Even if speaking the truth wasn't so important to her, she was aware more and more of the need to show Edmund how grateful she was to him for providing her with the means to be independent. It was the last thing she had dreamed would happen when she'd been compelled to agree to marriage. She doubted there were many men who would have taken the trouble to teach her.

"Look, Mama—the donjon is finished." Will's voice brought her back from her introspection.

"It's wonderful." She crouched to examine the gleaming steps, the hollowed out doorways and windows, and the jagged battlements. "What are those for?" She indicated a pile of snowballs heaped upon the top of the tower.

Will grinned. "For fighting off the enemy."

He seized a snowball and hurled it in her direction. There was no time to dodge; it struck her shoulder in a burst of glittering powder.

She squealed in mock rage and scooped up a handful of snow which she flung back. In moments, they were engaged in a full battle over the castle. Seeing Edmund standing to one side, a bemused frown wrinkling his brow, she dared to launch one of her snowballs in his direction. It hit him in the chest, but she had no time to savor her strike before he threw one back at her.

Will cried out, "Kill the Black Knight!" And flung a snowball which struck Edmund square upon his nose, eliciting a most unknightly curse.

Will gasped, his face turning as white as the snow. Saints preserve him, the poor boy must be expecting a beating. He had no way of knowing Edmund would never hurt him. Unlike Sir Roger. She made a dash for him, but before she could reach him, her feet slipped upon the packed snow, and she fell with a thump upon her back. She floundered to rise, watching the fear growing on Will's face.

"Will, it's—"

But her reassurance was interrupted by a most unexpected sound—Edmund threw back his head and laughed. Will, after a brief gasp of shock, joined in.

The years fell from Edmund before her eyes. His face lit with merriment, and the bleak shadow that had clung to him during his entire stay dispersed as though blown away in the breeze. "That was a fine shot, Master Will," he said, lines of laughter creasing the corners of his eyes. "You'll grow up to be a great warrior."

Then he strode up to Isobel and grasped her hand, raising her to her feet. Her heart fluttered. Was it her imagination, or did his clasp linger several heartbeats longer than was necessary? Part of her that still remembered the heady excitement of their trysts thrilled at the touch.

But there was a reason for Will's fear. A similar fear lurked in her own heart. She snatched her hand free and turned to Will.

"That's enough for today. It's time to get into the warm before we freeze."

She couldn't meet Edmund's eye as they trudged back to the solar. He had proved that he was ready to be a father to Will. It would be wrong to keep the truth from Will any longer. Yet she was afraid what that would mean for her.

Edmund had kept his word: he hadn't pressed her, hadn't told Will the truth without her consent. But now it was time to fulfill her end of the bargain.

The moment Agnes took Will to bed that night, leaving them alone in the solar, she said, "I need to speak to you about Will."

"What's the matter? I thought we got along well today."

"You did. I'm not criticizing. I don't want to lie to anyone about you any more, least of all to Will. You've made every effort to gain his trust, and I know it's not been easy."

Edmund's shoulders relaxed. "What do you want to do?"

"I want to tell Will you're his true father."

And after that, there would be no excuse for delaying the wedding.

Chapter Eleven

Today was a momentous day. At first light, Edmund climbed to the now familiar lookout point on the walls and regarded the western hills. In the soft light of dawn, they glowed a pale salmon. No more snow had fallen, but the cold was intense, preserving the huge drifts in motionless waves across the landscape. Only the foolhardiest of men would venture out, even if they weren't trapped inside behind a wall of snow.

No. He could stay in today with a clear conscience. If Cannington was in the area—and Edmund felt in his bones that he must be—he would be unable to make his escape for a few days yet.

Today was all about Will. Strange, then, that when he thought about yesterday's play in the orchard, all he could see was Isobel. When he had helped her to her feet, she had smiled up at him, the first unguarded smile she'd given. It struck him in the chest with more force than a crossbow bolt. For one heart-stopping instant, all he wanted to do was pull her into his arms and kiss her. It was a good thing Will had been there, or he might never have controlled himself.

Will. He should think of Will, not Isobel. Today they would tell Will the truth. It was high time. He had agreed to let Isobel choose when it happened, but already he'd caught Joss looking from Will to him with narrowed eyes. If they were to prevent unseemly gossip, they must be married soon. Telling Will was the first step.

Once the snow started to clear, he could resume his search and leave Molbren behind before Isobel could threaten his heart.

Isobel, Will, and Agnes were all in the solar when he walked in. Isobel paled, obviously worried how Will would react, but she set her mouth in a determined line and drew Will to her side.

"Come and sit with us for a moment," she said, settling in one of the fireside chairs and pulling Will onto her lap. She indicated that Edmund should take a seat opposite.

Agnes took a step toward the door, but Isobel held up her hand. "No—stay," she said. "You already know what we're about to say, and there's no reason to keep it secret any longer."

Agnes nodded, shooting a glance between Will and Edmund. It was clear to Edmund that she knew exactly what Isobel meant. How many others knew the secret? Were tongues wagging all round the castle and beyond? If so, it was best to tell the lad now rather than risk Will hearing the news from another source. Any lingering doubt that this was the wrong course fled, although how Will would take the news was another matter. The play in the orchard had gone a long way toward breaking down the barriers between them, but it would be a while before Will was truly comfortable with him.

Isobel placed a hand on Will's shoulder. "The truth is, this may come as a shock to you, Will, but Sir Roger wasn't your real father."

Will's face had been screwed up as he gazed up at his mother, but now it relaxed. "Oh, I already knew that, Mama."

Isobel bit her lip and hugged Will close. "You did? How?"

"One day I was in the solar playing with my horses, and he came looking for you. He trod on Dapple and said a bad word. Then he shook me and told me he was glad I wasn't his." Isobel pulled Will even closer, her fingers gripping the green wool of his tunic, her knuckles white.

Edmund fought the urge to close the distance between them and pull them both into his embrace. He hadn't been there for them then, but he would do all in his power to keep them safe from now on.

"He said as soon as he had got another heir on you, he would send me to a monstery. What's a monstery, Mama? Is it where monsters live?"

Isobel answered, her voice muffled against Will's hair. "He meant a monastery, my heart. It's where monks live. Why didn't you tell me?"

"He told me not to say a word to you, or he would send me away for sure."

Edmund's blood ran cold. No doubt if he had managed to get another heir, Sir Roger would have ensured Will never left the monastery. His heart burned to think of this sunny natured boy living under a shadow of fear. He knew only too well how it felt to fear the man who was supposed to be a father and protector. To think his own son had lived under that shadow and he'd never known.

Isobel's face had blanched. Guessing she was incapable of speech, he hastened to say, "I won't send you away, Will. You have nothing to fear from me. You'll stay with your mother until you're old enough."

Isobel shot him a look of gratitude, but Will stepped back from her embrace. "But who is my father, Mama?"

"It's Lord Edmund. We were married when we were young."

Edmund was glad she didn't attempt to explain any further. There was time enough when he was older and able to understand. For now all he needed was the bare facts.

"You're my heir, Will," he said. "You'll be Earl of Redmarch one day."

Isobel straightened up and gave Will an anxious look. "Do you mind, Will? I'm sorry I didn't tell you the truth earlier."

Will gave her a beaming smile. "I'm glad. I like Lord Edmund. We had fun with him yesterday. I never had fun with Father."

Edmund drew a breath, envying the boy his simple acceptance. He followed Will with his gaze as he went over to his toys and resumed play with his wooden horses, then turned to Isobel. "Considering what he's been through, he's remarkably unscarred. He has you to thank for that. You are a good mother, Isobel. I couldn't hope for a better mother for my heir."

Isobel gave a tight smile. "Perhaps, but I shall have nightmares about what he's just told me. I can't bear to think of him living in fear of being sent away."

Silvery tears clung to her lashes, and Edmund placed a hand on her shoulder. "I'm sorry I wasn't there for either of you before, but I am now. I won't let anyone else harm him or you."

A movement caught his eye, and he looked up to see Agnes nod at him with a smile and then leave the solar. He felt as though he had passed a test.

He lowered his voice so Will wouldn't hear, although a quick glance revealed the boy so lost in his make-believe world, he doubted Will would hear even if he sounded a hunting horn. "I've kept my word and haven't pressed you, but the longer I remain, the more likely people are to guess I'm Will's father. We must announce our marriage soon."

Isobel twisted her hands. "I know. I need a little more time, that's all."

"What for? I want to proclaim Will as my heir before folk start whispering lies about him. About us. Do you still doubt I'll make a good father?"

"No. It's…it's me." Then in a rush, "You're not the only one to carry scars from our time apart. Please…please leave. My head aches too much for a lesson today."

She called after him, halting him at the door. "But for what it's worth, I know you'll make a good father."

****

A good father. Isobel's parting words stayed with him all day and followed him into his dreams. He awoke with a jolt, the last wisps of nightmare still clinging to him. He flung back the rumpled blankets and sat up, gazing at a point on the bed hangings while he waited for his breathing to steady. He hadn't snuffed the lamps last night; most of them had burned themselves out, but two rushlights still gave off a smoky glow in their niches beside the door. It was enough to see that he was in the guest chamber at Molbren. Not the cramped chamber he'd been locked in after his father had rebelled.

God's breath, why now? He hadn't dreamed of his

time as a hostage in all the years he'd fought and faced the horror of war. Why should his nightmares return now, when he was in a place of safety?

He swung his legs out of bed and pulled on his clothes. It was pointless trying to sleep any more tonight. There were still three candles on the table that had a good half of their height remaining. He picked one up and lit it from one of the guttering rushlights. He would go over his maps again, see if he had missed anything.

He sifted through the documents scattered upon the table. Hellfire! The one map he wanted to study wasn't there. He must have left it in the solar. Isobel had hustled him out so suddenly he'd forgotten to pick it up. Of course, it had to be that map. It was the only one showing the area east of the castle, and he thought that might be the first area to search; the high hill where the castle stood had probably sheltered it from the worst of the snow. The question was, would he rather go back to his warm bed and risk more nightmares, or walk through the freezing courtyard in the dark?

Put like that, it wasn't a difficult choice at all. He pulled on his cloak and boots. At least the frigid wind might chase away his dark dreams.

A short while later, his toes freezing from the deep snow, he climbed the outer steps to the donjon and slipped inside. The guards were used to his presence by now, so he reached the solar unchallenged. His shadow danced on the whitewashed walls as he crept to the desk and searched through the scrolls and scraps of parchment.

A soft noise from one of the chambers on the far side of the solar made him pause. Was that a sob? It came again, and now he recognized Will's voice. Perhaps he should wake Isobel. She would know what to do. On the other hand, it would be a shame to wake her if Will was simply crying out in his sleep.

On silent feet, he made his way through the inner passageway to Will's chamber. At the sight of Will curled tightly on his side, hugging a pillow, Edmund's heart constricted.

He perched on the edge of the bed. "What's the matter, Will?"

Will's head whipped round, and the moment he saw Edmund he flung himself into his arms and buried his head in Edmund's stomach. "Bad dream," came the muffled reply.

Edmund hesitated, his hand hovering over Will's head. Then he brushed the tousled curls as he'd seen Isobel do. "It must be the night for it. I've been kept awake by nightmares as well. Would you like to come into the solar with me for a while?"

Will nodded, so Edmund wrapped a blanket around the boy's shoulders and helped him on with some light shoes, then took him by the hand and led him out of the chamber, cautioning him to be quiet so as not to wake Isobel.

After tossing more logs upon the fire, he sat on the settle and lifted Will beside him. "Do you often get bad dreams?"

Will glanced at him, his chin wobbling. Judging from his wary look, he didn't feel comfortable enough with Edmund to talk to him yet. Well, that was understandable. Edmund, too, felt out of his depth. Talking to the boy about horses or playing in the snow was one thing but sharing his deepest thoughts and fears was a step too far.

Remembering how they had got along when looking after his horse gave him an idea, however. What they needed was an activity to take their minds off the dreams. Casting about the chamber for inspiration, his eyes fell on the quills and ink upon the desk.

"Have you tried writing yet, Will?"

"Like Mama?" An eager smile transformed Will's face.

"That's right. Would you like to have a go?"

Will nodded. "Can you show me how to write my name?"

"If you like." He placed a thick cushion on a chair to raise Will to the correct height and then lifted him, blanket and all, onto the chair and pulled it up to the table. Then he took a seat next to him and inspected the quills until he found one cut into a sturdy, short nib less likely to split under Will's unpracticed hand. Finally, he chose a quill of his own and selected a scrap of parchment.

"Now, watch what I do." He dipped the quill into the ink pot and brought the quill over to the parchment and scratched out a large W. "There. That's the first letter in your name."

"Can I try?"

"Go on, then. See if you can write it below the one I wrote."

His tongue clamped between his teeth, Will jabbed his quill into the ink pot, causing Edmund to grab it before Will knocked it over and spilled ink over all the parchment. Then Will swung his hand across to the parchment. His face fell when he saw the splashes of ink trailing all the way from the pot. "Oh. That didn't happen to you."

"Don't worry. You'll make less of a mess with practice. Everyone does that at first."

"Even you?"

"Especially me. I remember my first lesson—I knocked the ink pot over and splashed ink all over the tunic of one of old King Henry's chief advisers."

Will giggled, and the last of the shadow left by Edmund's nightmare finally faded. He should remember that not all his time as a hostage had been dark. King Henry had seen to it that he had received an education, and his tutors had been kindly men. When he'd cowered away from the adviser whose tunic he had ruined, fearing a beating, the man had laughed, saying he'd worn his oldest clothes, expecting something of the sort. He remembered wishing the adviser had been his father instead.

He watched as Will scrawled a wobbly W upon the parchment, dripping more ink in the process and even managing to get a smear of ink on his nose. "Wonderful," he said, even though it looked more like a bird's footprint in the snow. "The next letter is easier."

They worked together until Will had managed to write his name in a wavering hand, punctuated by several large blots. Will beamed with pride. "I can't wait to show Mama in the morning." He flung his arms around Edmund. "Thank you, Papa."

Papa. Edmund froze, swallowing to clear the thickness in his throat.

Will raised his head, revealing furrows between his dark brows. The mirror image of his mother when she puzzled over a problem. "Can I call you Papa?"

He looked so worried that Edmund thrust aside his reservation. "Of course." He blinked to clear the sudden blur from his eyes. He must be growing tired. That would explain why his voice had become so husky.

Will beamed at him. "Thank you, Papa. I didn't know what to call you before, but Papa feels right."

Papa. He was a father. Will was his son. He'd been so focused on claiming Will as his heir that he'd not taken a moment to consider how he felt about being a father, having a son. His heart swelled until he was afraid it would burst from his chest.

He loved Will. The knowledge hit him like a mace. He had been so busy guarding his heart against Isobel, he hadn't considered the effect Will was having on him. And now it was too late. All he knew was a driving urge to protect Will and ensure his happiness. He couldn't bear the thought of leaving him.

Quite what it would mean for his relationship with Isobel, he didn't know. He needed time to think.

His attention was drawn back to Will when he yawned, revealing all his teeth.

"It's time I took you back to bed."

"Oh, but the bad dreams might come back."

"What do you usually do when you have nightmares?"

Will's brow crinkled. "Mama comes to talk to me. She tells me it helps to talk about them, to make them go away."

"Does it work?" Edmund had never breathed a word of his nightmares to a soul.

"Usually."

"Would you like to tell me about the dream you had tonight?"

Will's slate blue eyes fixed upon his face, as though assessing him. Finally he nodded.

Seeing his eyelids drooping, Edmund carried him back to the settle and sat him on his lap, wrapped in his blanket. "Tell me all about it."

"I dreamed about Father." Will's mouth quivered. "He was hurting Mama."

Edmund tasted bile. This was no nightmare that faded upon waking. It was all too real. He was familiar with that sort of nightmare himself and prayed Will wouldn't be haunted for years unending in the way he had.

"I wanted to go to her"—Will's voice hitched in a sob—"but I was scared and hid instead."

This time Edmund didn't hesitate but hugged Will close and answered the question he guessed Will had been too afraid to ask. "That doesn't make you a coward or a bad person, Will. I can promise you, your Mama would have far rather you stayed hidden and safe, than been hurt yourself."

"That's what she says, but—"

"No 'buts,' Will. You're too small to defend anyone. At the moment, it's up to your Mama and me to look after you and defend you, with our lives if necessary. When you're older, I'll teach you all you need to know about fighting so you can learn to defend those you love. But until then, trust us to take care of you."

A tremulous smile crept across Will's face. "Truly?"

"On my honor."

Will snuggled closer. "I'm glad you're my father."

Edmund's heart swelled. "I'm sorry I wasn't there

for you before, but I promise to be a better father from now on." As soon as the words left his lips, he wondered if he'd made a mistake. In effect, it was a promise to stay at Molbren; if he was to take his duties as father seriously, he had to be there for Will. But then he looked down at Will and knew it was the right thing to do. Whether Isobel liked it or not, either he stayed at Molbren, or Will and Isobel must come to Redmarch.

Chapter Twelve

"Look what I did, Mama." Will thrust a blotted piece of parchment into Isobel's hand the moment she stepped into the solar. "I wrote my name."

She looked at the blotched scrawl. "That's lovely, Will. Who helped you do that?"

"Papa."

"Papa? You mean Lord Edmund?"

He nodded, shaking his hair into his eyes. "I call him Papa now. He said I could."

Isobel wrinkled her brow. How long had she been asleep? She felt like a character from a bard's tale, returning to his village after a night spent in a fairy howe, only to find a thousand years had passed. "He did? When did this happen?"

"Last night. I had a bad dream, and he came and let me sit with him in the solar."

Isobel's heart twisted. "I'm sorry I didn't hear you, my heart. I would have come to you if I had."

"Don't worry, Mama. Papa must have already been up because I didn't cry for long."

At least it looked like Edmund was learning how to be a father to Will. That was good. Will needed a father he could look up to, emulate. She drew him close and hugged him, burying her nose in his hair, breathing in his familiar scent. "I'm glad he was there for you." It crossed her mind to wonder what he'd been doing in the donjon at night, but she dismissed it. It wasn't worth accusing him of taking liberties he had no right to. Besides, they would soon be married, and then the whole of Molbren would be his by right.

Will nodded and wriggled out of her arms. "I think he had bad dreams too, but he didn't say what about. I hope they don't come back."

He went to play in the window seat, and Isobel sank down beside her tapestry frame. She'd left the needle threaded with a deep green thread, ready to create ivy leaves twining around the trees, but she left it where it was, tucked into the edge of the canvas.

Edmund had done everything she'd asked of him and more. He needn't have gone to Will last night, but he had. And Will looked much happier than he usually did, the morning after a bad night. Whatever Edmund had said or done had worked. He was proving he could be a good father. In fact, there was no other man she would trust with Will.

All that remained was the wedding. Her stomach knotted. When they'd entered into their clandestine marriage, she hadn't felt any fear. But now…

She rose. Putting it off would only make the anticipation worse. She'd rather face up to her fear than let it grow out of proportion.

"Where is Lord Edmund now, Will?"

"I'm here." Edmund stood in the doorway. From his tousled hair and reddened face, she guessed he had been outside.

"Will tells me you were here last night." It came out in an accusatory tone she hadn't meant. Clearly it was going to take time to get out of the habit of shooting barbs at one another.

"I couldn't sleep and came to collect a map. I wouldn't have stayed, but I heard Will."

Now she came to study his face, she could see the shadows of a poor night around his eyes and mouth. Perhaps Will had been right, and he had also had nightmares. She waved away his unspoken apology. "It doesn't matter." She looked to see where Will was. Good. He was still playing in the window seat out of earshot. "I need to speak to you."

"About what I said yesterday?" Edmund also threw a glance at Will.

She nodded. "I thought about little else for the rest of the day, and what Will has just told me has made up my mind. You're right. It's pointless to put this off any longer, and we need to act to stop gossip." She was struck with the urge to laugh. Her practical reasoning was a cruel contrast to Edmund's impassioned declaration five years ago.

The corner of Edmund's mouth quirked, and she guessed the same thought had occurred to him. Strange how they could still share each other's thoughts even with the wide gulf separating them. "In that case there's no reason to wait any longer. If the men can clear the drifts from the gate, I'm going to search the manor beyond the village. I'll send word to the priest to perform the ceremony tomorrow."

"Tomorrow?" She'd been expecting a week's grace at least.

Edmund frowned. "Isobel, we can't afford to wait. Joss already has his suspicions. I don't like this secrecy. The sooner I can openly proclaim Will my heir, the better."

"Tomorrow." Isobel clutched her garnet cross.

One day, one week, what difference did it make? Her life was about to be bound to Edmund's again, and nothing would prevent it. At least she was confident he would be good to Will. "Tomorrow it is. I'll make the arrangements."

As soon as Edmund left, she sank upon a chair and gazed at her hands. So today was to be the last day of her independence. Then she glanced up at Will, lost in his imaginary world. This was for his sake. Edmund was right. Will did deserve to know his true father, to be Edmund's heir. And in these troubled times, her people would be reassured to know they had the might of Redmarch to defend them. She had been deluded to hope she could continue alone.

Drawing a deep breath, she rose to her feet. First she must tell Will, then there were preparations to be made. The people of Molbren hadn't had much to celebrate recently, but now their lady and new lord were to be married. She would give them a feast to remember.

****

Isobel hunched beneath her vair-lined mantle, only half listening to the priest as he spoke the opening words of the marriage service. Despite her servants having shoveled aside the snow from the chapel door, it was still up to her ankles and soaked through the thin leather of her boots, numbing her toes. She cast her eyes across the small crowd that had gathered to witness the marriage. For there would be witnesses to this rite. No one could force her to pretend it hadn't happened this time. The whole of her household was here, and even some of the villagers had struggled up the hill through snowdrifts. Several of them, including the priest, coughed and sniffled, but clearly had no intention of letting a minor head cold prevent them seeing their Lady Isobel become the Countess of Redmarch.

She caught sight of Will, standing beside Agnes. He was gazing wide-eyed at her, and she summoned up a quick smile to reassure him. He was the reason she was doing this. Marrying Edmund would make Will heir to an earldom. She was trading her independence for Will's sake, and it was pointless to regret what she had lost. Although if Edmund chose to spend as much time as possible away from Molbren, it would make life easier for her. The past five years had taught her that men invariably made choices to serve their own ends without considering the hurt to others. She wouldn't get close to Edmund only for him to let her down.

Edmund wanted his heir and his reward from the king. He didn't want her.

"Lady Isobel, do you freely consent to take Edmund Granville as your husband?" The priest's hoarse voice startled her to the present.

"I freely consent." This was the best thing for Will. She had to tell herself that. Focus on anything but the inevitable moment that loomed closer. Ever since Edmund had announced his intention to make their marriage official, she had learned to force the approaching event from her mind, focus on Will, her people, her tapestry. Anything. But this time her mind couldn't fix on anything else.

The priest droned on, although her mind refused to focus on the words. She shivered. Nothing to do with the cold: the source of this chill was deep in her core, and it spread through her body until every muscle and tendon was so tense and stiff she was afraid something might snap. If only she could come up with a distraction to take her mind off the images flooding her mind. Of Sir Roger, the reek of sour wine on his breath, the pain, the humiliation.

Edmund would never treat her like that, but even that knowledge couldn't chase away her fear.

"Place the ring on the book." The priest's words reached through her turmoil. The ring. Isobel clawed hold of the offered distraction. Edmund could hardly have come to Molbren prepared to marry. He wouldn't have a ring.

Edmund, however, didn't hesitate. He reached into the neck of his tunic and unclasped a silver chain, removing a ring that hung upon it. He placed it upon the priest's prayer book.

The painful memories faded. They would return, Isobel didn't doubt it, but she gratefully clung on to this new thread of memory. The ring was a delicate golden band set with seed pearls. It was all Edmund had been able to afford five years ago. It was the ring he had slipped onto her finger, vowing to love her until his dying day. Only a few days later, she had removed it to send with her messenger, begging him to come to her.

It was hard to believe one tiny object could represent so much love, hope, and pain. Even harder to comprehend why Edmund had kept it, when he thought she had rejected him. Her heart fluttering, she glanced at Edmund, but his face was turned toward the priest, his profile showing no more expression than a stone effigy.

****

As soon as the priest concluded the marriage ritual

with a final blessing, the chapel doors were flung open. Edmund and Isobel moved inside to celebrate their first Mass as husband and wife. Edmund stamped his feet to restore their feeling, then knelt beside Isobel at the altar. The priest might as well not exist for all the attention he paid to the man. No matter how Edmund tried to concentrate on the droning chant, his gaze kept sliding sideways to Isobel. His wife.

Not that she ever looked at him. Her eyes remained downcast, fixed on the gold and pearl band, which she twisted around her finger. Hellfire! What must she be thinking—that he'd kept the ring because he'd been pining after her for the past five years? Wearing the chain had become a habit, nothing more. He didn't love her, and the sooner he made that clear, the better.

If only he could get the message through to his body. As the service progressed the discomfort of the hard stone pressing into his knees faded into insignificance compared to the exquisite torment of having Isobel beside him. She knelt so close her hip pressed into his thigh with the slightest shift in position. Her rosewater scent teased him, and when she parted her lips to receive the communion bread… Blessed Jesu, would the torture never end?

But it only increased. When they processed through the great hall, the minstrels struck up a tune on pipes, shawm, and tabor. Men and women linked hands and flung themselves into a circle dance. Edmund's heartbeat sped up, chasing the pulse of the tabor, and the urge to sweep her into the dance flooded his veins. He had seen her dance before, remembered the dreamy look in her eyes, the flush highlighting her cheeks as she surrendered herself to the music. Would she respond the same way now?

He watched her as they walked to the dais. She wore her crimson gown, which hugged her body, emphasizing the curve of her breasts, the enticing sway of her hips. His mouth went dry. Blessed Virgin, he shouldn't feel this way. This marriage was for the sake of claiming his heir, nothing more. He must guard his heart. Concentrate on his mission for the king. Certainly not think about unlacing her gown, slipping his hand inside and feeling the heat of her flesh through her thin linen shift...

The minstrel playing the tabor beat a faster rhythm, matching the pounding of Edmund's heart.

They had just reached the high table when he caught a glimpse of her eyes. The fear in them doused his desire as effectively as the dash of cold water, but awoke his protectiveness.

"Sit." He guided her to her seat, then poured her a cup of mead and ladled a selection of food onto her trencher. While he picked at a dish of smoked eel, Isobel gazed across the hall with unfocused eyes, fidgeting with her ring. Her food remained untouched. If he didn't know better, he'd have thought her nervous about the upcoming bedding rite, but Isobel was no virgin. Surely she had no reason to fear.

The wave of jealousy caught him unawares. Isobel was his and had been for five years. The thought of her in Sir Roger's bed brought bitter bile to his throat. Not even a mouthful of mead could entirely chase it away. He was foolish to care. Their love had long since died, and he had no wish to resurrect it. He would never give way to the weakness of love again.

Isobel picked up her cup, her arm brushing his. He

sucked in an abrupt breath at the jolt of pleasure that shot down his spine. She shot him an enquiring glance, so he blurted the first thing that came to mind.

"Is something wrong? You've barely touched your food."

Isobel shook her head and pushed away her trencher. "I'm not hungry." Then after a pause: "Why did you keep this ring?" Her tone was abrupt, almost as though the words had slipped out before she could frame a more careful sentence.

Edmund grimaced. "Not here." This wasn't something he wanted to discuss in public. "Wait until we're alone." In the bridal chamber. The deepening flush on Isobel's cheeks told him her thoughts matched his.

She rose. "Then let's go now." Only the rapid rise and fall of her cross pendant and her hands clasped tightly against her stomach belied her calm voice.

The priest rose also. "My lady, you can't leave yet. There's the blessing of the bridal bed to—"

"No. Not...not that." She shot Edmund an anguished look which told him without words precisely how much she dreaded the bedding revels. Strange he should still read her thoughts so easily.

"But my lady—"

"You heard her." Edmund stared the priest down when he opened his mouth to protest. This was the first time Isobel had made a plea for help, no matter that it was silent. It awoke a deep desire to protect. "My wife and I can find our way to the bridal chamber without an escort." The priest hesitated then sank back into his chair.

Edmund took Isobel's hand and led her from the

hall. She didn't say a word, but her hand trembled in his. When the door closed behind them, it muffled the music, but the throb of the drumbeat followed them across the courtyard.

Even though there had been less than a day to prepare for the wedding, someone had found time to decorate the bridal chamber. In the absence of flowers, garlands of holly, ivy, and mistletoe twined around the bedposts. The glowing fire, herb-strewn floor rushes, and bright tapestries created a warm, welcoming atmosphere, but Isobel pulled her mantle closer around her and shivered. She looked down at the ring visible upon her clenched fist.

Edmund strode to a table which held a jug and two silver goblets. He picked up the jug and sniffed at the contents. Hippocras. Whoever had left it there clearly didn't know Isobel's tastes; she had always hated hippocras. He opened the door and summoned a servant.

"Fetch us a jug of mead." Then, remembering Isobel had eaten nothing during the hastily prepared wedding feast, he added, "And bring some marchpane as well."

When he turned back to the room, Isobel had seated herself by the fireplace, her hands stretched toward the heat.

This awkward silence between them was so unlike their previous wedding day. They hadn't had a bridal bed then, just their cloaks draped across a bale of hay. There had been no priest to bless them, or crowd of merrymakers to wish them well at their feast, but none of that had mattered. All he had cared about was the fierce flare of joy that came with knowing she willingly joined her life to his and nothing could separate them.

It just went to show how foolish he had been. Now, with all circumstances seemingly on their side, he had never felt further from her.

A soft knock at the door heralded the servant's return with a jug of mead and a platter of marchpane sweetmeats molded into delicate flowers. He took the tray and returned to the table to pour out two brimming goblets of mead. "Drink this; it will help."

She took a sip, and the tension eased from her shoulders. Then when he offered her the sweetmeats, a rosy flush crept up her cheeks. "You remembered I like marchpane."

She took a bite of a crumbly rose. The look on her face transported Edmund back to the day when he had gone to meet Isobel bearing a napkin wrapping a handful of marchpane treats left over from a banquet, knowing how she craved the costly sweets. She had closed her eyes in ecstasy as she tasted them, and Edmund had given in to impulse and kissed her. It had been their first kiss. To this day, he couldn't smell almonds without remembering how they tasted upon her lips.

Maybe Isobel remembered that day too, because her blush deepened. She placed the plate upon the table and twisted the pearl ring around her finger. "You still haven't answered my question. Why did you keep the ring all these years?"

"I became accustomed to wearing it; that is all. I forgot I had it most of the time." He would never tell her it had become a talisman, a reminder never to give his heart again.

When he had bought the ring from a stall at St

Giles' Fair, it had been all he could afford. But that hadn't mattered. The luster of the pearls reminded him of the glow of her milky skin. *Ma belle*, he had called her—my beauty. After her betrayal—no, not betrayal, he had to remind himself, despite what he had believed all these years. After their separation, he had kept the ring. At first he'd waited for her to send word to him, firmly believing he would soon restore it to her. When it became apparent no word would come, he had kept the ring on its chain, its constant weight over his heart a reminder never to be taken in by love again.

"I'm surprised you'd want a permanent reminder of that time," Isobel said. "I expected you to choose a different ring."

"Believe it or not, I didn't come to Molbren planning to marry. This was the only ring I had." But he had been glad to use it. Now if he weakened and forgot the wound his love had caused him—and the saints knew he was finding it difficult to ignore Isobel's allure—he had but to look at the ring on her finger to remember to guard his heart.

"Of course. I wasn't thinking," Isobel replied. "But it was a shock to see it. I thought…thought you were trying to punish me in some way."

"I wouldn't do that." But was it true? Could it be more than a reminder for him? Could he be certain that deep down he didn't want to goad her? Even though he knew she wasn't to blame, forgiveness didn't come easily. "If it seemed that way, I apologize." God's bones, this stilted conversation was so unlike the last time they had celebrated their marriage. They had been unable to stop kissing even while tugging off each other's clothes.

Heat pooled in his belly at the memory. Five long years of abstinence was making it increasingly difficult to think now they were alone. Alone in a chamber with a huge bed. He gulped down his mead, praying it would quench the burning within. Help him ignore the way the embroidered neck of her gown sagged a little, revealing the curve of her breasts.

Not that he was averse to tumbling Isobel upon the inviting bed—he didn't see why they couldn't take pleasure in one another, as long as he guarded his heart. It wasn't as though he hadn't already bedded her. But the cords of Isobel's neck stood out, taut as bowstrings. It was obvious she didn't want this, and he would never force her.

She took a sip of mead, then rose and ran her fingers along the garland spiraled around the bedpost, looking everywhere except at him.

He had to say something to fill the silence. "I'm surprised your servants found the time to decorate a bridal chamber, with a wedding feast to prepare in a hurry." Perhaps if they engaged in a harmless conversation, he could find a way to put her at ease.

"It's not that long since Twelfth Night. We still had food left over from the Christmas feasting. These, for instance." She took another nibble of marchpane and licked her lips.

Edmund looked away. By the saints, if she wasn't careful, he would lick the marchpane off her lips himself. Then he would be hard-pressed to stop himself from flinging her upon the mattress.

He cleared his throat. "Even so, it was kind of them to take the time to decorate the chamber."

"They are good to me. Protective." Then, in a voice

so low he doubted it was meant for him: "Although I wish they hadn't chosen this chamber."

"Why not?"

Isobel turned away, clutching the bedpost. Her knuckles stood out as white as the mistletoe berries. "It was Sir Roger's."

A chill crept down his spine. "Jesu, Isobel, I'm sorry." He remembered the way she had rubbed her arm when talking of Sir Roger before. "Did he beat you?"

"I don't want to talk about it."

That meant "yes," then. He picked up her cup and handed it to her. "Here. Drink this." It felt natural to slip his arm around her waist. She froze for a moment, then he felt her muscles relax a fraction. "We don't have to stay here; we could go to your chamber."

She blew out a shaky breath. "I told Will he could sleep in my chamber as a treat. He'll be asleep by now. Besides, this will be your chamber—there's no choice; it's the only one available. I can't avoid it forever."

Isobel twisted the goblet around and around, slopping mead upon the rushes. She muttered under her breath and put the cup down.

A fire burned in Edmund's belly. Sir Roger had had a lucky escape when he'd been killed at Shrewsbury. Whatever his feelings about Isobel, she was his wife. The woman he was sworn to protect. He almost regretted Sir Roger's death—he wanted nothing more than to hunt him down and feed him piecemeal to the crows. Whatever he had done to Isobel—and he had seen enough of the way victorious soldiers treated women after a siege to guess—had made a lasting impact.

"It might help to talk about it," he said, at a loss for

anything else to say.

There was a brief flash of the old, familiar fire in her eyes. "And have you told anyone about your nightmares?"

"How did you know—?" He coughed and took a sip of mead to cover his mistake. "What makes you think I have nightmares?"

"You told Will. If it's helpful to talk about your fears, why don't you tell me about yours?"

Of course Will would have repeated everything he'd said to Isobel. "It's not me who's trembling like a cat in a thunderstorm. I'm trying to help you."

"Let's change the subject, Edmund. I don't want to think about it, and I dare say you must think I deserve it after—"

Edmund slammed his cup upon the table, rattling the cups and platter. "Deserve it? Do you think so ill of me?" He spun her around, holding her slender waist between his hands. "Look me in the eye, Isobel." Blinking, she lifted her gaze to his face; he caught his breath at the pain and fear lurking in the depths of her eyes. "I admit this marriage isn't to my liking, that five years of resentment and bitterness can't be cast off overnight. But whatever my feelings about you—and for the sake of our son, I swear I'm making every effort to forgive you—nothing—*nothing*—would make me believe you deserved ill treatment. Trust me in this."

Her eyes widened, and she reached up to grip his forearms. At first he thought his words had reached her, but her fingers dug into the muscle of each arm and he could feel the tense quivering. Then she broke her grip and turned away, but not before he caught sight of silvery tears beading on her lashes.

"I was a hostage." He could scarcely believe he was speaking the words, but if there was any way to reach her he had to take it.

Her head whipped around. "What did you say?"

He sank into a chair beside the hearth and gestured at the opposite chair. Isobel sat down, her eyes fixed on his face. He'd finally found a subject to distract Isobel from the horror of this chamber, but now he had to think quickly, to decide what to reveal and what to keep locked away.

Chapter Thirteen

Shock punched Isobel in the gut. "A hostage?" The questions tumbled through her mind too fast for her to express them. Why had he never spoken of it before?

She raised her eyes to Edmund's face. It was expressionless, but she sensed deep turmoil beneath the surface. "When?"

"When I was four."

Sweet Jesu—Will's age.

"Why?" In her shock, the word came out as little more than a whisper.

"My father was involved in a failed rebellion against King Henry. When it was over, he was allowed to keep his title on condition he hand over a hostage."

"You?"

Edmund nodded.

"I can't believe it. To hand over a four-year-old child…" She shuddered. She could never allow Will to be used in that way. It was barbaric. She had always deplored the custom of using hostages to guarantee loyalty. Often these hostages were old enough to understand what they were doing and even volunteer themselves, but children were also chosen. It always filled Isobel with horror to think of a child being treated with no more regard than a pawn on a chessboard. Especially as a hostage lived under threat of death if the offense was repeated.

"Why did you never tell me?" She couldn't believe she hadn't known about such a huge and terrifying event in his life.

"It was a long time ago. I rarely think about it."

Somehow she doubted that. Such an experience couldn't easily be forgotten. She was prepared to wager the hurt ran deep, far deeper than the scar on his face.

"How long before you were allowed to return home?"

"I never went back." He clipped his words short. The pain it cost to utter each one evident.

"Never?" Neither of Isobel's parents had lavished her with love: to her father she had merely been a means of forging an alliance through marriage; her mother had been more concerned with obeying her husband than taking care of her daughter. Nevertheless, she'd had a home and been provided for. She'd been safe.

"Never. When I was old enough, I was released and allowed to serve as squire to Sir Gerald." The Marcher Lord whose service he had been in when they'd met, although Edmund had been on the verge of earning his knighthood by then. She'd never thought to question how he had gained his position. She'd assumed it had been arranged by his parents, in the same way they would foster Will out when the time was right.

She was struck by a wave of tenderness for the frightened boy Edmund must have been. "I can't imagine what you went through." Her vision narrowed until all she could see was his slate-blue eyes, framed with black lashes. Behind the pain of remembrance, she could also see concern.

He still cared for her! Enough to reveal the event that must have scarred him deeply.

For a long moment there was no sound but the spit and crackle of the fire. And the surge of her pulse in her ears.

She groped for words to cover her confusion. "Whatever you endured, it didn't stain your character. You grew into an honorable man. That shows great inner strength."

Edmund leaned forward and placed his hand over hers. Heat flowed between them, chasing away the last of the cold. "You have great strength too, Isobel. Never underestimate your courage."

She studied his face; there was nothing but sincerity in his expression. His confidence released something deep inside, and she found herself speaking, haltingly at first, but gathering assurance as she went on.

"Sir Roger...he never maltreated me in public, but when we were alone..." She clung to his hand, drew strength from the touch. "You have to believe I never went to him willingly. I took my vows as seriously as you, but he overpowered me." Her throat ached from the effort of holding back her sobs, but she couldn't stop now. She wanted—*needed*—to finish. "I fought him every time, but he was too strong. Until enough time passed that I could tell him I was with child. Then he left me alone until after Will was born."

She drew a hiccupping breath. There was more, but she hesitated to say it.

A muscle flinched in Edmund's jaw, and the words died before she could force them out. She couldn't face his revulsion.

Then Edmund gripped her hand more tightly. "Isobel, what Sir Roger put you through, that wasn't your fault. He forced you. There's nothing you could have done to stop him. You mustn't blame yourself."

"But I—" Then she heard a soft curse and strong arms wrapped around her and pulled her onto Edmund's lap. She couldn't hold back the tears any longer, and she buried her face against his chest and wept. Some of it was relief that he hadn't simply walked out and abandoned her again, but her tears were also for what she had lost. She doubted she had it in her to love again. Not after all she had gone through.

Edmund spoke, his soft voice rumbling against her cheek. "I don't blame you, Isobel. I'm sorry, so sorry I left you to endure that."

Then he slipped his fingers under her chin and tilted her face to his. He lowered his mouth to hers, and she gasped, her senses swimming. His kiss was every bit as potent as she remembered. Even after five years, he remembered exactly how she liked to be touched. Her heart hammered against her ribs. His every caress sent thrills through her body, making the muscles deep in her belly clench. When Edmund trailed hot kisses down her throat, she could do nothing but tip her head back and grip his shoulders, urging him lower.

In the back of her mind was a dim unease; if Edmund knew the whole truth, maybe he wouldn't be so forgiving. Oh, but she couldn't deny she'd missed this. Missed the comfort to be found in the act of love. More than anything, she craved oblivion in Edmund's arms. If she surrendered to him, he could make her forget the pain and humiliation Sir Roger had inflicted on her in this very chamber. In return, she could ease the heartache of his childhood.

Edmund slid one hand up from her waist to cup her breast. She gasped and arched into the caress which scorched her flesh even through the fine wool of her gown. But then the memory of Sir Roger's rough, cruel fingers invaded her mind, and she couldn't fight it off. Her breath came in short gasps and Edmund's arms, which had at first been a comfort, now caged her. She dug her fingers into his shoulders and pushed him away, then doubled over, hugging her stomach while she fought to drag air into her lungs.

"S-sorry. I can't do this." It was too soon, the dark memories too close. She braced herself for his anger.

Instead, Edmund shook his head. "I'm the one who should be sorry," he said. "I should have known." He eased her off his lap and went over to the bed. After tugging free one of the striped woolen blankets, he rolled it into a long strip and placed it beneath the covers, down the center of the bed. "I won't touch you until you tell me you're ready."

Long after Edmund's breathing slowed into the regular rhythm of sleep, Isobel gazed up at the canopy overhead. Edmund had shown a patience and understanding she hadn't expected. Marrying him had been the right decision.

But each time she dared to hope they might find a measure of happiness after all, her conscience gave her a jolt. It issued a sharp reminder that she hadn't told him everything. And when he knew the truth he might not be so kind.

****

It was a relief when the outline of Woodseaves manor came into view. Although it was less than two

miles from Molbren, the going had been tough.
Edmund was glad he had brought along one of the
grooms as a guide; without the man's help, they would
have long ago strayed off the road.

He could probably have waited another day or two
before venturing out this far, but Woodseaves lay on the
road between Cannington's last known location and
Welsh territory. What had piqued Edmund's interest
even more was gossip that Sir Geoffrey, the knight who
held Woodseaves for Isobel, had been outspoken in his
objection to surrendering Molbren to Stephen. In fact,
his brother was known to be in Normandy, having gone
there to pledge his support to the Empress. If anyone
was likely to be sympathetic to the fugitive Earl of
Cannington, it was Sir Geoffrey.

Of course, he'd had to put up with his squires'
unmistakable surprise at leaving his bride so early on
the morning after the wedding. He'd ignored it. After
all, he could hardly tell them waking with his face a
mere hand's breadth from Isobel's bare shoulder had
stretched his forbearance to its limit. He'd sprung out of
bed as though it burned him and left the chamber before
she awoke.

Even if Isobel hadn't confessed what Sir Roger had
done to her, there was no mistaking her fear when she'd
recoiled from his caress. It had been an instinctive,
visceral reaction. He desired her, by God, he couldn't
deny the fire she lit in his flesh, but he could never
force her.

Not like Sir Roger, may his soul rot in Hell for
eternity. Edmund closed his eyes against a wave of
remorse. No wonder Isobel had accused him of not
fighting hard enough for her. If he'd known the truth

when he'd come to her father's manor, he'd have drawn his sword and fought his way through to her.

But he hadn't. He'd fallen for her parents' deceit, and Isobel had paid the price for his weakness. Isobel and Will. Now he must strive to make up for his mistake and provide a safe home. Which meant obeying his king and capturing the fugitive.

As they neared the manor, Edmund spied a team of men shoveling snow away from the gates. Another man was directing them. His long, blue cloak revealed him to be a man of importance, most likely Sir Geoffrey himself. As soon as they were within earshot, Edmund hailed him.

"I would never harbor an enemy of the king," Sir Geoffrey said once Edmund had explained his mission. "I haven't seen the man, and you can be sure I'd tell you if I had."

Edmund wasn't entirely convinced by the knight's bluster. From the corner of his eye, he caught a glance shared between two of the servants; he'd wager his horse they knew something. However, he wasn't going to accuse a man based on vague suspicion. "Then you don't mind if I take a look around the manor?" Not that he had any intention of going away if Sir Geoffrey refused, but he would do him the courtesy of couching it as a question.

Sir Geoffrey made a wide gesture, encompassing the house and all the outbuildings. "Be my guest."

"He knows something," Joss murmured as they approached the house.

"I agree. I doubt Cannington's here now—Sir Geoffrey wouldn't be so quick to agree to a search if he were. But he's been here recently, I'm sure of it."

Edmund could only pray he hadn't escaped into Welsh territory before the snow arrived. "Question the servants. Maybe you can find someone willing to talk." It was unlikely, though. Servants depended too much upon their lords to risk their displeasure. "I'll speak to Sir Geoffrey's wife. If you see Sir Geoffrey approach the house before I finish, try and distract him."

He entered the manor house and found Lady Katherine doing her best to give instructions to a servant—her cook, judging from the sauce stains on his tunic—while scolding two children at the same time.

"I don't care what Griffith says, we still have a barrel of apples in the undercroft, and we must use those first." She spoke in a shrill voice, her face growing more flushed with every word. "The cider will keep until—Walter, Thomas—stop that at once!" The two boys, who were fighting over a spinning top giggled and ignored her. She dismissed the cook and took a step toward the boys, only to notice Edmund for the first time. "Yes, what do you want?" she demanded. Then she gasped, evidently taking in the quality of his sword and clothes and realizing he was a noble of higher status than her husband.

"Forgive me, my lord, I—"

Edmund held up his hands. "There's no need. I'm merely here to find out where the Earl of Cannington went when he left here."

"Oh, he went west, and—" Then she clapped her hand to her mouth. "Holy Mother, have mercy! It's supposed to be a secret. Please don't tell my husband."

Edmund, the memory of Isobel's confession still raw, felt a twinge of guilt at taking advantage of the woman's distraction. Sir Geoffrey looked like a man who would use his fists against anyone who disobeyed him, and he didn't want Lady Katherine on his conscience in addition to Isobel. "You have my word I won't tell him. Answer my questions, and I'll leave you in peace."

"Of course." She glanced toward the door, and Edmund hastened to reassure her. "My squires will keep Sir Geoffrey away. Now tell me when Cannington left."

"It was when the snow started. He was anxious to get out of the king's territory before he could be trapped here."

"Do you know where he was headed?"

"I don't know." She spoke with a slight hesitation and wouldn't meet his eyes. Was she telling the truth? "He wouldn't say. But the snow came down so hard and fast, he can't have got far, what with his wound as well."

This sparked Edmund's interest, and his suspicions eased. Lady Katherine certainly seemed willing enough to tell all she knew. "He was wounded?"

"Yes, my lord. He took a wolf bite to the arm. That's why he needed to shelter with us in the first place. Please don't be hard on my husband. He's a stern man, but he'd never turn anyone away who needed help. Especially as the earl had his young son with him."

A ripple of alarm shot down his spine. "He had a boy with him?" This was the first he'd heard of it. Cannington had a son of about Will's age, if he remembered correctly. Until now everyone had believed Cannington had left his son in the care of his late wife's relatives.

"Yes, poor mite. My heart bleeds to think of the lad out in this weather."

So did Edmund's. He couldn't help but remember how close Will had come to perishing of the cold, yet he'd been close to home. He prayed to all the saints that Cannington had found shelter and had been able to keep them warm through the endless blizzards. Maybe he wouldn't have felt this way before, but now he'd spent time with Will, he couldn't bear the thought of a boy the same age being in danger.

"You did the right thing by telling me," he told Lady Katherine. "I won't bring any trouble on you for letting it slip." And he would do all in his power to find Cannington before his son came to harm. But if Cannington was wounded... He remembered all too vividly the wolf that had threatened Isobel. It was most likely the same one. Its injured flank had probably been inflicted by Cannington in an attempt to protect his son.

Suddenly his mission wasn't just a matter of gaining his palatinate. Now he had a boy's life to save.

Chapter Fourteen

Isobel crossed the courtyard for the fifth time that morning. This time it was to ask the laundresses to wash the table linens now they had a day sunny enough to dry the cloths. Less than an hour ago, she had felt the urge to make sure she had enough stores of elderberry tincture to last out the winter's coughs and colds and before that she had visited the undercroft to see if they had enough wine, or if she needed to buy more from Ludlow market when the snow cleared. All these tasks could have been done by a servant, but Isobel felt the need to keep busy. Anything to keep her from dwelling on the previous night.

For once she couldn't blame Edmund. He had shown nothing but patience and kindness, even trusted her enough to reveal the pain of his childhood. Something he hadn't done when they had been in love, when she'd thought they'd had no secrets.

No, she was disappointed in herself. She'd always liked to think she wouldn't shy away from difficult situations, but here she was, the morning after their wedding night, and she'd failed to overcome her fear. She'd lain beside him in the darkness, every inch of her flesh aware of Edmund's nearness, quivering in anticipation of his touch. From his shallow breathing, she'd known he was awake, could sense the tension radiating from him. Her sensitized skin thrilled at the lightest brush of the sheets; her breasts felt heavy, nipples puckered to tight peaks. How she yearned for Edmund's caress! All she had to do was reach across the folded blanket. He wouldn't reject her advances.

But her fear had won. It whispered that Edmund could never make her forget Sir Roger's loathsome pawing. It still loomed before her, growing more insurmountable by the hour. Hence her need to keep herself occupied while she kept half an eye on the gates, both longing for and dreading Edmund's return.

"My lady, I understand I'm to wish you joy."

Isobel paused and greeted her steward. "Simon, when did you get back?"

"I've only just arrived. The castle is buzzing with your news. I'm sorry I couldn't be here to witness your wedding."

"I would have liked you to be there." Isobel decided to hint at the truth to assess Simon's reaction. "We decided not to risk gossip by waiting any longer."

"I am glad you have found each other," Simon replied. "It is good for Will to have a father once again."

Although he said nothing directly, it was his way of telling her he'd guessed the truth. Edmund had insisted they not reveal the truth about Will's parentage until he'd been able to inform the king, but Isobel knew Simon was also informing her of Molbren's support. There would be no unseemly gossip.

"Thank you, Simon," she said, feeling the anxiety she'd had on Will's account drift away. "It's good to see you back. How is your sister's husband?"

Simon gave a broad smile. "It's a miracle, my lady. He's well on his way to recovery. I never thought it possible, but he improves by the hour."

"I'm glad to hear it. If there's anything else I can do, you must let me know."

"You've done more than enough. I'll never forget the care you've shown for me and my sister. If there's ever anything I can do for you in return, you have but to ask."

Edmund returned shortly before the noon meal. It was strange to welcome him into the solar. She had to remind herself that this was Edmund's home as well now. Having the three of them together in the solar gave her a warm glow. They were a real family now. It made her all the more disappointed in herself for allowing her painful memories to get the better of her last night. However, while she helped Edmund remove his boots, letting her fingers linger on his firm calf muscles, the same twinges of fear mingled with the yearning.

No. This couldn't continue. She refused to be governed by fear. In fact, she would not allow Edmund to leave for Redmarch until they had consummated the marriage.

When Agnes led Will off to get his meal, Isobel stopped Edmund before he could follow. "Have you decided when you're leaving for Redmarch?" Now she'd set herself a challenge, she needed to know how long she had to prepare.

Edmund smacked his forehead. "Forgive me. I came to a decision a few days ago, but between the wedding preparations and the hunt for Cannington, I forgot to tell you."

"What decision?" Judging from Edmund's frown, she wasn't going to like it.

"I'm staying at Molbren even after the thaw. When I return to Redmarch, you and Will are to accompany me."

"But we agreed—"

"We agreed I am to be a father to Will. I can't do that if I'm living miles away. We've missed four years, and I won't waste a moment longer."

"When did you decide this?"

"After Will's nightmare. I promised him I'd always be there for him when he needed me. I can hardly keep my promise if I'm in Redmarch and he's here."

"And you decided this without me? Despite your promise I would have the final say over both Will's upbringing and Molbren?" The fragile glow of warmth that had surrounded her all morning dissipated, leaving her chilled and trembling. After his kindness last night, the blow struck doubly hard.

"We're married because of Will, Isobel. So I could be a father to my heir. I found myself trying to fulfill two conflicting promises, and I had to put the one I made to Will first."

"But why make it in the first place when you knew it would undo our agreement?" For the first time that day, she didn't regret letting her fear get the better of her last night. It was far easier to be angry with him without that intimacy between them.

"Because he was frightened. Do you know what he dreamed about?"

Isobel shook her head.

"He dreamed Sir Roger was beating you, and he was too frightened to stop him."

Isobel clutched her cross, her anger draining away as fast as it had overtaken her. "Blessed Mother! Please tell me he doesn't blame himself. He was far too young to do anything."

"That's what I told him. But I also know that as he gets older he must have confidence in himself. He will need to believe he is strong enough to defend those he loves and strong enough to hold Redmarch against all enemies. I can teach him, but I must start now if what he went through isn't to have a lasting effect. I know what it's like to have your confidence knocked and the sooner he learns to face his fears the better."

Isobel flinched. Was that an oblique reference to last night? But she dismissed the thought as unworthy. Edmund had promised not to pressure her, and she knew he'd keep his word. He was focused fully on Will.

"What do you know about loss of confidence?" Edmund had always displayed a self-belief bordering on arrogance. Then she remembered his confession of the night before. "Is this to do with being a hostage?"

A muscle in his jaw flinched, but Edmund shook his head. He indicated the scar on his face. "I was thinking about how I got this."

"Didn't you get it in battle?" She hadn't asked him about his experiences of war. None of the men she'd known had seemed willing to speak of what happened on the battlefield. It was a world women were excluded from.

Edmund gave a twisted smile. "Nothing so noble. This happened not long after I arrived in the Holy Land, when our forces freed a hill town from the Saracens. In my innocence, I thought freeing the inhabitants was reward enough, but for many it wasn't. They were in it for plunder. Not long after the battle I saw three knights accost a young woman—one of the inhabitants we'd been fighting for. They demanded her gold and attacked her when she refused."

A shadow settled over Edmund's face. It struck Isobel then that he'd experienced his own share of horrors after their parting. "What did you do?"

"I was such an innocent. I believed because I was in the right, I could take on three seasoned knights and not suffer any ill effects. Instead I got this scar."

"But did you save the woman?"

"Yes, but the narrowness of my escape left me badly shaken. I'd survived my first battle, only to come close to meeting my end at the hands of my own men."

"How did you overcome it?"

"It took a long time. The knights escaped with only flesh wounds, and I avoided them after that, afraid they would finish what they'd started. It was only after another battle when I saw them attack another innocent woman that I had to make a choice."

"You stepped in and saved her, even though you were scared." It wasn't a question. Edmund's honor was what had drawn her to him from the first. It was why it had taken so long to believe he'd abandoned her.

"I did, and this time I made sure they weren't able to walk away. But, Isobel, until that moment I felt so alone. I had no one to guide me. I hate the thought of Will having to go through that kind of experience on his own. I want to be there for him. Mentor him. I can't do that if I'm not here."

Isobel couldn't argue with that. "I want the best for Will, too." She couldn't force him to leave. If she was honest, she didn't even want him to leave. "But I need to know you trust me to run Molbren without interference."

"Of course. I need you here. And even though I'll be with Will as much as possible, I'll still be called away. The king will make sure of that. I can only see this conflict getting worse."

For some reason, Edmund's assertion that he only planned to stay at Molbren for Will's sake gave Isobel a hollow ache in her chest. It was foolish. They had both agreed their marriage was for Will alone. Clearly she'd read too much into Edmund's tenderness last night. He saw her as Will's mother and the mother of his future children. And she was happy with that. Truly, she was. There really was no reason to object to Edmund's decision to spend more time with Will. He was right to consider what was best for Will and act on it.

If it was in Will's best interest to be with Edmund as much as possible, she would just have to find a way to get used to it.

****

After the meal, Edmund took Joss and Ancel up onto the donjon roof to discuss where their search should lead them next.

"Woodseaves is over there." He pointed east to where a smudge on the horizon showed the tree line and the rough location of the manor. "Cannington left at roughly the same time as we were out searching for Will. How far do you think he went? We have to assume he's taken shelter somewhere." Edmund prayed it was so, and they wouldn't find a pair of corpses when the thaw came. He had to find them before the boy came to harm.

He tried not to think of what would happen to the child after reaching King Stephen's custody.

Joss swept a patch of snow from the parapet and leaned against the exposed stone, his breath misting in the air. "I can't see him covering more than a mile or two. We had enough trouble getting between here and the village, and we had several men at our disposal. A wounded man and a small boy…if Cannington had any sense he'd have taken shelter in the first place he could find."

Ancel joined Joss and peered out across the white landscape. "But there isn't a manor or village between here and Woodseaves, and we know Cannington's not here."

Edmund's pulse quickened. "Not a village or a manor, but I do remember something marked on the map." He frowned, trying to bring the details to mind. "Yes, shepherd's huts. According to the steward, they're used at lambing time."

"So they should be empty for another few weeks," Joss remarked. "I bet that's where he is."

"If he's still there." Edmund glared across the snowscape, as though wishing could make his quarry magically appear. "If we've been able to get out, we have to assume Cannington has as well." He scanned the land running between the river and the forest and realized that a group of humps he'd previously dismissed as burial mounds could in fact be snow-bound huts. They were less than a mile away, easy enough to walk. He glanced up at the sky. "We still have a good four hours of light left. Let's make the most of it. Come with me." He ran down the steps. If there was any chance Cannington was still there, he had to search the huts today.

****

There was only one bridge crossing the river within several miles. Edmund inspected it carefully before they crossed, but although their own tracks from yesterday remained, there was no trace of any other footprints. Cannington and his son had yet to reach the Molbren side of the river. Nevertheless, as Ancel was a good tracker, Edmund set him to walk ahead to see if he could pick up any trace of Cannington.

"I'm surprised you're so keen to spend so much time out of the castle the day after your wedding," Joss said as they followed.

Edmund gritted his teeth. "I don't expect this kind of talk from my squire."

"What about your cousin? I wouldn't address you so familiarly if Ancel was closer, but as he can't hear us…"

Edmund sighed, but in truth, it might help to confide in him. Not that he'd betray Isobel's confidence, but it might help clarify his thinking to explain some of their history. "I'm sure you've guessed much of it already," he began.

"If you mean guessed that Will is really your son, then yes I have. He looks a lot like you. I doubt anyone could mistake the resemblance once they see the two of you together."

"God's blood, is everyone talking about it?"

"I've heard one or two people speculate, but with no malice behind it. The people of Molbren are staunchly loyal to your lady and won't permit anyone to spread gossip. From what I hear, her late husband was a harsh man and not liked by his people. They're only too happy to discover he was rearing a cuckoo."

"Will's no bastard. He's my rightful heir." Edmund

described the circumstances of his first marriage, and how Isobel's parents had contrived to separate them.

Joss whistled. "So that's what happened. I could see you had a shared past, but that explains everything. I'm glad you've found each other again."

Edmund toyed with the idea of confessing that he and Isobel were only together for Will's sake but decided that was revealing too much.

Then there was no time to say any more, because they were approaching the shepherd's huts. Edmund's blood thrilled. If Cannington was there, they would have him trapped. He signaled his squires to circle around to cover the rear, then he dismounted and strode to the nearest entrance. Any occupants would have a clear view of him outlined against the snow, so he made no attempt at concealment but drew his sword and flung back the door.

The hut was empty but had recently been in use. A straw pallet, set against the rear wall, still bore the imprint of a body. Charred wood and ashes lay in the central hearth. He touched them; the stones beneath were warm. His pulse quickened: the fire must have burnt out only that morning. Whoever had been here couldn't have got far.

He dashed outside and examined the ground for prints. His own prints were clear, deep prints in the snow, but Edmund could also make out two sets of fainter ones, one set so small it could only have been made by a child. They were blurred by the wind and would only grow more indistinct.

"My lord!" Ancel called from within the hut. Edmund ran back to see the squire holding up a strip of linen between finger and thumb. It was stiff with blood.

"This explains why he didn't leave until now. He must be in a bad way if he's still bleeding." Ancel dropped the cloth with a shudder and wiped his hand on his tunic. "I wonder what made him leave."

"Probably because the weather looks set to hold for a day or two at least. I expect he's desperate to reach safety." And desperate to prevent his son from being used as a hostage. Edmund's stomach clenched, but he did his best to ignore his feelings. If Cannington was wounded and out in the ice and snow with his young son, he needed help. Surely the boy was better off in captivity than risking death from the cold and wild beasts? He refused to feel guilty about doing his sworn duty to the king.

"There are some faint tracks out there," he said. "See how far you can follow them, Ancel."

In the end, the tracks didn't lead far. Just to the edge of a stretch of boggy ground. There was still snow cover but frequent pools and clumps of tufty grass broke up the trail until it was impossible to see where a disturbance was made by a man or whether it was made by other animals.

They abandoned the trail and returned to the bridge. Much to Edmund's confusion, there were still no tracks there apart from their own.

"You don't suppose they fell into a pool?" Joss asked.

Ancel shook his head. "Their struggles would have left signs none of us would have missed."

Joss peered over the bridge, down to the river. "Could they have crossed on the ice?"

"I wouldn't want to risk it," Edmund replied. "The river's too wide and fast flowing to freeze easily." He crossed to the other side and dug out a hefty stone from the road's verge. He tossed it onto the frozen surface. With a crack, it plunged through the ice. "That was a big stone, but nowhere near the weight of a man." It was clear the only way Cannington could have crossed the river was by bridge. Edmund had studied enough plans of the area to know this was the only bridge within ten miles.

"This is pointless," he said. "They clearly haven't crossed, and there's not enough light to go back out and search. We'll carry on tomorrow." Cannington was wilier than Edmund had given him credit for. It was beginning to look like he'd laid a false trail. Perhaps he'd known someone was after him, and he'd since doubled back to the huts. For the boy's sake he hoped so.

"Let's return to the castle. Report to me in the great hall. You could both use more sword practice."

****

The sun was sinking toward the hills when Isobel crossed the bailey. She was on the point of going into the kitchens when the clash of steel upon steel drew her into the great hall. She stepped through the door and saw a group of men forming a rough ring at the end of the hall usually reserved for dancing. In the center two men sparred, their swords reflecting a myriad points of light from the overhead chandelier. It was Edmund and Joscelyn.

Edmund had stripped off his usual calf-length tunic and wore a form-fitting gambeson that ended at mid-thigh. Every thrust and parry revealed the muscles across his back and arm. Each move had the control and grace of a cat on the prowl.

Isobel's mouth went dry. A twist of longing curled deep in her belly. Unbidden, memories of stripping his tunic and chemise returned. Her fingers tingled as though they traced the muscles his gambeson emphasized rather than concealed. His form had filled out in the five years they'd been apart. Then, he'd been on the cusp of adulthood; now he'd reached the peak of manhood. She shivered. What would it be like to lie in his arms again?

A flutter of fear returned, but it wasn't the sharp stab of last night. Now it was more like the apprehension of their first time, the fear mixed with the longing. She wanted him. She wanted to recapture the joy of their first time. He was nothing like Sir Roger. Edmund had shown her nothing but patience and compassion.

Sharing a bed with Edmund wasn't a trial to be endured, but a pleasure to be enjoyed.

As she watched, Edmund ducked to avoid his opponent's attack, then whirled beneath the blade until he was behind his squire. With an economy of movement that looked more like a dance, he pressed the tip of his sword between Joscelyn's shoulder blades. The squire's chest heaved with exertion, yet Edmund showed no sign of tiring. The only expression he showed was a crooked smile tugging at one corner of his mouth.

She had a flash to the snarl, the fury blazing from his eyes when he'd flung himself between her and the wolf. Strange how he had taken that attack so personally when until that point, all his anger had been directed at her.

Edmund lowered his sword, and Joscelyn gave him

a mock bow. "I yield this time," he said. "Next time you won't best me so easily."

"So might a lion cub snarl at its sire." Edmund slammed the sword into its scabbard.

Isobel swallowed. These past days had shown a side to Edmund she hadn't seen before: his power and confidence, yet tempered with compassion and a grim humor. It was seductive. Irresistibly so. She wanted him. Almost as much as she had wanted him their first time.

She shrank into the shadows beside the doorway, wanting to study him without being seen. Was this wanting, this yearning, enough to overcome the fear instilled by Sir Roger? Only yesterday she would have thought she could never desire a man's touch again, and still the thought of any man but Edmund touching her curdled her stomach. *Any man but Edmund.*

Dare she do it? Edmund had said he'd wait for her, wouldn't press her, and he would keep his word. He would keep his distance unless she told him she was ready. Was she? Was this desire truly strong enough to overcome her fear?

There was only one way to find out.

Chapter Fifteen

"What's troubling you?" Isobel put down the chemise she was embroidering and frowned at Edmund. After coming to her decision earlier, she had waited with increasing agitation for Agnes to take Will to bed, but even though she and Edmund were now alone, there had been no opportunity to bring up the subject. Edmund's sparring match with Joss clearly hadn't burned off his energy, and he'd barely stayed in one place for more than ten heartbeats ever since he'd returned to the solar. He'd leafed through his maps, fidgeted with the chess pieces, and now he'd given up all pretense of occupation and simply paced, deep lines scoring his brow.

His restlessness undid all her efforts to calm her nerves. She had retreated to the window seat seeking peace and a chance to work out how to invite him into her bed, but his incessant pacing made concentration impossible.

Eventually, after a final circuit of the solar, Edmund sighed and climbed into the opposite seat. "Did you know Cannington has a son?"

Puzzled, Isobel replied, "Now you mention it, I do remember something about a boy. I met the earl briefly when he visited Sir Roger." She thought back to the visit with reluctance. Most of her memories of that time were overshadowed by her fear of displeasing Sir Roger and incurring his punishment. Not a memory she wished to occupy her mind, considering her intentions. She needed to forget Sir Roger and hold on to the desire that flared even now as she studied his hands, imagining them caressing her bare flesh.

The heat of a flush rose from throat to cheeks. "Yes, I remember now." Her voice croaked. She had to concentrate! She cleared her throat. "His wife had recently died, and his son was very young, so he was sent to live with his mother's kin."

Edmund's brow furrowed. "Cannington's wife. She came from Staffordshire, didn't she?"

"I believe so."

"I think I begin to understand what happened— why it took Cannington so long to reach these parts. He must have gone to Staffordshire first, to collect his son."

"Holy Mother!" A chill snaked down Isobel's spine. "Do you mean Cannington is fleeing with his son?"

"That's what it looks like."

"What kind of man would risk taking his son away into the wilds in the dead of winter?" That didn't match with her impression of Cannington as a kind, thoughtful man.

"There are worse things you can do to a child." Edmund's hard tone reminded Isobel of his confession.

"You mean Cannington didn't want his son to be used as a hostage?"

Edmund nodded. "If Stephen had taken the boy, Cannington would have had no choice but to give himself up."

"I can't see Stephen harming a child. He's not a

cruel man."

"Are you sure of that?"

"I'm certain."

"Enough to wager the life of your own son?"

Isobel shifted. That was different. She didn't trust anyone with Will apart from herself. And maybe Edmund now. "Perhaps not."

Edmund's lips twisted into an expression partway between a grimace and a smile. "Nor would I. Believe me, I would go to any lengths to ensure Will was never used as a hostage, including fleeing into the wild."

He wasn't talking about Cannington now, she knew. "Was being a hostage really as bad as that? I thought hostages lived as part of the household."

A muscle flinched in Edmund's cheek. "They do, for the most part."

"Then why—?"

"Cannington and the boy are out there in the snow. Why do you think I'm worried? I'm not heartless, Isobel. I don't want them to suffer, yet I can't see either of them surviving long in this weather." He was deflecting her question. She could swear his worry was rooted in his own experience, but from the set of his jaw, there was as much chance of persuading him to explain as there was of Will voluntarily tidying his toys.

She dared to place a hand on his arm. Holy Mother, even that slight contact sent pleasurable tingles through her flesh. The air thickened between them. Edmund's gaze dropped to her hand, then shifted to her mouth before locking with hers. His pupils stretched wide, drowning nearly all of the blue. Her body swayed closer, drawn by a need to lose herself in those depths.

She licked lips that were suddenly dry. "You've

done everything you can, Edmund. You've gone out in conditions I would have thought impossible for traveling. And you'll go out tomorrow and look again. No one can fault you for not finding him. Tomorrow, take some of the garrison so you can broaden the search."

And tonight…her heart pounded. Yet how could she introduce the subject? It had hung in the air between them all evening, and she didn't want to hesitate any more. Edmund's compassion for Cannington's son—a boy he didn't even know—proved that if there was one man she could trust, it was Edmund.

Edmund rose. "Whatever happens, I've a long day ahead of me. It's time I retired."

Isobel drew a breath. "Edmund—"

At the same moment, Edmund said, "I hold to what I said last night. I'll wait until you're ready. Will's back in his own chamber so you can—"

"Wait, Edmund. Let me say something first." If she didn't speak now she doubted she'd ever find the courage. Yet she refused to let her fear win; if she said nothing now, it would only increase day by day until it became an unbreachable wall.

Edmund nodded and returned to his seat. The fact that he was prepared to listen and not interrupt gave her the courage to continue. It struck her then that he was the only person apart from Agnes she felt able to confide in. And she had never told Agnes what she was about to say now.

She moistened her lips again. "I didn't tell you everything last night, because I was afraid. Afraid you'd never want to look at me again." But she would tell him now, and she would know from his reaction whether she could trust him enough to lie with him. Desire alone wasn't enough; there must also be mutual trust.

She paused, gathering her courage. Edmund said nothing but kept his attention fixed on her. The only sound was the wind rattling the closed shutters and the crackle of the fire.

"I told you Sir Roger didn't touch me after I told him I was with child."

Edmund nodded again, the slate-blue gaze not leaving her face.

"What I didn't tell you..." She swallowed to clear the thickness in her throat. "I didn't tell you that after Will was born things changed. Sir Roger...he threatened Will. Said if I didn't submit, he would hurt him."

She looked away, unable to face Edmund's revulsion. Her stomach churned as memories of lying passively while Sir Roger pawed at her forced their way into her head.

Edmund leaned forward. "What are you saying, that you stopped fighting him because he threatened Will unless you submitted?"

It was obvious he was repulsed by her confession. She couldn't blame him. If she had fought him every time, she could at least claim that she'd been faithful to her vows in her heart even if not in body.

She studied the tiny pearls studding her wedding band, unable to meet his eyes, see the revulsion. Her attempt to speak produced no more than a whisper. "When you told me you'd remained faithful all these years, I knew you must blame me. I thought you might be able to forgive me if I'd resisted, but knowing I gave in…willingly broke my vows…"

Edmund rose. To walk away, she presumed. Her heart swooped when instead he sat next to her and slipped an arm around her shoulders.

"Isobel, he gave you no choice. You didn't break any vows. It would have been a sin to sacrifice Will to salvage your pride. If you'd done that, I'd have had a hard time forgiving you, but as it stands, there's nothing to forgive. You took the tough choice, the right choice, and you were deeply wounded by it. Yet you're acting as if I should be angry."

He wasn't angry? She dared to lift her head and search Edmund's face for any sign of rejection. There was nothing but compassion and tenderness.

Relief flooded her body. She sagged in Edmund's hold and let herself relax, believe that maybe Edmund would always be there for her, that she could rely on him. With her cheek pressed against his chest, she breathed in the comforting scent of woodsmoke and leather that always seemed to cling to him. It was like coming home. She could hear the thud of his heartbeat, steady at first, but then his hand tangled in her hair and the tempo increased.

Quite when their hold changed from comfort to something more, she wasn't sure, but she gradually became aware that it wasn't just Edmund's heart beating a rapid tattoo. Her own pulse raced, and heat coursed through her veins, nothing to do with the blazing fire. This was a heat generated by her own desire.

She lifted her head and wrapped her arms around his neck, pulling his face down to hers and pressing her mouth to his. Whereas last night their kiss had been about comfort, this was molten fire. She tangled her hands in his hair, reveling in his nearness, all her senses ablaze as she drank in his taste, the scratch of his stubble against her jaw, a pleasing contrast with the smooth silk of his lips.

With a gasp, he broke the caress and stilled her questing fingers in his grip, gazing at her with eyes that were almost black. "Isobel, is this what you want?"

"Yes." She wove her fingers with his, and he circled her palm with his thumb, sending jolts of lightning down her spine.

He slipped his free hand around her back, moving lower, caressing her hip, down to her thigh.

She flinched, remembering rough fingers, digging in to tender flesh.

Edmund removed his hand. "I'm sorry. You're not ready."

She shook her head and took his hand, placing it back on her waist. "I am ready. I want you to make me forget him. Remind me how it used to be between us."

"Then tell me what you want, *ma belle*. Tonight I'm yours to command."

It was his use of the old endearment, together with his willing ceding of control, that gave her the confidence to continue. Remembering how she had felt watching him spar with Joscelyn, the yearning to see the muscles his clothes only hinted at, she whispered, "I want to see you."

She put her hands on his belt, unable to resist letting her touch linger, feeling the muscles in his taut abdomen twitch. She undid the buckle, letting the heavy belt slide to the floor, then she sat back. "Take off your tunic."

The ghost of a smile tugged at Edmund's lips as he pulled the tunic over his head and sent it to join his belt. Now he wore nothing but a thin linen chemise, hose, and braies. She glanced down and giggled, another layer of fear evaporating. "I think you should take off your shoes next."

Once his shoes and hose were gone all laughter died, burned to a cinder by the flare of desire. Any other man would look foolish, vulnerable even, wearing nothing but chemise and braies. But there was nothing vulnerable or remotely foolish about Edmund. His clothing had only concealed his powerful muscles. Isobel licked dry lips, running her eyes over the toned thighs and calves now revealed. Gone was the boyish, wiry strength of the Edmund she had known. This was the sculpted form of a man, a soldier. A hero from a bard's song.

"What next, *ma belle*?"

The craving intensified. "Take off your chemise."

She sucked in a sharp breath as he raised the hem of his chemise over his head, revealing the play of muscle with every movement. Not only were the muscles more defined than she remembered, there were new scars: one running from his shoulder down his upper arm; another snaked down from his waist, disappearing beneath the ties of his braies. She yearned to trace the lines with her fingers, discover the feel of this new, more mature Edmund. But of course, Edmund had put her in control. She could do whatever she wanted.

Hesitantly at first, then growing bolder, she traced the scar on his shoulder, following the ridge of raised flesh. Her fingertips tingled and even that light touch set the blood thundering in her ears. A wave of desire threatened to engulf her, and she fought it, struggled to retain control.

"How did you get this?" she asked, tracing the scar again. Maybe talking would help her cling to sanity.

"I don't remember the exact moment. I led a charge to break a siege. When it was all over, I discovered I was bleeding, but I felt nothing at the time."

"Didn't you feel any pain?"

"Only when I saw the wound. Then it hurt like fury."

"What about this one?" She traced the line of the second scar down to the top of his braies.

He sucked in a breath; his muscles clenched beneath her fingers. Isobel relished the power she had to affect him with just one light touch.

"That was due to a lapse in concentration. I was so busy watching a Saracen's sword, I forgot to look to see what he held in his other hand. He managed to slip his knife behind my shield."

She didn't ask if he'd felt any pain that time; the memory of it was all too clear in his eyes. Overcome with sudden anger that he'd been forced to put himself into such danger, she leaned down and planted a line of kisses along the scar on his upper arm. Not anger at him, this time; anger at her parents for forcing their separation. As much as she wanted to burn away the memory of Sir Roger's brutality, she hoped tonight would also destroy the ghost of Edmund's ordeal.

"I'm so sorry," she whispered. "So sorry you had to go through such pain."

Then, listening to her desire, she trailed kisses along his collar bone to his throat, then his lips. One thing hadn't changed, and that was his taste. She parted her lips and their teeth clashed, tongues tasting. She pressed her body to his, her blood singing. Edmund groaned against her lips and wound his arms around her, pulling her closer until she felt the ridge of his arousal pressing against her belly.

Suddenly his arms were a cage, and she pulled away, a sob catching in her throat. "I'm sorry."

He shook his head. "You've done nothing wrong. We can stop any time you like."

It was this assurance, given when his body so clearly cried out for fulfillment, that gave her the confidence to continue. Sir Roger had never considered her, only seeing the need to gratify his own desires. "I don't want to stop."

"Then tell me what you want."

She pointed at his braies. "Take those off."

Edmund shot a glance at the door. "Are you sure you don't want to retire to your chamber?"

She shook her head, trying to put her misgivings into words. "My chamber is too…enclosed. You can't lock us in here." There was more than one exit: the one leading to the sleeping chambers and the other door leading to the stairs. Although she knew Edmund wouldn't hurt her, the fearful part of her was reassured by knowing she could always leave. She smiled. "Unless you're worried someone will walk in and see us."

Edmund unlaced his braies and kicked them off, a slow smile curving his lips. "I have nothing to be ashamed of."

That was certainly true. Isobel allowed her gaze to linger, drinking in the sight of him. Until this moment she had kept her bliaut on, needing the shield of her clothing, highlighting the difference from her encounters with Sir Roger, when he had invariably remained clothed while stripping her. Now, however, her clothing felt too tight, constricting her breathing.

"Name your next command, *ma belle*."

"Take off my gown."

She raised her arms, allowing him to unlace the side of her gown and pull it over her head. She considered removing her chemise as well but rejected the idea. Being completely unclothed would remind her too much of being with Sir Roger.

Her voice husky, she said, "I want you to touch me."

Edmund's eyes glinted as his gaze caressed her form. "Tell me where."

She couldn't force the words through the tightness of her throat, but she took his hand and placed it on her waist. Its heat burned through the thin linen of her shift. Even freed from the constriction of her gown, she still couldn't get enough air into her lungs. She sobbed for breath as Edmund's thumb traced teasing circles, sending shivers through her flesh. Yearning for more, she pulled his hand up to cup her breast. Whether by accident or design, his thumb brushed her nipple and she gasped, arching her back into the touch. She couldn't stop herself now. She straddled his hips and seized his mouth in a devouring kiss.

"Touch me," she gasped again when the need to breathe forced her to part their lips.

"Where?"

"Everywhere."

Then his hands did her bidding, trailing fire in their wake, first over her shift, then beneath, branding her with his passion. By this time her braids had unraveled, curtaining them both with her tresses. She couldn't wait any longer. Every inch of her body cried out for him. Shifting her hips, she eased herself onto him.

With a groan, Edmund clutched her hips. "Are you sure you want this?"

"Yes. Oh, yes."

Then while he supported her, she lowered her hips, gasping, until he was fully inside her. Even now, as he groaned her name, he let her set the pace and she cried out at the bliss of their joining. There was no fear any more, just the fire of his touch, the thunder of his heartbeat and the feeling of homecoming at the sound of her name on his lips.

Edmund had released her from Sir Roger's ghost.

****

Isobel woke to the light shining in her eyes through the unshuttered windows. She stretched languorously, wincing a little at the unaccustomed aches, then gave a slow smile. She rolled over, and the last vestiges of sleep fell away when she found the other side of the bed empty. Recalling Edmund's worry about Cannington and his son, her disappointment faded. Judging from the brightness of the room, the morning was far advanced, and Edmund wouldn't let a sleepless night prevent him from resuming his search.

She went through her morning duties in a daze. Edmund had chased away all lingering fear last night. Rather than being something to endure, his lovemaking had taken her back to a time before she'd ever met Sir

Roger, to a time when she had believed their love was strong enough to endure all hardships. Nothing had existed save the feel of his hands, his lips, the glide of flesh upon flesh and his voice murmuring reassurance.

It almost made her believe they could love again.

She caught her breath. Was it possible? Oh, not to return to the innocent love they'd shared before; they were both too changed for that. But maybe they could forge a new love from the ashes of the old.

Yes. A new love. That was what she wanted.

She renewed her tasks humming merry tunes, looking up with pounding heart every time she heard booted feet approach.

"Mama!" Will ran up to her when she returned to the solar to warm up before the noon meal. "Where's Papa?"

It did her heart good to see how Will had accepted Edmund into his life. "He's gone out, looking for someone lost in the snow." No need to say that person was a wanted outlaw.

Will's face fell. "I wanted to ask him to play with me in the snow again. We had fun last time."

Suddenly the solar felt too cramped to contain her overflowing high spirits. "Will I do? I might not be able to build as good a snow castle, but I'll play with you if you like."

The beaming smile on Will's face was all the reward she needed, and she left the donjon with a spring in her step, Will's hand in hers.

She paused beside the orchard gateway, breathing in the crisp air. Funny how she hadn't noticed before how the orchard wall had tumbled slightly where it was choked beneath trailing ivy. She must have a word with the steward to ensure it was fixed as soon as the snow cleared.

"Look, Mama, I'm making the first footprints ever made in this snow." Will ran through the orchard gate and set a trail that wound around the tree trunks. In fact they weren't the first footprints—a trail by the door of the hut showed that Simon Fitzgifford must have been here earlier, checking on the fruit stores.

Isobel strolled around the orchard, enjoying its peace and pristine beauty. The world had an extra sparkle to it today. She shivered, a delicious thrill, in anticipation of Edmund's return and how they would pass the night. They might be too old and wise for love, but even the Church preached on the necessity for a wife not to deny her husband his conjugal rights, except on fast days. Who was she to go against the teaching of the Church?

After a while, a glance back through the gateway revealed folk making their way to the great hall. The morning had flown by. "Will," she called, "it's time for the meal."

There was no answer, and Isobel couldn't see where he was hiding. "Come out, Will. There's no time for games."

No answer. Isobel sighed. This was a game Will had played last time it snowed: she would have to follow his trail to his hiding place.

It didn't take long for her to see a trail of small footprints leading to the hut. She hurried to the door, then stopped, her heart pounding as it finally dawned on her what she should have noticed right from the start. The large footprints she'd thought were Simon's didn't lead from the orchard gate, but from the tumbledown section of wall. Then the next warning sign punched her in the stomach: there were no return prints.

The blood roared in her ears. Heaven have mercy on them—whoever had gone to the hut was still there. And Will was with them.

Will! She couldn't force her thoughts into order. All she knew was her son needed her. She strode to the door and flung it open.

"Step inside slowly and shut the door," a voice snapped. A man's voice speaking Norman French with an accent that revealed he'd been born into the nobility. "Don't make a sound—I have the boy."

Every bone in her body heavy with dread, she shut the door and waited for her eyes to adjust to the dim interior. Gradually—an agony of heartbeats—she made out a tableau of shadowy forms.

A tall man stood near the back of the hut, holding a much smaller figure in front of him. Will! The child drew sharp sobbing breaths. With dawning horror, Isobel saw the faint gleam of lamplight upon steel. The man had a knife.

Chapter Sixteen

Edmund didn't have to go beyond the threshold of the shepherd's hut to see Cannington hadn't returned. The hearth was stone cold, and nothing had been moved since last time they had looked. Hellfire! How was it possible for a grown man and a boy to disappear so completely? He could almost believe Cannington had been snatched away by the Fair Folk.

"Where now?" asked Joss with a grimace. "God's bones, every time I close my eyes, all I see are mile upon mile of empty, snowy wilderness. I don't think I can face another futile traipse through this cold. I've forgotten what summer feels like."

"Check the other huts, although I doubt we'll find any sign of them there. After that we'll return to the castle and rethink our plan. It's pointless making another attempt to track them from here. Any trail will be over a day old."

To think he had left Isobel's bed for this. Still, anticipation of the night to come would lighten the journey home.

Home. He had a home. It was the first time since being snatched away as a terrified four-year-old that he had felt this way about any place. The huge, bleak castle in Redmarch was the seat of his earldom, nothing more. But something about Molbren beckoned to him, welcomed him. It could only be Isobel.

A slow smile spread across his face as he recalled last night. The memories were so heated he half expected the snow to melt into a vast pool around his feet. Besides the desire, though, the memory also awoke a feeling of profound gratitude. After the years of heartache caused by lies and broken faith, Isobel had demonstrated enough trust in him to confide her most deeply felt doubts and fears. It had been no easy thing for her, and the fact she'd been able to open up to him was a sign the rift between them was healing.

Maybe it wasn't too late for them. Maybe they had both finally closed the door on the past. It was time to look forward to a future together. Acknowledge their past mistakes, but no longer dwell on them.

Maybe, just maybe, he could let Isobel into his heart once again.

The faintest whisper niggled at the back of his mind. Love could lure you in. Entrap you. And before you knew it, you were paying the price for your foolishness with your head in a noose.

He ignored it. That was in the past. He and Isobel had proved the past no longer ruled them.

Of course, their future would be assured if only he could find Cannington. The moment he arrived back at the castle he went to the solar to consult the maps again. Neither Isobel nor Will was there, but that was no surprise. Isobel was probably busy, and now it had stopped snowing, Will would be out playing. He would spend time with them in the evening. Right now, he needed to concentrate on pinning down exactly where Cannington might have hidden himself.

****

"Will!" Isobel lunged toward her son.

190

"I said stay there!"

Isobel froze. It felt as though a clawed hand squeezed the air from her lungs.

"Now take a step to your right, so I can see you."

Isobel moved into the circle of light cast by a smoky tallow candle, her eyes fixed on Will. "I'll do whatever you want, but don't hurt my son." The man had to be an outlaw, driven to take shelter from the cold. Her mind whirled and she glanced frantically around. What could she offer in exchange for their freedom?

The outlaw gave a shuddering sigh. "Lady Isobel. I thought it was you, but I had to be sure."

What was going on? The man spoke as though he knew her, but it was impossible. She strained her eyes against the gloom.

Now she could make out more than shapes. The man's appearance didn't match his voice at all. His hair was a wild tangle, his jaw sprouting a good week's growth of beard. His clothes looked fairly new; she guessed he'd found somewhere to provide a fresh change of clothes. However, what snagged her attention was a bloodied strip of bandage around his right arm.

Then she spotted another huddled form by the man's feet: a boy about the same age as Will. Realization dawned.

"Cannington!" She slowly held out her hands so he could see they were empty. "Let my son go. I promise not to call out. I just want to talk." Dear God, don't let him have discovered she'd wed the man hunting him, or he might never let Will go.

Cannington swayed. Whether from exhaustion or his wound she couldn't tell. It was obvious he was at the end of his endurance and in no condition to put up a fight. Time was on her side, not Cannington's. The knowledge calmed her.

She stepped closer. "I want to help, but I won't do anything while you have my son."

For an agonizing moment, all she could hear was Cannington's harsh breathing and the thump of her own heart. Then the man's shoulders slumped, and he released Will, who hurtled into Isobel's arms.

"I would never have hurt him." Cannington's voice was a hoarse croak. "I just had to be sure it was you. I couldn't risk you bringing the entire castle garrison down on me."

Isobel hugged Will, breathing in Will's scent and reassuring herself he was unhurt. "How could you be so sure I wouldn't turn you in?"

"I remember watching you with your son last time I was here. When Sir Roger was alive." The tone of his voice expressed his disdain for her late husband. "Forgive me if I'm speaking out of turn, but I could see how you did all you could to protect Will. I can't see you allowing anyone to harm a child."

From the sympathetic tilt of his head, it was clear Cannington had guessed at the abuse she'd suffered. Only a short while ago, the mere hint at what Sir Roger had done to her would have brought back all the painful memories, but now it felt as though Cannington were speaking about someone else. Edmund had done this, had released her from the stomach-churning fear.

Edmund. Who was at this very moment out searching for the man who stood before her. Blessed saints, what was she to do? Her conscience refused to allow her to turn in a man with a young son, but if she sheltered him she was acting against the man she loved.

The man she loved. She swayed on her feet as though struck with a physical blow. God help her, why had she only woken to the truth now, when she contemplated betraying him? But now she saw she had never stopped loving him. Her love had been smothered beneath layers of anger and bitterness, twisted out of shape, but always there, nevertheless. Edmund's care and patience these past days had gradually released it and breathed new life into her heart.

No. She couldn't think about that now. Mustn't think of Edmund at all. Her focus had to be Will.

He was looking between her and Cannington, his eyes wary. Needing to protect him from the turn the conversation had taken, she bent down. "The earl's son looks hungry." She gave him a reassuring smile. "Why don't you take him to the back of the hut and show him where the apples are stored?"

"You won't leave, will you?"

"No. I'll be right here."

Still Will hesitated, casting a sideways glance at Cannington.

Seeing Cannington's son, hunched and shivering under a thin cloak, gave her an idea. She unpinned her cloak and draped it around the boy's huddled form. "That should help. What's your name?"

"John."

"Well, John. Are you hungry?"

A nod.

"This is Will. He'll show you where to find the apples." She gave Will a small push. "Go on, my heart. We're quite safe, and poor John won't find the apples on his own. I'm sure he'd like your help." Not only would it give her a chance to talk to Cannington privately, but it would keep Will out of reach should Cannington turn violent.

After a last look back at her, Will took a hesitant step forward and took John's hand. Together they ambled to the shadowy reaches of the hut, and in no time they were chattering and giggling.

"The resilience of the very young," said Cannington, his lips twisting into a wistful smile. Then he staggered, clutching his arm.

Isobel sprang forward to steady him. With an arm around his shoulders, she eased him down upon a stool. "You'd better let me look at your arm. Is it your only wound?"

He nodded. "A wolf bite."

"What about your son? Has he taken any harm?"

"No. He's just cold."

It was clear that Cannington was in no condition to leave. It gave Isobel time before she had to decide what to do. Whether to tell Edmund.

She pointed at Cannington's knife. "Hand that to me, then I'll tend your arm."

Cannington tightened his grip on the hilt. "You'd leave me unable to defend my son?"

"You're taking shelter in *my* castle. If you want my help, you must trust me. And if I'm going to trust *you*, I need you to hand over your knife. You have my word no harm will come to you or your son while you're here."

He hesitated a moment longer, then flipped the knife over in his hand and offered her the hilt. "I hope I don't regret this."

The tightness in her chest eased, and she took the

knife and tucked it into her belt. "So do I. Now hold out your arm." She unwrapped the stiffened bandage, sucking in a breath when she saw the puncture marks. "This looks nasty."

Cannington grimaced when she prodded at the wound. "It seemed to be improving. We found shelter after the attack, and the lady of the house treated the bite. I thought it was healing, but it flared up again after we left."

"It needs a poultice." Ribwort would draw out the poison and reduce the inflammation. "I have everything I need in my stillroom. I can bring you food and drink as well."

"How do I know you won't fetch your men-at-arms?"

"Because I gave my word you wouldn't be harmed. If you won't let me help, why did you come here?"

Cannington gnawed his lower lip, then gave a grudging nod. "As I said, I remembered your kindness, and you've given me no reason to doubt that's changed, even though you have ceded Molbren to Stephen."

"Your allegiance means nothing to me. As long as you don't threaten us, I'll treat you just like any other traveler needing shelter." And remembering Edmund's sufferings as a child hostage, she couldn't conceive of allowing Cannington's son to be taken captive. All she could do was pray Edmund never found out what she was doing.

"I should warn you, though. You might change your mind when you know." It was best she was honest with Cannington from the start. If he discovered the truth another way, he might think she'd planned to trick him.

"Know what?"

"I've recently remarried. To Edmund Granville."

Cannington's eyes had been drooping from weariness but now they flew open. "The Earl of Redmarch? But he's the one who's been sent to capture me." He staggered to his feet. "I must leave."

"No." She pushed him back down. "You're not well enough. I can't in good conscience let you go out into the snow and ice in your condition. You have your son to consider as well. If I don't treat this wound, you'll only get worse. You're already feverish."

Her decision crystallized in her warring mind as she spoke. Even though the prospect of lying to Edmund, denying him his prize, was a spear to her heart, she knew she had to hide Cannington from him. Besides, she'd seen how conflicted Edmund had become when he'd discovered Cannington was with his son. If she told Edmund where Cannington was, she would only be passing the dilemma to him, forcing him either to take a boy captive or defy his king.

By hiding Cannington she was protecting Edmund. If she told herself that often enough, she might start to believe it.

"Trust me," she said. "I won't betray you to my husband."

But she was betraying Edmund.

Cannington closed his eyes briefly and muttered what sounded like a swift prayer under his breath. "Very well. Fetch what you need." He shot a glance at the boys. "But leave your son here."

Over her dead body. She drew herself up to her full height. "I don't think you understand your position. All I have to do is call out, and my men will be here. Either take me at my word or leave, but Will comes with me."

Cannington rubbed his temples as though forcing himself to think. Isobel guessed the fever must be making his thoughts chaotic. Her heart went out to this man, who'd had to endure weeks of cold for the sake of his son.

She crouched down and touched his shoulder. Even through the cloth of his tunic, she could feel how his flesh burned. "If you won't think of yourself, think of your son. Supposing you get too sick to travel, what then? Who's going to take care of him? Who's going to get him safely to your kin?"

He nodded slowly. "Very well. But promise me you'll keep your son away from the garrison until I'm well away from here. If he talks about me, I'm lost."

"I'll confine him to his chamber. You have my word he'll tell no one."

Clutching Will's hand, she left the hut, going limp with relief as soon as the door closed behind them.

After leaving Will in his chamber, impressing upon him how he mustn't breathe a word of Cannington's presence to a soul, she rushed to the stillroom on shaky legs. Once inside, she snatched up a basket and flung all the supplies she might need into it and covered it with a cloth. The bright yellow and red stripes were a cruel contrast to her bleak mood. With the basket under her arm, she dashed into the bailey, only to run straight into Edmund.

Edmund caught her around the waist to save her from crashing onto the icy cobbles. "Careful, *ma belle*. Anyone would think you were running from a blaze."

Ma belle. Hearing the old endearment slip so easily from his lips sent an ache through her heart. She leaned into his embrace, breathing in his scent, painfully aware he would push her away if he knew the truth. Was it only this morning she'd woken with a heart lighter than she'd known for a long time? And it had all been down to Edmund's care and patience. Yet now she held a secret that would shatter their fragile trust if he ever found out.

Edmund frowned. "Isobel, what's wrong?"

She forced a smile. It was the hardest thing she had ever done. "Nothing at all. I'm afraid I'm in a hurry, though. One of the servants has hurt his arm, and I'm on my way to treat him."

"Do you need help?"

"No, I've got everything under control. I expect you need to get on with your search." Her throat ached from the struggle not to weep. Lying to him—and a huge, ugly lie at that—just when she had started to hope they could find happiness together...it was too cruel. He would never forgive her if he found out. Never return her love. But then she thought of Cannington's son—that fearful, half-starved boy no older than Will. If she didn't help him, who would? She would never forgive herself if he came to harm.

Feeling as though she were tearing her heart in half, she prised herself from his arms and hurried away, only just remembering in time not to head directly for the orchard gate. She veered toward the blacksmith's forge. Pausing beside the door, she looked back and saw Edmund disappearing through the door to the great hall. With a whispered prayer that he wouldn't come out again, she ran through to the orchard and back to the hut.

She slammed the door behind her and slumped

against the rough wood. Her legs were so weak she had to pause to gather the strength to cross the room.

She found Cannington still slumped upon the stool, his son curled in his lap. Seeing the love and trust between them firmed her resolve, and she pulled out some bread, cheese, and a handful of hazelnuts from her basket and handed them to John. "This should make you feel better."

The boy snatched the food and tore off a chunk of bread and crammed it into his mouth. Isobel wondered how long it had been since he'd eaten anything but apples.

A quick rummage through the items jumbled at the rear of the hut produced a second stool, which she dragged in place beside Cannington's. Then she sat next to him and unpacked the rest of her basket. "Drink this," she ordered, producing a corked flask of willow bark tea. Thankfully she'd made it only the previous day, so it had only needed warming. "It's for your fever. I'm going to put a ribwort poultice on the bite to draw out the poison, but first I need to clean out the wound with this." She drew out another flask, this one filled with strong wine. "It will hurt."

It would be best if John didn't witness his father's pain. She handed him a couple of thick blankets, saying, "There's a pallet against the back wall. It would be a great help if you could make up a bed for you and your father. You'd both feel better after a good sleep."

"I'm sorry," she murmured after John had disappeared, "I know it's cold out here, but I can't risk bringing you into the castle. This is the safest place for you both."

Despite her firm belief that hiding Cannington

from Edmund was the only sane option, a lump came to her throat as she bathed Cannington's wound. It wasn't Cannington she saw beside her, but Edmund. Edmund who hadn't abandoned her, as she'd once thought; Edmund, who had flung himself in harm's way to protect her; Edmund, who, instead of taking away her independence had encouraged it. Edmund, who had, chip by patient chip, broken through the stone barriers she'd erected around her heart.

Edmund, whom she was betraying.

Tears welled up. She dashed them away with trembling hands before Cannington noticed.

"Have you given any thought to how you're going to get into Wales from here?" she asked, clearing her throat when her voice shook. "My husband has the immediate surroundings closely watched. Evading him will be difficult."

"Then we must leave tonight. If you would be willing to provide us with enough food and drink to last two or three days, we'll leave the way we came in— over the wall."

"Tonight? You're not well enough to go anywhere tonight."

"I'll manage."

Isobel crushed the ribwort leaves and spread the resulting paste upon a piece of linen and placed it over the wound. Her mind buzzed with conflicting ideas as she wound a bandage around Cannington's arm to hold the poultice in place. After she'd tied off the bandage she said, "Very well. If you can walk to the door and back without stumbling, I'll consider you fit enough."

Cannington rose and took three confident strides before swaying and clutching at a shelf, bringing a wooden crate crashing to the floor. Isobel hurried to his side and caught his arm.

"Do you still think you are well enough to walk out in the freezing cold with a young boy in your care?" She guided him back to his stool.

Cannington slumped across the table and rested his head in his hands. "My son," he choked. "If it was just me I wouldn't mind, but I won't see my son taken into captivity."

If any doubts lingered, they were gone now. Cannington was a good man trying to save his son. No matter the cost, she couldn't surrender him to Edmund. She imagined herself in his position: so close to freedom, yet his chances of escape fading by the hour.

She placed a hand on his shoulder. "Listen to me. You have to stay here another day at least. If you leave tonight in your condition, you'll be going to your death. Yours and your son's. I might be Stephen's vassal now, but I'm also a mother. I won't do anything to harm your son. If there's any way I can get you safely away, I'll find it. You have my word." She resolutely thrust all thoughts of Edmund from her mind.

Cannington raised his head and gazed at her with red rimmed eyes. After a long pause where he seemed to be assessing her, he nodded. "It seems I have no choice, but I think I can trust you."

"You can." She straightened up. "I have to go before I'm missed."

She would spend half the night thinking of a way to help Cannington escape. The other half she'd spend praying Edmund never found out.

Chapter Seventeen

Another day, and he was no closer to his quarry. Edmund rose from the steward's desk and stretched with a groan. How Simon could sit in that instrument of torture he called a chair day after day, Edmund couldn't imagine. A glance out of the window showed him the light was fading. There was nothing more he could achieve here. Tomorrow. He had to believe he'd find Cannington tomorrow. For now, it was high time he returned to the solar and Isobel.

Isobel! Images of the night in her arms had followed him all day: her soft gasps, the look on her face as she'd lost herself to pleasure, the feeling of homecoming that came with being buried deep inside her. Flashes of memory that kept him warm even out in the bitter wind.

With a stack of the steward's lists under his arm, he climbed the stairs to the solar with an extra spring in his step. But he stepped through the door to find the chamber empty. Where were they? He'd never known Isobel or Will to be away from the solar at this hour. Strange he should feel so bereft, when only a short time ago he'd welcomed his own company.

Before he knew it, he was pacing in front of the fire, casting ever more impatient glances at the door. He caught himself with a curse. God's blood, this would never do. What was he—a leader of men or a moonstruck maid with nothing better to do than swoon over love poetry? He flung himself into the chair beside his desk and forced himself to focus on a sketch Simon had made for him. It showed Woodseaves and the local area. Maybe he'd see something he hadn't noticed in the last thousand times he'd examined it.

Taking up his quill, he marked on the approximate line of the tracks they had followed from the huts. It didn't make sense. If they continued in a straight line, they would eventually come to the river about a mile south of the castle. There was nothing there. On the other side of the river was a tiny settlement—no more than a few houses—called Rhyd yr Hen. Edmund puzzled over the unfamiliar words. If he was going to spend more time here in the Welsh Marches, he should probably learn the language. But that was beside the point. There was no bridge, and he'd already proved the river wasn't sufficiently frozen to cross on foot and too deep and swift of current to ford.

What about a boat? He cursed himself for not thinking of that before. Even so, with the amount of ice on the river, it would be a tricky crossing, and how would Cannington have known where to find a boat even if it was possible?

He tapped Woodseaves Manor with his quill. Unless Lady Katherine hadn't been as honest as he'd thought. Maybe he'd been directed to cross the river at Rhyd yr Hen because they knew he would find a boat there.

He poured himself a cup of mead and moved to one of the fireside chairs with a groan. It looked like he was going to have to return to Woodseaves if he was to have any hope of picking up Cannington's trail.

The door opened. His heart stuttered as Isobel entered, her cloak pulled tight around her, emphasizing rather than hiding her curves. He rose and smiled a greeting, but instead of giving an answering smile, she wouldn't meet his eye. She avoided the welcoming fire and toyed with the maps instead.

Edmund waited for Will to dash in full of tales about his day. Instead there was silence, leaving a void that surprised him. He had only known Will for a few short days, and already his absence was a tangible ache. "Where's Will?"

A deep flush colored Isobel's cheeks. "He's in bed, fast asleep. He was out playing in the orchard earlier and tired himself out." She still wouldn't meet his eye.

"Is something wrong, *ma belle*?"

"Nothing at all. Why do you ask?" Turning her back to him, she bent over the chess table, setting each piece in place with painful precision.

She was hiding something, he could feel it in his bones. Edmund studied her in silence for a moment, puzzled and hurt. "You seem out of sorts," he said finally. Are you sure nothing's happened?"

She smiled, but it didn't dispel the lines of tension around her eyes. "Only the usual frustrations of managing the household." She poured herself a cup of mead and sank into one of the hearth-side chairs. "It's good to be able to rest and enjoy the peace."

Edmund sat in the opposite chair and studied her. He couldn't get over the suspicion that something had happened since he'd left her sleeping that morning. Why wouldn't she tell him? After last night he'd felt sure they'd begun to trust one another, and here they were only a few hours later and already Isobel was hiding something.

Yet he still hid secrets from her. The nagging voice whispered in the back of his mind, and he couldn't deny it was true. There were some things he doubted he'd ever feel able to confess to another; the betrayal, the sense of helplessness was too close. It had nothing to do with Isobel; he had every intention of locking away the memories and never revisiting them.

Of course, if he was allowed to hold back, he could hardly fault Isobel for doing the same. And he shouldn't be surprised if she was still nervous; one night's tenderness was never going to completely dispel the shadow of years of suffering. He mustn't try and rush her, but let her talk, put her at ease. "What have you been doing?"

Her answering laugh had a brittle edge. "Nothing out of the ordinary. Just all the castle business that's been at a standstill for days because of all the snow and the wedding. What about you? Have you found any sign of Cannington?"

"Nothing. It's like he's disappeared into thin air." He gave a quick summary of his day. "I don't know what to do next, Isobel. I must have missed something, but what? I've gone over and over his last known whereabouts and nothing makes sense." He took a gulp of mead, willing it to relax him, help him think.

Isobel gazed down at her cup, twisting the stem between her fingers. "Is finding Cannington really so important to you?" She studied the contents of her cup as though it contained the answer to the world's deepest questions. "Would it be so terrible if he got away? What has the poor man ever done to you?"

"It's not what he's done to me. I have nothing

against him. But I've sworn to do my duty to the king and if I succeed, having Redmarch proclaimed a palatinate would be a huge benefit to all my people. We are living through volatile times, our borders open to attack from all sides. If Redmarch becomes a county palatine, I'll have far greater authority to organize our own defenses. The Welsh have been taking advantage of England's turmoil, and I've seen far too many settlements attacked and burned in the short time since I was named earl. The king has promised to add Cannington's land to Redmarch as well. With the extra forces and power, I'll be able to make Redmarch strong, keep its people safe. A rich inheritance for Will, with land to spare for more heirs."

"I see." The mead still appeared to hold her attention. "Then I'm sorry. I…I wish I could help."

"You are helping, *ma belle*. Just being able to talk it through is a help. I know this is late in coming, but I'm glad we've found each other again. Not just for Will, but I'm glad to be back with you."

To his shock, Isobel's eyes brimmed with tears. He reached out a hand. "Come here, *ma belle*."

With a sob she grasped his hand, and he tugged her forward to sit on his lap. She buried her face in the crook of his neck, and he traced gentle circles on the small of her back, fighting the sudden rush of desire. "What's wrong?"

She shook her head. "It's nothing." She fingered the ties at the throat of his tunic. "It's been a trying day, and you weren't here."

Then it struck him. He'd left her this morning before she'd woken up. He'd been so intent on resuming the hunt, he hadn't considered what that might mean to her. Was she worried that she'd somehow displeased him?

"I missed you, too." Then his lips found hers, and he pulled her close, striving to show her with his actions what he'd failed to put into words. For a breathtaking moment, he reveled in her taste, the scent of rosewater, the softness of her breasts against his chest.

Gasping, he broke the kiss and rose to his feet, keeping his arms locked around her waist. "Come with me, then, *ma belle*. Let me show you what I missed doing this morning." He would leave her in no doubt what last night had meant to him.

****

Blessed Mary, Edmund's touch felt so good! When he pressed his lips to the side of her throat, lightning sparks shot down her spine; she molded her body to his, arching her neck to give him greater access. He backed her toward her chamber, and she thrilled at the promise in each of his kisses, every caress. Heart pounding, she allowed him to steer them through the door, then turned her face to his, seeking his lips. For several glorious heartbeats, all thought fled and she was aware only of his taste, his touch, and a frantic need to feel his skin against hers.

But the clatter of the latch as Edmund kicked the door closed brought cold reality crashing down. She couldn't do this. Making love with Edmund was an intensely intimate experience, one that involved the utmost trust. As much as her body yearned for him, it felt wrong…*deceitful*… to share her body when her heart and mind were guarding a secret. A huge secret that could ruin him.

And if he found out…

She broke the embrace with a gasp, the image of Sir Roger, his hand raised, flashing in front of her eyes. She staggered back to sink down upon a chair, hugging her arms to her chest. "I'm sorry. I…I fear I'm more tired than I realized."

Edmund blew out a breath, then perched upon the edge of the bed. "There's nothing to apologize for, *ma belle*. I'm not Sir Roger. I won't force you to do anything."

No. He wasn't Sir Roger. So why had that terrifying thought occurred to her? Tears pricked her eyelids. "It's not…not that. I've already told you: I had a trying day."

"Won't you tell me about it?" Then Edmund frowned. "Is this why you were so lost in thought when you ran into me earlier? Tell me what's happened. I can't help if I don't know."

Isobel found she was fidgeting with the cross at her throat. She lowered her hand to her lap and clasped it. She studied Edmund's face. Drank in the strong lines of cheekbones and jaw, tried not to let her gaze fall on his mouth. The years had etched their suffering upon him, scarred him, but experience had taught her that he was still honorable and kind at heart. Nothing like her former husband.

An almost overwhelming urge swept over her to confess, tell him Cannington was here. She hated having this secret between them, threatening their happiness. Edmund had shown over and over in the past days that he was a good father. Knowing of his own experiences as a hostage, surely she could trust him to save Cannington's son from a similar fate.

But the memory of Sir Roger refused to leave, a lingering miasma.

She forced a smile. "Honestly, there's nothing to tell. Things didn't go to plan today, that's all."

Edmund rose, a furrow scored deep between his brows. "Very well. As you're tired, I'll leave you to sleep." He hesitated, his hand on the latch. "I'd hoped you were learning to trust me. If you won't confide in me, I can't help."

He didn't slam the door; even so, the chill he left in his wake made his displeasure plain.

Too heartsick to bear her maid's company, she removed her veil and gown herself, then crawled into bed, shivering. She was doing the right thing. She had to believe it. Tomorrow, if Cannington had regained his strength, she would find a way to help him to safety. After that, there would be no more secrets. Nothing more to fear.

But heaven help her if Edmund ever learned what she had done.

****

He had to get away, back to his mother and safety. He looked for her, twisting this way and that, but all he could see was a forest of legs. Strong hands gripped him when he tried to break free. Then he was lifted onto horseback and he saw her. She had come to take him back! But why was she waving?

Then he was in a narrow chamber. Outside the window he could hear the hammer of a mallet upon wood. The shutters blew open, and the noise grew louder. Heavy with dread, Edmund climbed on his bed until he could reach the bars and pull himself up to look out into the courtyard. In the middle stood a gallows.

As he watched, a workman slung a rope across the high beam. Then he turned and beckoned to Edmund.

Edmund's eyes flew open. Blessed saints, when would these nightmares end? He sat up and gazed at the unfamiliar bed hangings, trying to work out where he was. As the fog of his dream cleared, memory returned. Dawn light shone through the gaps in the shutters, revealing his chamber in Molbren.

It was a good thing he hadn't slept in Isobel's chamber; he'd hate her to have witnessed his nightmares. Above all, he couldn't bear the prospect of having to explain them.

Not that she had a right to expect answers when she refused to confide in him. Because she had been hiding something from him, he was sure of it. He tossed back the covers and pulled on his clothes. His irritation made him clumsy, and he knocked his water pitcher to the floor, soaking the rushes. God's blood, he had to get out of here before he took out his mood on Isobel or Will. He fastened his cloak and stalked out, looking for his squires.

Once out on-horseback, however, the fresh air cooling his ire, he found himself trying to see things from Isobel's point of view. He was probably overreacting. After all, he couldn't deny running Molbren kept her busy; she probably had been exhausted last night. Just because he'd returned tired and dispirited from yesterday's futile search, it didn't give him a right to expect Isobel to act exactly as he wanted.

He'd missed her, though. He'd lain awake for hours, listening to the night sounds—the screech of an owl, the distant yelp of a fox. All the while, a strange, hollow ache gnawed at his chest.

The ache had had nothing to do with the lack of lovemaking. Or not entirely. The realization struck him as they clattered over the bridge. No, it was the sharing of confidences that he'd missed. How odd that when he'd contemplated taking Isobel as his wife again, it had been the prospect of sharing his bed that had enticed him the most. It only now struck him how he valued her opinions, how confessing what had happened to him as a child had eased the burden on his heart.

He gave the reins a sharp tug as the truth dawned brighter than any sunrise: he wanted more than just a bed-fellow and mother to his heirs. He wanted a true companionship of shared thoughts and hearts.

He wanted love.

"Is something wrong, my lord?" Joss's voice brought Edmund back to awareness of his surroundings, and he saw that Al-Ashab had come to a halt.

He coaxed the stallion to move forward. "All's well," he said. "Keep going."

In heaven's name, they'd better pick up Cannington's trail quickly, because now he knew what he wanted, he refused to waste any more time. As soon as he returned to Molbren, he would lay siege to Isobel's heart until she opened up to him. He would lay his heart at her feet and settle for nothing less in return.

An hour later, he was once again approaching Woodseaves with Joss and Ancel. Lady Katherine greeted them in the manor's great hall. "I'm afraid my husband is out hunting."

"Actually, it's you we came to see."

"Me?" She suddenly became engrossed in studying

the rings on her fingers. "If this is about the Earl of Cannington, I've already told you all I know."

"Maybe not everything. When he left here, where was he headed?"

Silence. Lady Katherine twisted a band of red and blue enamel around her finger.

It was time to apply a little more pressure. "Need I remind you that I can make things very difficult for you?" Not that he planned to tell her husband about her blunder, but he would use any weapon available to get her to talk.

She frowned as though struggling to remember. If they were ever short of mummers at Molbren, he'd recommend Lady Katherine. "He was trying to get west into the Welsh hills." Her glance slid sideways before returning to his face. She was definitely hiding something, but what?

"Let me be more specific. In order to reach the hills, first he would have to cross the river. Where?"

She shook her head. "I can't say."

Edmund addressed Joscelyn. "Ready the horses. We're going to find Sir Geoffrey."

"No, please don't! I'll tell you. He was going to cross the river at Rhyd yr Hen. That's all I know, I swear. Now please leave before my husband returns."

She was telling the truth this time, he was certain. "Thank you for your cooperation. We'll leave you in peace. I trust you'll be more forthcoming in future, should I ever need your help again."

The oblique warning delivered, he signaled his squires to leave.

****

"I don't understand," said Joss as they rode south

toward Rhyd yr Hen. "There was no crossing marked on the map. How could Cannington get to the Welsh side?"

"The only thing to do is go and look," replied Edmund. "I'm sure Lady Katherine was telling the truth this time."

He couldn't help comparing Lady Katherine with Isobel. Isobel would never have given in and revealed a secret. She had an inner strength that her experience with Sir Roger had refined, not broken. It might bring them into conflict from time to time, but he knew who he preferred. Isobel would never endanger someone under her protection.

Unlike his parents. Shivering from the memory of his nightmare, he spurred Al-Ashab into a gallop.

It didn't take long to cover the distance to the river. On the opposite bank he could see the cluster of squat, thatched dwellings comprising the settlement of Rhyd yr Hen. But what about the crossing? From their approach, the river was hidden behind a low thicket, and the track wound around the edge.

When they finally reached the bank, Edmund drew rein and swore fluently. The river was wider and shallower here. The ice creaked and groaned as the sluggish current beneath swirled around thick slabs set upon the river bed. It was clearly a ford.

Joss expressed Edmund's feelings perfectly with a string of oaths that, from the sound of it, he'd picked up in a Jerusalem bawdy house. "All this time we've been searching the wrong side of the river. Cannington must have crossed yesterday."

In his heart, Edmund suspected that Cannington was out of reach in the Welsh hills by now, but he had to continue to do his duty and investigate every possibility. He urged Al-Ashab into the ford. "Let's see what the residents have to say."

The first piece of information he gleaned wasn't related to Cannington, but it did reassure him that he hadn't been the victim of a conspiracy to conceal vital information. Wisps of smoke rising through the thatch of the nearest house—more a hovel—encouraged them to try there first.

"But everyone knows there's a ford here," the woman who opened the door told them in answer to Edmund's question. "That's what the name means—Rhyd yr Hen: Old Ford. This was the crossing long before the Normans came and built the bridge up by their castle." Isobel's steward must have assumed Edmund, whose county bordered on Wales, would know enough Welsh to understand. In fact, having left Redmarch at four and only returned a few months ago, he'd never had the opportunity to learn the language.

"Did you see a man and a boy cross here yesterday?"

"Oh, yes. I see everyone who comes across. I was right surprised to see them cross in this weather, but the man told me he'd been caught out by the blizzard and forced to take shelter until it cleared. He said—"

"You spoke to him?" Edmund's pulse raced.

The woman nodded. "He came here asking for shelter. I had to turn him away, even though I felt sorry for the poor mite of a boy. He *said* he was unwell, but if you ask me he was an outlaw and had been wounded. We've had a fair few of them in these parts since—"

"Did you see where he went?" It seemed that, unlike Lady Katherine, his problem here was going to be how to stop his witness from talking.

"Well, as I was just saying, he said he wasn't well enough to travel far. I sent him up to Molbren village. 'They're not too particular there,' I told him. 'You'll be bound to find someone who—'"

"Molbren! God's bones—he must have been under our noses all night." Edmund thanked the woman and gave her a coin.

"We've got him this time." He sprang into his saddle. Then he pointed Al-Ashab's head at the village and set off at a gallop.

Chapter Eighteen

Isobel had woken before dawn; the bed felt empty without Edmund. They had only shared a bed for two nights, and already Isobel missed him when he wasn't there. The sooner she got Cannington away and healed the rift with Edmund, the better.

Unable to face him until there was no longer any need to lie, she remained in her chamber until she could be sure she wouldn't run into him. When Edmund's voice drifted up from the courtyard, she wrapped a shawl round her shoulders and peered through the window. Her heart thumped when she saw him, sitting tall on Al-Ashab's back. A cloak swathed his upper body, but the sight of his long, muscular legs made her mouth go dry with longing. In the light of day, her fears that he would punish her as Sir Roger had seemed foolish, yet they lingered, like the memory of a nightmare, no matter how many times she reminded herself of Edmund's kindness.

Today. If Cannington was fit, she would send him away today. Then she could go to Edmund, if not with a clear conscience, at least knowing she would never allow any more secrets to come between them.

The moment the gates closed behind Edmund and his squires, she hurried out to the orchard hut, bearing more food together with fresh linen and herbs to dress Cannington's wound. Although he was heavy-eyed, his fever had dropped. When she unwound the bandage, she saw his wound had lost most of the swelling and redness. The tightness in her shoulders eased.

"Thank the Lord—you're well enough to travel." She placed a fresh poultice upon his arm. "I'm sure my husband suspects I'm hiding something. It's not safe for you to stay any longer."

After a quick glance at John, who was only just stirring from a deep sleep, she bandaged the poultice in place. "Climb over the orchard wall and hide yourselves. I'll fetch horses and more supplies as soon as I can." Thank Heaven both Cannington and his son looked much better after food and a good night's sleep. She could send them on their way with a clear conscience.

The trouble was, how was she to get the horses? She pondered the question as she returned to the donjon. She could ask the stable master to saddle them up for her, but he would insist on providing an escort. Not for the first time, she cursed the limitations laid upon women. Edmund could have taken two horses with no questions asked. She, on the other hand, although mistress of Molbren, was unable to walk away with so much as a donkey.

She tilted her head to the skies. *Blessed Virgin, show me what to do!*

As if in answer to her prayer, her steward's thanks sounded in her mind. He'd vowed he was her man if she ever needed help. She quickened her pace and directed her steps to the donjon. Not only had he pledged his support, his sympathies lay with the empress, so there no fear of him feeling honor-bound to tell Edmund. This would work! Only a short while now, and all her problems would be over. She could offer her heart to Edmund with a clear conscience.

She sprang up the donjon stairs and flung open his door. Thank the saints, there he was, scratching some notes with a swan's feather quill.

He rose to his feet. "My lady Isobel, how can I be of service?"

"Simon, you promised your help should I ever need it. Well, I need it now." As briefly as possible, she explained the situation.

Simon's eyes opened wide, but he rose and picked up his cloak without hesitation. "Leave it with me, my lady. I'll meet you behind the orchard wall."

Only pausing to collect more linens in case Cannington needed to apply a fresh dressing, she hurried out to the meeting place, managing to slip unobserved through the main gate. Cannington and John were already there. True to his word, Simon appeared shortly after, leading two horses, packed with supplies. "It only occurred to me after I left," he said, "but I can't go back through the main gate. Not when I've been seen leaving with the horses."

Isobel cursed. How were they to get away with this when snags continually threatened to trip them up? And they were running out of time. If Edmund came straight back from Woodseaves, he wouldn't be away long. She glanced around, half expecting to see him ride into view. Holy Mother, she had to be inside the castle before he returned.

Her glance fell on the tumbled sandstone blocks at the base of the orchard wall. "Climb over here. Quick!"

"But—"

"Do it! Don't let anyone see you cross the courtyard and stay in your office for as long as you can."

After throwing her an agonized look, Simon hoisted his robes around his knees, revealing skinny calves. At any other time, Isobel would have giggled at the sight of her steward losing all dignity as he scrambled over the wall with Cannington's help, his robes riding up dangerously close to his backside. But all she could do was pace, praying Edmund didn't return.

At last Simon made it to the other side and Cannington sprang down. Isobel turned to leave when she remembered one last thing. "I nearly forgot this," she said, removing Cannington's dagger from her belt. "I pray you won't need it."

Just as Cannington's fingers closed around the hilt, she heard a twig snap behind her. She whipped around, her heart hammering her ribs. "Who's there?" she cried, fighting to keep the tremor from her voice.

"It's me!" Then in a flurry of snow, Will was there, flinging his arms around her legs.

"Will." Shaky with relief, she took his hand. "What are you doing here?"

"I followed you, and you never noticed! Why did Simon climb over the wall? He looked funny. I can't wait to tell Papa when he gets back."

The words had barely left Will's mouth when Isobel caught a flash of steel from the corner of her eye. Her mouth opened in a scream, but terror closed her throat. In a nightmarish blur of movement, Cannington grasped Will's free arm and jerked him away from Isobel.

"I'm sorry, but I can't let you return to the castle. Not now. Don't cry out, or you'll regret it."

Isobel's knees shook; she clung to the wall for support. "For the love of God, let him go."

"I can't do that. Believe me, I didn't want this to happen, but you promised your son would stay out of sight. There's no way you can guarantee he won't tell what he's seen."

"I can. I'll confine him in his chamber until—"

"That's what you said last time, yet here he is. If it were just me, I'd risk it, but my son's fate hangs in the balance, and I'll do anything to ensure his safety. You and your boy are coming with me."

Cannington lifted Will up onto the saddle of the larger horse, all the while keeping between Will and Isobel, giving her no chance of snatching him to safety. "Get up on the other horse," he ordered.

She struggled to think of a way out, but Cannington had Will at his mercy; she daren't risk crying out. She climbed into the saddle, her mouth dry.

Unbidden, her fingers found her garnet pendant. She glanced down, a desperate hope forming. It was her only chance. While Cannington's attention was focused on settling the boys in front of him, she jerked on the slender chain to snap it and flung it to the ground, praying Cannington wouldn't see.

At Cannington's command, she followed him, not taking her eyes off Will. All she could do now was pray Edmund would find the necklace, work out what happened. And above all she prayed he would forgive her betrayal and come to find her.

****

Edmund strode up the hill, leading Al-Ashab,

kicking at any rock or lump of ice that dared get in his way. Where in God's name was Cannington? He'd been so sure he would find him in the village, but after a wasted morning turning the place upside down, he had to concede the man had outwitted him.

So much for being able to devote more time to Isobel; they would have to ride out again after the briefest of dinners if they were to have any hope of finding him.

"My lord, look!"

Edmund glanced back at Ancel, who had stopped and was pointing at a spot some distance from the path. It looked like a patch of churned up snow. "Is that a trail?" His pulse quickening, he left Al-Ashab on the path and jogged toward the spot.

He stopped dead when he got there. It was a clear trail through the snow, showing that two horses had ridden away from the castle.

"These tracks are fresh," said Ancel, who had knelt to examine them. "No more than two hours, I'd say."

Leading away from the castle, the trail soon disappeared behind a cluster of trees. But why would anyone leaving the castle not take the track? It was less steep and far safer.

In his bones, Edmund felt sure this had to do with Cannington. But he had been led astray too many times in the past days. He had to be sure. "Let's see where the trail starts."

They followed it up the hill and soon came to level ground beside the orchard wall. And thanks to a freshly fallen section, the wall could be scaled with little trouble.

Edmund's senses tingled. "This has to be it.

There's a hut just over the wall, if I remember correctly." A hut where a fugitive and his son could take shelter. "Come with me, Joss."

Leaving Ancel to take care of the horses, Edmund led the way over the wall. The first thing he saw on the other side was a trail leading from the hut. He flung open the door, and what he saw confirmed his worst fears. He noted the apple cores and nut shells on the floor and examined the blood-stained bandages on the table. "Cannington was here." He kicked over a stool. "God blast him to hell, he was here all along. Come on."

He was in the process of scaling the wall again, when Ancel called to him. "Come quickly, my lord. You have to see this."

He scrambled down and ran to where Ancel was kneeling, peering at more tracks. "What is it?"

Ancel pointed. "A child's tracks."

"We've confirmed this must be Cannington, so this has to be his son's tracks. We have to go."

He made to rise, but Ancel stopped him. "There's more." He pointed to another set of prints. "These were also made by a child, but a different one."

A chill that had nothing to do with the snow tricked down his spine. "Are you sure?"

"Positive."

They weren't necessarily made by Will. There were other children living in the castle. It could be any one of them.

Then a glint of red and gold caught his eye. The breath whooshed from his lungs when he saw a gold chain dangling from the branch of a nearby bush. Suspended from the chain was a cross made of tiny garnets set into gold. He'd seen that cross too many times to have any doubt who it belonged to.

He snatched the chain off the branch with fingers that trembled. The chain had snapped.

For a sickening moment, the ground rocked beneath his feet. He couldn't think, couldn't see anything except the glittering garnets, winking at him. Mocking him. Only the experience he'd gained in the Holy Land enabled him to push aside the fear and think again.

He turned on his heel and grasped Al-Ashab's bridle. "At least he had the manners to leave us a clear trail this time. Let's go."

Edmund mounted and spurred Al-Ashab to a gallop he'd have described as reckless even in good conditions. But he couldn't afford to let Cannington get away. The king's favor and Redmarch's palatinate status meant nothing to him. Isobel needed him, and this time he wasn't going to give up until she was safely back in his arms.

Chapter Nineteen

Until now, Edmund had loved the hills and woods around Molbren. Now he missed the open desert, where he could see for miles. Isobel and Will must be somewhere ahead, but each time Edmund crested a hill, standing in his saddle to scan the horizon, another hill loomed ahead, blocking his view. Was he closing in on his quarry? Did he have any hope of reaching them before they left Molbren lands? There was no way of knowing.

Will and Isobel needed him, just as Isobel had needed him five years ago. He had given up too soon before, but this time he would never give up. Not even if it meant riding alone into Welsh lands and tearing down any walls standing between him and his family. It's what he should have done five years ago but hadn't. He wouldn't make the same mistake twice.

Joss pulled level. "How much farther before we enter Welsh territory?"

Edmund tried to visualize all the maps and written descriptions of Molbren's boundaries. "It can't be far. If I've remembered correctly, there's a river valley beyond the next ridge. That marks the boundary." It was hard to speak when the motion made his teeth rattle, but he pressed on, raising his voice to make sure Ancel also heard. "I won't stop at the boundary, but I don't ask you to come with me." There was a danger the Welsh would see them as raiders and attack on sight. He wouldn't order his squires to take that risk.

"You don't have to ask," Joss called back. "We're coming. Don't try and stop us."

Ancel shouted his agreement. Encouraged, Edmund spurred Al-Ashab up the next slope and strained his eyes for signs of Isobel and Will.

This time his view was impeded by a line of oaks atop the ridge. He ground his teeth with impatience, desperate to see into the valley beyond. When, after what felt like a hundred years, he emerged from the trees, he looked out with pent breath. At first he saw nothing more than the steep hillside shrouded in snow; at the valley bottom, a meandering line of alders marked the course of the river. The edge of Molbren's territory. Then he caught movement from the corner of his eye, and he focused upon the clump of trees beside the track about a quarter of a mile away. There! Two horses emerged, both carrying riders. One seemed to have smaller forms in front—children? He let his gaze linger on the crimson cloak of the rider at the rear. Isobel!

Joss saw them at the same moment. He cursed. "We'll never catch them before they reach the river."

Edmund traced the path of the track. It wound down the hill in a series of traverses. Isobel and Cannington were already halfway down. "I will if I take the direct route."

Joss's despairing voice followed as Edmund galloped down the hill, ignoring the much longer track. "That's insane!"

Nevertheless, a quick glance behind showed him that both his squires were following.

The wind roared in his ears. Snow sprayed from Al-Ashab's hooves and whisked into his eyes. This was his last real hope of stopping Cannington. He'd meant it when he said he would follow Isobel into Welsh territory, but in his heart he knew that would mean a lengthy captivity or death. The gradient increased. Edmund struggled to keep his balance in the saddle and guide Al-Ashab around obstacles at the same time. This was the most reckless thing he'd done since flinging himself between those knights and their intended victim in the Holy Land. Well, he'd survived that, so he could only pray he'd survive this too.

He aimed for the last bend in the track. If he timed it right, he would arrive at the same time as Cannington. He glanced across to locate the crimson cloak. Perfect. At present they were facing away from him and wouldn't be aware of his approach. Up ahead there was a line of trees to afford him some cover. Cannington wouldn't see him until it was too late.

They were behind the trees and fast approaching the track when Al-Ashab must have stepped into a concealed dip. He stumbled and fought to right himself but couldn't find purchase in the treacherous conditions. Pulse hammering, Edmund flung himself forward, fighting to control his horse and cling on at the same time. But with a lurch of fear, he felt Al-Ashab slip on the icy trail, and he knew there was no saving them. Casting up prayers to all the saints he could recall, he swung his leg across the cantle and flung himself clear, hitting the ground with a force that knocked the breath from him. He struggled to draw air into his lungs, ears ringing. Then a terrified squeal from Al-Ashab alerted Edmund to his horse, sliding, looming over him. His heart slamming against his ribs, he rolled away just in time. A mere heartbeat later, the horse collapsed onto the spot where he'd been lying.

****

Isobel struggled to keep pace with Cannington. Only a short distance away was the ford marking the end of her lands, where Cannington had agreed to set her and Will free. She wished he had allowed Will to ride with her, but he'd insisted on carrying both boys on his horse, in case Isobel had been tempted to make a break for freedom.

A horse squealed away to their left, making her horse shy. She fought to regain control and shot a glance in the direction of the noise. It seemed to be coming from a small copse. Cannington pulled his horse to a halt so abruptly it reared. "What was that?" His hand went to the hilt of his dagger.

Then a figure dashed from the trees. His hair was disheveled, his gambeson torn, and blood streamed from a cut to the forehead, but Isobel's stomach swooped. It was Edmund. He had come for her.

Her joy only lasted a brief moment before reality sank in. Cannington had Will. If Edmund tried to take Cannington by force, Will could be hurt. She had to stop him.

Edmund ran straight for Cannington, drawing his sword. With a cry, Isobel scrambled out of her saddle and ran to intercept Edmund. Her boots slipped on the snow, impeding her progress. Edmund was going to reach Cannington before she could get there. Trembling in her haste, she found an extra burst of speed and flung herself in front of Edmund. "Edmund, stop! He's got Will."

Edmund skidded to a halt. His gaze flicked to Isobel and then back to Cannington. "Did he hurt you, Isobel?"

"No, I…" A brief glance at Cannington showed him slumped in the saddle, lines of exhaustion and defeat adding twenty years to his age. A sudden image came to her of their positions reversed, of Edmund the one defeated, faced with the loss of Will.

She couldn't do this. No matter how it damaged Edmund's opinion of her, she couldn't stand passively by and watch a man and his son taken into captivity. A man whose only crime was to hold to an oath others had abandoned.

She reached up for her cross, only to encounter bare flesh. Needing something to hold on to, she bunched her fists in her skirts. "I won't let you harm them, Edmund. I gave my word I wouldn't allow them to be taken captive. Let them go."

"Don't be a fool, Isobel. He's dangerous. He took you and Will, for heaven's sake. There's no way I'm letting him go." Edmund advanced, his sword pointed at Cannington's heart.

If she was to have even the slightest chance of saving Cannington, there was only one way she could think of doing it. She had to tell Edmund the truth.

"He's not dangerous, Edmund, not if you don't threaten his son. Don't you see? I *chose* to help him. I knew he'd taken shelter in the hut. I tended his injury and fed him. He only took me and Will to prevent us from giving him away."

Isobel saw the precise moment her words sank in: Edmund's face drained of color. He faltered, his sword-arm dropping to his side.

It was only a momentary hesitation, but it was enough. Cannington pushed past her, dagger in hand, his mouth contorted in a snarl. "You won't have me, or my son!"

Isobel could only watch in horror as he flung himself against Edmund, bowling him over and knocking his sword out of his hand. What had she done? She'd meant to persuade Edmund to let Cannington go, not render him vulnerable to attack. She held her breath as Edmund rolled aside and staggered to his feet. He sidestepped neatly when Cannington lunged, then drew his own dagger.

"Don't be a fool, Cannington." Edmund adopted a defensive stance. "Look at you. You can barely stand upright."

Cannington shook his head. "What do I have to lose?" With a sudden lunge, he tried to slip beneath Edmund's guard. Edmund parried then sidestepped; Cannington's momentum carried him past Edmund and toward the squires who now drew their swords.

But Isobel's relief was short-lived. With a strangled cry, Cannington whirled around and charged Edmund, his dagger aimed at Edmund's throat.

Isobel's heart stuttered. A scream forced its way out of her throat. She wanted to fling herself at Cannington before he could reach Edmund, but her muscles were locked tight.

With a movement too swift to follow, Edmund ducked beneath the blade and jabbed his elbow into Cannington's wounded arm. Cannington dropped his dagger and staggered to his knees, clutching his arm.

Giddy with relief, Isobel could only watch as Edmund and his squires overpowered Cannington.

229

Cannington, slumped in defeat, offered no resistance as Edmund's squires marched him toward his horse. Finally the life returned to her limbs, and she approached the group. She desperately wanted to go to Edmund, explain her actions. Discover if she had destroyed all hope of winning his love. However, Edmund kept his back turned to her, busying himself with ensuring Cannington was securely bound to his horse. The rigid set of his shoulders, the clenched jaw, told her as clearly as any words that she was to stay away.

At least Will needed her. It gave her the strength to assume a cheerful mask. She ran to him as fast as her shaky legs could carry her and pulled him into her arms. "How are you, my heart? I hope you weren't too scared."

"I was at first, but then the man promised he wouldn't hurt me. I don't think he was a bad man, really."

Isobel pressed her cheek to the top of his head, reassuring herself he was well. "No, I don't think he's bad. He's just trying to help his son."

She glanced across to see how John fared. Her heart swelled to see him hunched over, clinging to the saddle's cantle. Tears trailed down his cheeks. "What are those men doing with Papa?" he asked, his voice wobbling.

Isobel released Will and hugged the frightened boy. "I won't let anyone hurt him, I promise."

Although how she would manage that when she had lost Edmund's trust, she couldn't say.

The crunch of feet on snow sounded behind her. She knew without turning it was Edmund.

"Are you both well?" His voice was flat. Expressionless.

She turned on leaden legs. "We're unhurt." An awkward pause, then: "What about you? How did you cut your face?"

He grimaced. "Al-Ashab fell, but it's nothing. We're both none the worse for it."

"I'm glad."

Holy Mother, was this what they had come to? Exchanging empty phrases as though they were complete strangers? She fought back a sob. Only two days ago, Edmund had been so patient, lavishing her with care and love, and dispelled her deepest fears. She'd dared to hope that was how life would be from now on.

Throat aching, she reached out a trembling hand, as though she could cling on to that hope. "Edmund, you must let me explain. I—"

"Not now, Isobel. I…I must keep watch on Cannington."

He turned away sharply, but not before she saw the tightness around his mouth, the lines of pain etched between his brows. It gave her the strength to grasp his sleeve and halt him. It wasn't the time or place to plead for herself, but she would do all in her power to fulfill her promise to Cannington and his son.

"Cannington was never going to hurt us, Edmund. He's only trying to do what is best for his son. You'd do the same for Will. What do you mean to do with him?"

"I have no choice, Isobel. I have a sworn duty to the king. We'll return to Molbren tonight, but tomorrow I must take him to Shrewsbury and hand him over to the castle garrison."

"But what about his son? I promised Cannington I wouldn't allow his son to be taken. The king only gave you orders regarding Cannington. Please let his son go free."

Edmund turned away from his contemplation of the fire, his brows scoring a black "V" above his eyes. "You think I would send a boy into captivity, knowing what happened to me as a boy? You accused me before of not believing in you. Not fighting hard enough. But I did this time. I believed you wouldn't act against me, and I fought to win you back. Only to find it was you who failed to believe in me. Did you truly think I would put my own gain above a boy's wellbeing? He'll stay here until I can arrange an escort to his family."

He jerked his arm from her grasp and strode away without a backward glance.

****

The sun set long before they rode through the gates of Molbren. Thankfully it was a full moon and the skies were clear, although the temperature plummeted. By the time she and Edmund were alone by the solar hearth, Isobel was so chilled in body and heart, she doubted she would ever feel warm again.

Edmund flung himself into a chair and gazed into the flames. Isobel poured some wine, then fiddled with the cups upon the table, arranging them into a perfect square. What should she do? Was there anything she could say to make him understand?

Finally, Edmund spoke. "Tell me the truth, Isobel. I need to know what happened. Why didn't you alert the guards when you found Cannington?"

Lying to Edmund last night had been painful. No

matter how much it hurt, she would tell the truth. Their first attempt at marriage had been torn apart because of trickery and lies. Any further deceit could destroy it beyond redemption.

She sank into the chair opposite his. "I felt sorry for him."

"You felt sorry for him." Disbelief dripped from every word. He leaned forward in his chair, grasping the arms so hard, his knuckles turned white. "You betrayed me, lied to me, because you felt sorry for him? Did you think of me at all?"

Isobel's throat ached with the effort of holding back the tears. "I did think of you. I thought of you all the time. I hated that what I was doing might harm you, but Cannington was injured, hungry, and needed my help. Most of all, I couldn't bear to think of what would happen to his son if I turned them in."

"So instead you put Will in danger. Risked his life."

"Edmund, you have to believe me, I tried to keep Will away. He must have followed me. He—"

Edmund thumped the arm of his chair, and she flinched. "It doesn't matter *how* it happened. If you had done the right thing and turned Cannington over to me, he could never have got his hands on Will in the first place."

The fight drained out of her. "I know that. Don't think I don't blame myself, because I do. If anything had happened to Will, I'd never have forgiven myself. But in truth, I don't think Cannington would have harmed Will. He was just doing whatever he could to save his son."

"That's precisely why you shouldn't have trusted

him. Do you think if he'd been forced to choose between your lives and that of his son, he would have hesitated for even a moment? Everyone is out to protect their own interests, and to hell with everyone else."

"That's not true."

Edmund gave a harsh laugh. "Oh, isn't it? Try telling that to my parents."

The moment the words were out of his mouth, his face turned ashen, and Isobel knew he'd never intended to say them.

She leaned forward. "Why? What did your parents do?"

"That's irrelevant. The point is—"

"It's completely relevant. If you're going to punish me because of something your parents did years ago, then I have every right to know."

Edmund gazed at her for a moment, then his shoulders slumped. "When I was sent as a hostage, my parents told me all would be well, because they would never do anything to risk my life." Edmund brushed his hair from his eyes. With a shock Isobel saw his hand trembled. "And do you know what happened next?" he continued, his voice bleak.

She shook her head, her throat too tight to speak.

"My father only waited for enough time to gather his supporters, then he rebelled again. He used me to get what he wanted. That's all I meant to him."

Her muscles contracted in shock. Cannington's hardships...her own fears, everything paled beside what Edmund had endured at such a young age. "How could he do that to you?"

He turned his face away. His neck cords buttressed his throat, rigid as stone. "All too easily. The king demanded he surrender, or risk losing his youngest son. Can you guess how he responded?"

She shook her head before realizing he wasn't looking at her. "No." Her voice was a dry croak.

"He said he already had two other sons. Had no need for a third."

Isobel couldn't take it in. How could anyone be so callous? "He can't have meant it. He must have given himself up in the end to save you."

"My survival is no thanks to him. He continued his rebellion for months until they came to terms. They locked me in a cell and built a gallows in the courtyard. I could hear the hammering from my cell."

Cold nausea seized her, making her head spin. She couldn't comprehend what he must have suffered. "How…" Isobel couldn't complete her sentence. Such behavior was beyond the bounds of her experience or imagination. It was impossible to put into words how she felt about a man who would sacrifice his own son. "Why weren't you hanged?" she asked finally.

"King Henry took pity on me. He said he hadn't become king to murder children. Even though I was useless as a hostage from then on, he kept me at his court, provided tutors, and saw to it that I received weapons training when I was old enough." His lip curled. "He defeated my father and only allowed him to keep his lands on the payment of a crippling fine and the provision that he swore oaths to support Maude after his death. And you saw how faithfully he held to that. He went to Stephen before the dust had settled on Henry's tomb."

She blinked, looking down at her hands, twisting the gold and pearl band around her finger. She didn't want to look at him, see the pain in his eyes. "Why did you never tell me any of this when…when we were together the first time? I thought we had no secrets back then." Although she shouldn't be surprised. After all, they'd managed to amass plenty of secrets now.

"You never told me about your parents. Perhaps you should ask yourself why."

No. Not that she'd experienced anything that remotely compared to Edmund's trials, but the way her mother had never defended her to her father had worn her down. She hadn't told him because she'd wanted to put her past behind her and begin her life afresh with Edmund. She could hardly blame Edmund for wanting to do the same. It was a pity neither of them had possessed the wisdom to see that they couldn't run from who they were. They had both been molded by their experiences. Isobel could see now that even if her parents hadn't managed to separate her and Edmund, the foundations of their love would have been shaky. The first storm might well have caused cracks to appear.

Just as they had now.

She let the silence grow between them. What good were words against the shell of bitterness Edmund had erected around his heart?

A wave of exhaustion swept over her, and she pulled herself to her feet. "It's probably good advice. I'll think on it, if you promise to do the same."

"What do you mean?"

She was too tired to measure her words; they tumbled out, and she was unable to stop them. "What happened to you as a child is the reason you refuse to forgive me…love me. You'll never know peace until you've come to terms with your parents' betrayal." Tears pricked her eyelids, and she addressed her last words to her clasped hands. "I hope you do, because I can't bear the thought of you carrying this burden all your life."

She dared to shoot a sidelong glance at Edmund; his face was an expressionless mask. When it was clear he had no reply, she moved to the door. She had to get out, before she did even more damage.

Halfway there, she stopped. It was no good. She had to know now, or the question would burn into her thoughts all night. "What do you mean to do about me, Edmund?"

After an agonizing silence, he replied. "I mean to grant you your dearest wish. You wanted your independence—to run Molbren without interference. Well, that's what you'll get. After I've delivered Cannington to the king, I'll return to Redmarch. I was a fool to think—" He cursed under his breath.

Fighting to control her quivering mouth, she took a step toward him, then stopped when her trembling legs threatened to give way. "Edmund, please, you have to trust me, I—"

"That's the trouble, Isobel. I can't trust you anymore." The anger had left his voice, leaving only defeat and deep sadness. "You lied to me. Betrayed me. I'll be gone at first light. Tell Will I..." His brows convulsed as though from sudden pain. "Tell him I'll see him when I can."

He made an abrupt move toward her, and for one brief instant she saw not Edmund, but Sir Roger, his face contorted in fury. She flinched. The moment lasted less time than it took to blink, then Sir Roger was gone and he was Edmund again, his expression not one of rage, but pure anguish. Without waiting for her answer, he strode past her to his chamber. A latch rattled, and he'd shut her out.

Isobel staggered to her chamber and curled up on her bed, hugging her knees to her chest. What had just happened? Edmund would never hurt her, so why had the fear returned? A fear she'd thought gone forever.

Her stomach churned. Would she never be free of Sir Roger's ghost? Would she always return to this point whenever they disagreed? If so, Edmund was right. They'd be better off apart.

****

On silent feet, Edmund climbed the winding donjon stairs to the top of the tower. The cold sucked the breath from his body when he stepped out onto the open platform, but even that couldn't make him forget the pain in his heart. Over the past days he had come to trust Isobel to the point where he'd told her things he'd believed he'd never reveal to another. When she'd confided in him in return, he'd allowed himself to believe they were learning to love again. That this time it would be different. He should have known things would never change. He could never truly trust another.

He leaned against the cold stone parapet and gazed at the stars, fading in the pre-dawn light. General wisdom would have him believe his future was written up there if only he knew how to interpret the movements of those remote pinpricks of light. Try as he might, he could see nothing but the past. A boy running to his mother, begging her not to let the soldiers take him away. It had been years ago, but still her reply haunted him: *Trust me. All will be well.*

The door creaked open; he pressed back into the shadows, straining his eyes in the dark to see who disturbed his solitude. A slight figure, cloaked and hooded, formed a brief silhouette against the torchlight in the stairwell before the door slammed shut. Edmund didn't need the glint of moonlight catching the curls escaping from the hood to tell him it was Isobel.

"So you couldn't sleep either."

Isobel froze mid-step. She turned her head, roving the shadows until she found him. "I thought you'd be up here. I...if you want me to beg, I'll do it. I know I was wrong. I betrayed you. But please don't take Will away from me. You've got everything else you wanted. Please leave me with Will."

"Everything I wanted?" He gave a bark of a laugh. "Maybe that is what I wanted at first, but then I changed. You changed me, led me to believe I could love you again. I thought there was one person in the world I could—" He stopped himself. He wouldn't provide her with any more weapons.

Isobel swayed on her feet as though pulled in two directions. Now he could see her eyes were red and swollen. "You changed me too, Edmund. I thought I'd never be able to love again, but you fought for me, proved I could trust you."

Trust. "Then why didn't you?" He recalled her agitation of the previous day, when she must have known Cannington was in the orchard hut. Was it only yesterday? It felt like a lifetime ago. "Do you know how much it hurts to know you thought I would harm a child? Why didn't you trust me to do right by Cannington's son?"

"I..." Her shoulders slumped. "I don't know. I've

been thinking about it all night. If I can't understand myself, how can I hope to—?"

Overcome with the urge to comfort, he reached out toward her. She flinched. A knife through the heart would have hurt less, but he had his answer. His anger drained, leaving nothing but weariness and sorrow. If he'd had any doubt he was doing the right thing, she'd just made up his mind.

He dropped his arm. "If I need to confront my past, then so do you."

"I…I don't understand."

"Don't think I didn't see how you cringed away from me just now. After all the patience and care I've shown you, you still can't trust me. It's better for both of us if we lead separate lives."

He heard Isobel's half gasp, half sob, but he couldn't bring himself to look at her. He pushed himself away from the wall and flung open the door. He paused on the threshold, clutching the latch so tight it bit into his palm. He braced himself for her to call him back. Was he strong enough to resist when his heart cried out to go to her and pull her into his arms?

But she remained silent. Instead of relief, leaden disappointment seeped into his veins. Loathing himself for his weakness, he tore his hand from the latch and clattered down the steps. First his mother, now Isobel. He wouldn't make the same mistake again, would never allow another woman close enough to hurt him.

Chapter Twenty

The first rays of sunlight were scarcely slanting above the eastern horizon when Edmund marched into the great hall in search of his squires. He needed action now. Anything to cast Isobel's stricken face from his mind's eye. Anything to forget her words.

What happened to you as a child is the reason you refuse to forgive me...love me.

If clamping his hands over his ears would have kept out Isobel's voice, he would have done, but it was a lethal arrow driven deep inside his skull and there was no dislodging it.

Because she's right.

No! God's blood, he couldn't think about this now, not when he had a difficult task to do.

Ancel approached. "The horses are ready, my lord. Joss is with the prisoners."

Edmund forced his mind to focus on the present and handed over his bags. "Await us at the gates. I'll escort the earl with Joss."

The earl was hugging his son when Edmund stepped into the chamber where they had been quartered. The boy clung to Cannington's neck, his face crumpled and wet with tears. Edmund felt sick. The sight was far too much like seeing himself as a boy being taken away from his mother. The difference was, it was clear the earl loved his son and clutched John

241

almost as tightly as the boy held him.

A wave of nausea washed over him. He couldn't do this. Isobel was right—about this, at any rate. Not about—no. He wouldn't think about that. He would concentrate on the here and now. The poor boy shouldn't be separated from his father. If he tore father and son apart, he was no better than his parents.

"Are we ready to leave, my lord?" Joss stepped forward. Behind him, the Earl made a choking sound.

"Yes. Escort Cannington to the gate. The boy will ride with me."

Joss frowned and at the same time Cannington whipped round, eyes blazing. "But you said—"

"I know what I said, but I find I was mistaken. Move."

It was only when the road from the castle met with the Shrewsbury road and he turned to the west that Joss spoke. "My lord, this is not the way to Shrewsbury."

"I know." Edmund turned in his saddle and addressed Cannington. "You will direct us to your kin in Wales."

Cannington had been slumped in his saddle, but now he raised his head, hope chasing confusion and despair. "I…my cousin lives near Hay. But I don't understand."

"Neither do I, but it turns out I can't separate you from your son." Edmund felt as though he was standing outside himself, looking on. When the king learnt he had let Cannington slip through his fingers, not only would he never be awarded a palatinate, he was in grave danger of having his lands and title stripped from him. Was he being every kind of fool?

One look at Cannington's glowing face, the

dawning joy and wonder in his eyes as he looked at his son, told Edmund if he was being a fool he ought to be foolish more often.

It was Isobel's fault. Loving her had changed him, and now she had betrayed him he didn't know how to fill the gaping hole in his heart. Before their reunion he had thought overseeing his lands and serving the king would provide him with all the fulfillment in life he could want. Now it all felt empty. Futile.

You'll never know peace until you've come to terms with your parents' betrayal.

Isobel's voice bored through his mind and refused to be ignored.

****

Isobel stood at the open window in her chamber, heedless of the icy blast whipping the tears from her cheeks. The gates had long since swung closed, and now she couldn't tear her gaze from the bend in the road, the last place she'd seen Edmund.

She'd gone up to the roof last night to clear her head, work out if there was anything she could say to persuade Edmund to stay. Instead, her instinctive reaction had proved to Edmund that there was no hope for them. It had convinced her, as well.

She was deaf to the shouts of the people going about their work in the courtyard; all she could hear were Edmund's parting words. It was all she'd heard since he'd uttered them.

"If anyone's too afraid to confront their past, it's you. Don't think I didn't see how you cringed away from me just now. After all the patience and care I've shown you, you still can't trust me. It's better for both of us if we lead separate lives."

Isobel sank onto a chair and buried her head in her hands. He was right. If she couldn't trust Edmund after all his kindness, what hope was there for their marriage? She'd thought he'd dispelled Sir Roger's ghost, but at the first sign of tension between them, it had returned, stirring up the old fear, even though in her heart she knew Edmund would never hurt her.

No wonder he hadn't been able to bear looking at her. He'd taken such care of her, shown her nothing but tenderness and consideration, and she'd flinched the instant he'd taken a step in her direction.

They couldn't live like that. It was bad for them both and damaging for Will. They were better off apart.

It might be true, but it didn't stop her heart from breaking.

****

Four days later, Hay a day's ride behind them, Edmund reined in his mount at a fork in the road. By this time Cannington and his son were safely with their kin. Now all that was left to do was confess to the king. The south-easterly fork would take him to Oxford, where the king was known to be. Edmund eyed the other fork, the one that led to Molbren. Then he turned to his squires.

"I'm going to be in ill favor with the king. I'm not dragging the pair of you into this. Return to Molbren. Protect Isobel if Stephen decides to take retribution."

"And leave you to travel alone through enemy lands? I could never live with the shame if I deserted you now." Joss's voice was high with indignation.

"It's not desertion. These are my orders." He doubted the king would punish Isobel for Edmund's misdeeds, but he had to be certain. If anything happened to her or Will while he was in the south, he would never forgive himself.

"I don't like to leave you, my lord. You face a dangerous road, and Molbren Castle is well defended. The risk to yourself is far greater."

Ancel nudged his mount forward. "Joss speaks for me also."

"It seems the pair of you need a lesson in obedience. Nonetheless, I thank you for your loyalty." A reluctant smile tugged at the corner of his lips. It eased his heart to know he had such faithful squires. "Very well. This is what we shall do. I won't leave my wife unwarned. Joss, you can come with me on the provision that Ancel rides to Molbren. As we're not far from Ludlow, it will be a safe enough journey to make alone." He pulled out his money pouch and tossed a few coins to Ancel. "That will pay for board and lodging in Ludlow. From there it's a short journey to Molbren."

As soon as Ancel disappeared over the brow of the hill, Edmund turned to Joss. "I didn't want to bring you into this, Joss, but I admit I'll welcome the company on the road." He kicked Al-Ashab's flanks, and they moved off.

It was time to face the king and pray freeing Cannington wouldn't lose him all he had worked to build. Isobel might have destroyed their marriage, but she couldn't take Will from him. From now on he would work to build Redmarch into a strong inheritance for his son.

And maybe one day he would stop hearing Isobel's words. *You'll never know peace until you've come to terms with your parents' betrayal.*

Chapter Twenty-One

"He did what?" Isobel stared at Ancel in disbelief. The hem of his cloak was splashed with mud from the road, and his cheeks were reddened from the cold, but he had insisted on being brought straight to her in the solar to deliver his news.

"He escorted the Earl of Cannington and his son to his kin in Wales." Ancel edged closer to the fire. "He bade me tell you that he's now on his way to the king in Oxford. He wanted you warned in case King Stephen sent his forces here to take retribution."

Isobel sank upon the settle. "Why would Stephen punish him?" The king might withhold Edmund's reward, but nothing worse, surely. If he punished every noble who made a mistake, he'd have no supporters left.

Ancel tugged at the neck of his tunic. "I fear he's going to do more than tell the king the earl escaped. Knowing my lord, nothing short of the complete truth will do. I think he's going to confess that he freed Cannington."

"Has he gone mad? Why would he do that? He's been obsessed with earning the king's favor." But on reflection, she knew Ancel was correct. Edmund was sworn to serve King Stephen. His integrity would forbid him to keep such a transgression secret. He would feel honor-bound to confess what he had done.

He wouldn't be the man she loved, had he acted otherwise. How could she have doubted his honor and feared he would separate the earl from his son?

"When we thought we hunted Cannington alone, it was no problem." Ancel stretched his hands to the fire. "But when we learned his son was with him—a boy who had recently lost his mother—both Joss and I could see how much it troubled Lord Edmund. It didn't surprise me one jot when he announced he wouldn't surrender the boy to Stephen. Even though I was shocked when he freed Cannington, I can see now it was for the same reason: he couldn't bear to part father and son." Ancel shot Isobel a brief smile. "I think we have your influence to thank for Lord Edmund's change of heart."

After Ancel left to warm himself in the great hall, Isobel returned to the table she'd been working at before the interruption. But she'd lost the will to continue with the written lists her steward had provided, even though just a short while before she'd felt proud of her ability to decipher them. Before she realized what she was doing, she'd opened the box containing the bestiary and removed it. She opened it with care and leafed through the pages. Her eyes blurred when she saw the picture of the turtle dove. She couldn't see it now without thinking of Edmund.

Edmund. Who had believed so strongly in their marriage he'd remained chaste all those years. Who believed in her enough to teach her to read, give her what she'd wanted so badly as a child and been denied. Who had allowed her to grow into the woman *she* wanted to be. Who had fought for her.

Unlike her mother. Edmund's words came back to

her: *You never told me about your parents. Perhaps you should ask yourself why.*

Too late, the answer came to her. Thinking about her parents made her uncomfortable, painfully aware her mother had never fought for her. It was only now she knew how it felt to have someone on her side, prepared to stand up for her, that she could see the effect her mother's behavior had had on her.

She had grown to believe she wasn't worth fighting for. The lie had seeped into her soul, poisoning her confidence. As a result, she'd been too quick to accept the loss of Edmund's love. Twice.

Worst of all, it had whispered in her heart that she deserved to be punished, had reawakened her fear of Sir Roger. Now she knew the source of that voice, she could see it for the lie it was. Could lay Sir Roger's ghost to rest once and for all. But too late.

The hollow ache in her chest expanded, and the tears that had never been far away since Edmund's departure sprang to her eyes. It was ironic that now she had gained her independence, she no longer wanted it. Not if it meant losing Edmund.

A small hand tugged her sleeve, jolting her back to awareness. She brushed away the tears from her eyes and smiled down at Will. "What is it, my heart?"

"Why are you crying? Is it because Papa's gone away?"

She nodded. "I miss him."

"I miss him too. I hope he comes back soon."

He would come all too soon. To take Will away from her. But what could she do? She had tried her best to change his mind, but she might as well have asked the sun to stop its daily travels through the sky.

Will scrambled into her lap and picked up a quill. "Mama, please write Papa a letter. He'll come home if you ask. Ancel said you helped change his mind about the earl and John. Please change his mind about coming back."

Will's words were a ray of light across her soul. If she had persuaded Edmund to help Cannington, maybe there was hope. Edmund had accused her before of not fighting hard enough for their love. If she gave up now, wasn't she doing the same, and letting her parents defeat her all over again?

Will pushed the quill into her hand. "Go on, Mama. Write a letter."

She ruffled the feather between her fingers. Even if her writing was good enough to express the words in her heart, she doubted a letter would be enough to change his mind. No, if she wanted to show Edmund how much she loved him, she would have to go to him. Preferably before he took all the blame for Cannington's escape on his shoulders.

She put down the quill and held Will close. "I promise to do all I can to bring your papa home, but it will mean going to Oxford. Would you mind staying here with Agnes, if it meant you could spend more time with your papa in future?"

Will nodded, his hair falling into his eyes in his enthusiasm. "Yes, I want him to stay here always."

"Well, that wouldn't be possible, my heart." No matter how much she now yearned for it. "He is at the king's command. But when he can...I will try to persuade him."

"Promise? I want him to come home."

"I promise. I'll leave at first light. Pray that we'll

both be home soon." And that she could persuade Edmund of her love, because he'd been so mired in bitterness when he left she feared she had lost his love forever. All she could do was make the journey and pray Edmund would listen to her this time. Because Molbren was a barren place without him.

****

Edmund shifted in his saddle with a wince, trying to find a position that eased his aching muscles. This was the second day after parting ways with Ancel, and now they skirted Gloucester. A haze of woodsmoke hung over the rooftops, and he thought with longing of the hot fires and hearty dinners the townsfolk must be enjoying. He swore he could smell the scent of roast meat drifting through the air. His stomach growled.

"I suppose you plan to sleep in another barn tonight." Joss brought his horse alongside Edmund's and regarded the town with a wistful expression. Not that Edmund could blame him. Last night had been so disturbed by the scrabbling of rats and mice in the moldering straw of a long-deserted hovel that he had scarcely managed an hour of sleep.

He regarded the Oxford road with a frown. There was an alternative to a barn, but personally he'd prefer the vermin. He would sleep better on stinking straw, if only Isobel's parting words would leave him in peace. They had gnawed at the fringes of his consciousness throughout the journey until he feared he would lose his mind.

What happened to you as a child is the reason you refuse to forgive me...love me. You'll never know peace until you've come to terms with your parents' betrayal.

The answer to Isobel's challenge lay little more

than two hour's ride down that road. If he chose to seek it.

Joss removed his gloves and blew into his hands. They were reddened and swollen, his lips chapped and bleeding. Edmund could almost hear Isobel's voice: *Are you truly prepared to let Joss suffer because you're too proud to accept I might be right?*

He urged Al-Ashab into a walk. "We can do better than a barn tonight; we're not far from Stephen's territory. We won't have to go far along the Oxford road before we find manors in friendly hands." One in particular, although he would hardly describe the lady of the house as a friend. But she wouldn't turn him away.

He clicked his tongue, and Al-Ashab increased his pace. He kept a wary eye on the road for signs of soldiers, but clearly the townsfolk weren't anticipating trouble on a cold winter's day, with the sun past its zenith.

The sun lit the western clouds in a gaudy display of golds, salmon pink, and purple by the time Edmund found the track he was looking for. Thank the saints—it meant they were now safely out of the empress's territory, although there was an equally formidable woman to face at the end of the track. "This way. Only another mile or two and we'll be in front of a warm fire."

"Where are we going?" Joss asked.

"One of my manors."

"Who lives here?"

"My mother." Edmund ignored Joscelyn's raised brows and urged Al-Ashab onward.

He wasn't doing this because of Isobel. His mother

just happened to live on his route, that was all. However, he had to admit it would give him satisfaction to prove Isobel wrong, see her reaction when he told her of his visit and how it had made no difference to his feelings. Of course, he would have to return to Molbren to tell her so.

As they approached the manor, his thoughts drifted from Isobel to his mother. He hadn't spoken to her—hadn't laid eyes on her—since he'd left for the Holy Land. When he'd returned to take up his title, his mother had already retired to the manor at Sherbrook, and he'd had no desire to seek her out. His gut twisted at the prospect of what he would say to her now.

He didn't have long to consider. All too soon they rode into the courtyard at Sherbrook. The manor consisted of low, thatched buildings occupying three sides of the courtyard with a high wall on the fourth side. Behind the manor was a mound topped by a stone tower. If Sherbrook came under attack, the inhabitants could take refuge there; although it had no strategic worth, its flocks brought in a good price for their wool and the land was productive. His mother—the Lady Cecily—might have chosen to retire to an out-of-the-way manor, but she had chosen one of his richest properties.

Servants hurried out to take their packs and horses, then an elderly woman dressed in an emerald-green gown emerged from the great hall. Her shoulders were stooped, and when a gust of wind whipped her veil behind her, it revealed iron-gray braids coiled around her ears. Edmund glanced at her and dismissed her as one of her mother's ladies until a second glance revealed bright, slate-blue eyes.

"Mother." He did his best to hide his shock. He had imagined her unchanged, was unprepared to see how she'd aged.

She pressed her hands to her chest. "Edmund? Is it truly you?" The act of a mother long separated from her child was so convincing he was almost taken in. Almost. However, he bit back his retort, having no desire to create a scene in front of the entire household.

"Forgive my surprise visit. I didn't know I'd be passing by until it was too late to send word." He stooped to kiss her cheek. Her skin was as soft as he remembered, and her rosemary scent transported him back to the days when he'd been Will's age and longing for her attention.

He straightened, fighting to retain his composure. "I apologize for the inconvenience. We only require lodging for one night. I have urgent business with the king and leave for Oxford tomorrow."

Cecily gave a gracious smile. "Of course you're welcome. You must excuse my abrupt greeting—your arrival took me by surprise. I'll have a chamber prepared."

Later, from the comfort of a steaming bath tub, Edmund wondered if age and loss had mellowed his mother. She had certainly provided a much warmer welcome than anticipated. Not only had he been shown to a warm chamber with a large, canopied bed and a glowing brazier, but servants had arrived with this tub and ewers of hot water without him having to send for it. Cecily also sent word bidding him to join her in the solar for a meal as soon as he was ready. It had never occurred to him that his mother could change. Had he been wrong? Was it possible she regretted her actions and this was a belated attempt to atone?

Isobel's words continued to nag him, and he could no longer avoid the knowledge that the past she urged him to confront centered around his mother. Could he make peace with the woman who had knowingly sent him into danger? At this point, he would do anything to quieten Isobel's voice.

He rose from the bath and prepared to face his mother. He would confront her and demand an explanation. Nothing she could say would change his mind, but at least he'd have answered Isobel's challenge, proved her wrong. Then maybe he could silence her voice, and the raw and bleeding mess that had once been his heart would start to heal.

He found his mother in the solar, sitting beside the fire. She beckoned him to the opposite seat and summoned servants to bring food.

"I trust you are recovered from your journey," she said, ladling venison stew into his trencher. His mouth watered at the aroma of the rich wine and juniper berry sauce.

"I'm quite rested, thank you." He took a mouthful of the stew and chewed in silence. It was all very well for Isobel to challenge him to confront his past, but when that past was an elderly woman he scarcely recognized, he didn't know where to begin.

The silence dragged out while he ate. Cecily threaded a needle and worked on an embroidered girdle. Only when Edmund ladled another spoon of the stew onto his trencher, did Cecily speak again. "You say you're on your way to the king?" When he nodded, she said, "You must do all in your power to gain his confidence. Your father, may God assoil him, never understood the need to win royal favor. If you learn from his mistakes, you have the opportunity to be an influential voice at court."

The stew curdled in his stomach. Was that what this was about—plying him with comforts so she could enjoy the advantages an influential son could provide? There was an easy way to find out.

"I doubt I'll enjoy the king's favor once he's heard my news." In a few, brief sentences, he explained about Cannington.

She pursed her lips and narrowed her eyes as the tale unfolded. "Have you taken leave of your senses?" she snapped when he finished. "You'd be mad to reveal the truth to the king. Tell him you lost Cannington in the blizzard—you can't be held accountable for the weather. If you order your squires to hold their tongues, you may yet salvage the situation."

Not so much the repentant mother now. It gave him no pleasure to see he'd been right about her all along. "I refuse to dishonor myself by lying to my sworn liege."

"Honor? What use is honor? Will honor provide you food, clothing, and shelter when the king seizes your lands?"

"Perhaps not, but it will allow me to sleep with an easy conscience." Was that how Isobel had felt when she'd helped Cannington, even though she'd feared what he might do? Not a comfortable thought.

"And what of those depending on you? Did you never consider them before deciding to play the noble crusader?" Cecily flung her embroidery aside and leaned forward, gripping the arms of her chair. "It took years for Redmarch to recover from your father's foolishness, and now you want to throw it all away."

Foolishness? Not how he would describe the reckless action that had nearly cost him his life. A criminal betrayal was closer to the mark. He wiped his eating knife with trembling hands and put it away. Suddenly he'd lost his appetite.

He shoved the table aside and rose. This was a fool's errand—his mother was never going to change. Never going to apologize for the horror he'd endured. He'd leave at first light.

He'd only taken a step toward the door, when an image of Isobel appeared in his mind's eye, her brows raised in challenge. If she found out he'd failed to confront Cecily with her failures as a mother, she would accuse him of cowardice again. Well, he was no coward. He sank back upon the chair with a sigh.

"In the unlikely event the king seizes Sherbrook, you have my word I'll provide for you."

"That's not what I meant, Edmund. I'm more concerned about the poor folk who have nowhere else to go."

This was too much. "If you'd ever shown any consideration for others before, I might believe you."

Cecily folded her hands in her lap and looked Edmund in the eye. "It's clear you've come here to say something, Edmund. After so many years of you ignoring my approaches, forgive me if I'm skeptical about your motives for visiting now. If you have a charge against me, please do me the courtesy of saying it to my face instead of casting groundless accusations."

Edmund thumped the arm of the chair. "Groundless? You sent me as a hostage to the old king, knowing full well Father would continue his revolt. You sent a four-year-old child into danger. No one in their right mind could deny my accusation is justified."

Cecily drew a breath and nodded. "I feared that's how you would view it."

"What other way could it possibly be viewed? Do you deny it? Or does it keep you awake at night, knowing how close you came to sending a child to his death?"

"Of course it does. I'm not the monster you seem to take me for, Edmund."

Edmund had been prepared for denial, had a scathing attack hovering on his lips. Now all words failed him, and he could only sit in silence and wait for her to explain.

Cecily picked up her embroidery, but it seemed to be an automatic action because she didn't take up her needle. Instead she turned the girdle over and over in her hands, her head lowered as though studying each minute stitch. Edmund, too, was transfixed upon the pattern of green and silver ivy leaves. For some time the only sound was the crackle of the fire and his mother's harsh breathing. If he didn't know her better, he'd think she was struggling against tears.

Eventually she spoke, addressing her words to the girdle. "Why else do you think I came here the moment I heard you'd returned to England?"

"To get your hands on my richest manor." He didn't know what game she was playing now, but he refused to be taken in.

"I came here because I was afraid to see you. Because I knew it would be like this. I knew you would blame me."

"Why shouldn't I? I had to watch while they built a gallows for me. A four-year-old boy! And you sent me there."

"I don't expect you to believe this, but I sent you to the king for your protection."

A bitter laugh burst from his throat. "You're right. I don't believe it. You'll be telling me next you thought Father would turn into a dutiful vassal, remain at Redmarch, and commission a bard to compose praise poems for the king."

"Of course not, but I never dreamed he would rebel again."

"I find that hard to believe. How could you not know what your own husband was planning?"

"Believe me." Now Cecily looked up. Her mouth was taut, quivering. The first inkling of doubt crept into Edmund's mind. His mother's betrayal had been the pillar supporting all the perceptions of his childhood, and now a wave of dizziness swept over him as cracks formed in his most basic beliefs. "Your father knew I disapproved of the sway he held over your brothers, how he dragged them into his intrigues. He kept me in the dark regarding his plans so I couldn't warn them against him."

"Then why were you adamant I should be used as a hostage, not one of my brothers?"

"It was already too late for them—they refused to listen to my warnings. But you..." Cecily's face convulsed. "You were still mine. Still young enough not to be of interest to your father. I didn't want you to leave, but I thought you'd be safer with the king than with your father. I was trying to protect you."

"By sending me to the gallows?" But Edmund's heart wasn't in the barb. Ironic that it should be Cecily, in his eyes the antithesis of motherhood, who could explain Isobel to him. Isobel, whose every action was to protect Will. Who had been forced to make a difficult choice to protect a motherless child. A choice Edmund had refused to understand.

"By sending you away from your father, to learn from men who weren't so blinded with avarice, they couldn't see they were charging toward their own destruction. I wanted you to learn the wisdom you would never find in your father. If I'd known he'd planned to rebel I'd have killed him myself, before he'd had the chance to threaten your life, but he sent me to a distant castle. The first I knew of the revolt was when the king's men came to lay siege to it."

Edmund studied her but could find no trace of a lie. Now the words that had haunted his dreams took on a new meaning: *Trust me. All will be well.* If Cecily spoke the truth, then the act of sending him away had been one of sacrifice and love, and the outcome an unforeseen tragedy. So many years of heartbreak, of running away from love, and nothing he'd believed had been true. It was on the tip of his tongue to ask why she'd never tried to explain, but when he thought about it, he knew he'd never given her a chance. He'd refused to read the few letters she had sent, and each time she'd attended court, he'd always slipped away whenever she approached.

"There's nothing more I can say," Cecily concluded. "It's up to you to decide, but upon my oath, it's the truth. Everything I did was for your protection, and seeing you now, I know I made the right choice."

Edmund swallowed. "I...I don't know what to think." It was too much to take in all at once. A lifetime's pain couldn't be healed in one day. Even so, his heart was noticeably lighter. "I promise to think on it."

Not just on the effect this revelation had on his relationship with his mother, but what this meant for his marriage. If he could have made this huge mistake regarding his mother's feelings and motives, what about Isobel's? Had she really betrayed him, or was his belief colored by his mistaken feelings about his mother? He owed it to her to find out.

Chapter Twenty-Two

Oxford, February 1139

Edmund paced about the herb garden, pausing every now and again to kick stray pebbles off the path, sending them ricocheting off the low stone walls and at one point chipping a lump off a clay pot that held the last withered stumps of a mint bush. Four days. In Heaven's name, surely the king ought to have reached a decision by now.

When he'd arrived, saddle-sore and chilled to the bone, he'd insisted on speaking to the king straight away. In front of the whole court, he had confessed to escorting the Earl of Cannington and his son to safety.

"I see." Stephen's voice was mild, although his fingers clenched the arms of his chair. "You defied my direct orders. Why?"

"I couldn't in all conscience deliver a four-year-old boy into captivity when he had done nothing wrong but be born Cannington's heir."

"I asked only for the earl. You could have delivered him to me and kept the boy safe."

"He had recently lost his mother, your Grace. I hadn't the heart to separate him from his father as well."

The king eyed him closely for several painful heartbeats. "I need to think on this. Remain in Oxford;

I'll summon you when I'm ready to pass judgment." He waved a hand in dismissal, and Edmund had walked out of the great hall on shaky legs.

He had expected to learn his fate the next day at the latest, yet here he still was, pacing from herb garden to orchard, from orchard to bailey and back to the herb garden until he was surprised he hadn't worn down the cobbles. God's bones—what was taking the king so long? Any punishment he could mete out had to be better than this agonizing wait.

At least the delay had given him time to think. Consider what his mother had said. Gradually the bitterness had faded, replaced by deep sadness. All these years he had refused to see his mother, believed she'd betrayed him, but it was all due to his mistaken perception of events. His mother had loved him every bit as deeply as Isobel loved Will.

Isobel. He yearned to return to her. Beg her forgiveness. If only the king would make up his mind and release him.

He must have taken another dozen turns around the garden before Joss appeared. "The king has sent for you."

His stomach twisting, he strode into the hall, only to stop dead when Ancel entered the other door; judging from his tangled hair and mud-spattered garb, he'd only just ridden in.

"Ancel, I thought I told you to—" Then his eyes fell on the figure standing behind him. From the height and slight outline, it was a woman, but the hood of her mantle was pulled over her head. His mouth went dry. It couldn't be her.

A slender hand reached up to tuck a wayward

tawny lock beneath the hood. A hand with a pearl band upon her ring finger. His heart faltered, then pounded, the blood roaring in his ears.

He forgot everything. Forgot the king awaited him. Forgot he was angry with her. He only knew she was here, and he didn't want her embroiled in any punishment King Stephen was determined to dole out.

He shoved Ancel aside and took her arm, then pulled back her hood. "Isobel!" He should scold her, get her to safety, but all he could do was trace the elegant line of her cheekbone with his knuckle and drink in the sight of her. Even in a travel stained riding gown of a dull moss green, her lips chapped from the bitter cold, she was the most beautiful woman of the court. How he had ever imagined he could live without her, he'd never know.

Isobel closed her eyes and leaned into his caress. They stood there for the space of several heartbeats. Edmund didn't care if they kept the king waiting. All he cared about was that Isobel was here, in his arms, when he'd feared he would never hold her again. He breathed deeply, the mingled scent of rosewater and rosemary making his senses reel. She was truly here!

Then Ancel coughed, bringing Edmund back to reality, aware the eyes of the court were on them. He could only breathe a prayer of thanks that the king was in deep conversation and had not noticed their embrace. "Isobel," he said again, savoring her name, "what in Heaven's name are you doing here?"

Isobel straightened and glanced around the hall, a delightful rosy blush stealing up her cheeks when she saw the curious looks aimed their way. "Ancel told me of your addle-pated plan to confess all to the king. I decided you needed rescuing. Tell me I haven't arrived too late to stop you."

"I told him the moment I arrived. Now go. He's yet to pass judgment, and I want you safely away before he includes you in my punishment."

"No. He'll hear my side of the tale before he pronounces his sentence."

Before he could stop her, she swept past him and approached the dais, kneeling in a deep curtsy when she had the king's attention.

Stephen ordered her to rise with a wave of the hand. "Lady Isobel. What a pleasure to see you, although I don't recall summoning you."

"Yet you summoned my husband."

The king frowned, and his glanced flicked from her to rest on Edmund. "Your husband? Redmarch, in your haste to confess your misdeeds, you neglected to mention a marriage."

Edmund reined in his impatience. He was anxious to learn his fate, and now he would have to explain the details of his marriage—in front of the whole court, no less—before he could learn the king's decision.

"Forgive me, Your Grace. It was a marriage contracted in secret when we were younger, when I was still but the third son of my father."

Whispers and murmurs eddied around the great hall.

Stephen leaned forward, pinning Edmund with his gaze. "And the boy—the heir to Molbren?"

Edmund strode to Isobel's side and clasped her hand. It trembled, but he was heartened when she clasped his in return. He should be angry with her for disobeying him; instead his heart sang. She had chosen to stand by his side. She believed in him enough to face the king's displeasure and suffer whatever punishment Stephen decided to hand out.

He wouldn't let her down again. He would prove his love to her, prove her trust wasn't misplaced, no matter how long it took.

"He is my son. My legitimate son, born in wedlock."

"And so not the heir to Molbren after all." Stephen scowled. "And the legitimacy of the boy is a matter for the Church to decide. Nevertheless, this leaves Molbren without an heir precisely when we need our borders to be strong. I must consider this further. But as to your punishment for freeing the Earl of Cannington, I—"

"If I might speak, Your Grace?" Isobel's voice rang out clear and proud. The king's eyebrows shot up, and the murmurs of his courtiers rose in volume, but Isobel raised her chin and looked Stephen in the eye.

Before she could say more, Edmund pulled her close and murmured into her ear. "Isobel, you must stay out of this. Think of Will if not for yourself. What good will it achieve if we both anger the king?"

She shook her head. "No. I have to do what's right." She addressed the king again. "I beg you consider what I have to say before passing judgment on my husband."

The king gave a wave of the hand. "Very well."

Edmund had no choice but to bite his tongue and pray for the king's leniency.

****

Isobel's knees quaked. For the duration of the mad ride to Oxford she had been so intent on getting there before the king passed judgment, she hadn't considered what to say when she got there. Then she felt Edmund's fingers weave with hers, and it gave her the strength to continue. Even if his show of support was just that—a show put on for the benefit of the court—she took comfort in it. It gave her hope she could still salvage their marriage.

"Before you pass sentence on my husband, you should know it was I who gave the Earl of Cannington and his son shelter. I hid him from my husband because I knew Lord Edmund desired to carry out your orders."

"That does not explain why your husband should then escort Cannington to safety in defiance of those orders."

So Edmund had told Stephen the truth. As much as she loved him for his honor, she couldn't help wishing he'd let the king believe Cannington had evaded Edmund and escaped. There was only one thing she could do to put this right.

"Your Grace, there is a perfectly good explanation."

"Tell me."

"My husband is a man of honor."

"Hardly honorable if he defied his sworn duty. How am I to trust him again?"

She drew a breath, only to falter when Edmund shot her a glare. *Keep quiet!* it said, and his desire to protect her only bolstered her determination to save him.

"That depends, Your Grace. Do you wish to have men close to you who blindly obey your every word, without thought to the long-term effects that will have on your authority? However, if you are looking for a strong man to hold the borders of your kingdom against both the Welsh and the empress's forces, who will reflect honor upon you and bring more men flocking to your banner, then you can do no better than my husband." The words poured out with scarcely a thought. Although she looked at the king, all her senses were focused on the man who stood beside her, the man who, as her husband, had the right to silence her, banish her from the court. Yet far from stifle her, he nurtured her independence, cherished it.

Her heart swelled, ached with love as she concluded, "If that's the case, then Edmund should be rewarded, not punished."

"Heartfelt words indeed." Stephen addressed his next words to Edmund. "I'm glad to hear your wife thinks the same way I do. I had already come to the same conclusion, but it is good to know she shares my opinion."

Isobel's heart swooped with relief. "You mean—?"

"I will overlook your failure to follow orders in this instance, Redmarch. Since your arrival, I have received a message from the Earl of Cannington's family, saying that thanks to the kindness and mercy you showed, they will now support me. Your help has strengthened my borders considerably. As it would be foolish of me to hand Molbren over to anyone else, even though I am well within my rights to do so, you may add Molbren to your holdings. In addition to making Redmarch a county palatine."

Isobel gasped. "Thank you, Your Grace." So her actions hadn't lost Edmund his prize after all.

Only the knowledge that Edmund might still be angry with her prevented her from flinging herself into his arms in front of the whole court. She longed to speak to him, discover if there was any way she could win back his love, but she had to curb her impatience while Edmund, face glowing, bowed and expressed his own gratitude.

However, now that her dreaded ordeal was over, the aches of the journey made themselves known; a wave of tiredness washed over her. Her knees trembled, and she staggered.

A strong arm wove around her waist, lending her strength. She breathed in the scent of leather and woodsmoke, leaning against Edmund's hard body. Now her knees shook from an altogether different reason.

"Your Grace, you have my word to do all in my power to uphold your trust. Now my wife is tired, and I wish to take her to my chambers to rest." Most men would have left their wives to fend for themselves rather than risk displeasing the king by excusing themselves before he had concluded their business, but not Edmund. Stephen gave him an indulgent wave of the hand, and Edmund guided her out of the great hall, his arm a secure support around her waist.

Isobel felt dizzy with his nearness after fearing him lost to her forever. She rested her head against his shoulder, and pleasurable prickles surged through her veins when his hand dropped from her waist to her hip. She did her best to suppress her need for him—she had begun her fight for his love, but there was no guarantee she would win. There was still much to be said.

"I can't believe you came all this way." Edmund guided her across the courtyard to the castle gates. "I wasn't able to get lodgings within the castle, I'm afraid, but there's not far to walk. Once we're there, we have to talk."

Anticipation speared her in the gut. Back in the great hall she had been sure of his support and hoped that meant she also had his love. Now doubt crept in. Maybe he had simply wanted to spare her the humiliation of a rejection before the court. Fear closed her mouth; all she could do was nod and allow him to guide her through the tangle of streets to a large house. Once inside, he opened a door and ushered her into a spacious chamber. A huge canopied bed stood in the center; Isobel tore her eyes away from that to take in the rest of the room. Arranged beside a lit brazier was a pair of chairs with swans carved into their backs; a coffer painted in greens and reds stood against the foot of the bed.

She fumbled at her throat for her cloak pin, but Edmund brushed her hands aside and unclasped it. The light touch of his fingers upon her collar bone set her flesh alight as he eased her cloak off and flung it upon the coffer.

He took her hand. "Come and sit by the fire."

She sat and twisted her hands in her lap. No matter that he had poured a goblet of wine for her and ordered the maid who had come scurrying at his call to bring food, she couldn't help but be afraid this was his way of breaking it to her that he would never return to her.

"I'm sorry if my coming made you angry," she said, when she could bear the tension no longer. "I know you wanted me to stay in Molbren, but I couldn't allow you to be punished for my actions."

Edmund's expression softened, and he sank into the chair opposite. "I was angry when I saw you, but not because you disobeyed me. I didn't want the king to turn his anger on you." He smiled. "That was a brave thing you did, *ma belle*. Not many women could face down a king. I was proud to stand beside you. Now more than ever, I know we belong together."

Her insides swooped. "Then…you'll come back?"

Edmund groaned and in a flurry of movement that left her breathless, she found herself sitting upon his lap, his lips caressing her brow, her jaw, her lips. "I will if you can forgive me."

"Of course I—" but he silenced her with a lingering kiss that set her insides aflutter and warmed her far more thoroughly than the brazier.

"Let me speak first," he said when he ended the kiss.

Isobel's heart hammered so hard against her ribs she doubted she could have spoken anyway. She nestled her head in the crook of his neck and fingered the silver clip decorating the tip of his tunic lace.

"You were right." His voice rumbled against her cheek. "I should have spoken with my mother long before now. I went to see her on my way here, and I've come to realize that all my beliefs about her were wrong. She was acting out of love." He related his conversation with Cecily.

Isobel listened in dawning understanding. "I'm so glad, Edmund. I found it hard to believe a mother could be that callous." She stroked his cheek, thrilling at the way he leaned into the caress. "I'm so happy you've discovered the truth."

"I couldn't accept it right away, but I've had days to think of little else. The more I thought about it, the more I could see it was true. It's frightening to think I believed the worst of her for so many years."

He pulled her close. Holy Mother, it felt good to be

in his arms again. "The greatest tragedy is how that affected us," he continued. "You saw it before I did. I was so blind. If you hadn't challenged me, we'd probably still be apart. For all this time, I believed my love and trust for my mother nearly led me to my death. I believed love made me weak. When I discovered you'd concealed Cannington, had lied about it, it brought back all those feelings of betrayal. You were the first woman I'd allowed myself to trust since my mother, and when I found out about Cannington, I couldn't bear that you'd turned my trust against me."

"I'm so sorry, Edmund. I was at my wits' end, I hated myself for doing it."

He silenced her with a kiss. She closed her eyes and clung to him, her heart swelling with gratitude that he still loved her, wasn't leaving her. She slanted her mouth against his, parting her lips, reveling in his taste, the caress of his tongue. Soon they were both breathing heavily.

Finally, he broke the kiss with a gasp and pulled her against his chest. They sat in silence for a while, Isobel listening to the thud of his heart, Edmund's fingers tracing maddening circles on her back.

"You've nothing to reproach yourself for," Edmund said after a time. "You were in an impossible situation, but you acted with more integrity than I did. You protected an innocent man and his son, even though you must have been afraid of what I would do if I found out. That's why you're so good for me, *ma belle*. You stand up to me. You're not afraid to tell me when I'm wrong. I love you, but I need you, too. I'm a lesser man without you."

Isobel swallowed the lump in her throat. "I won't

have you take all the blame. What you said about my parents…it made me think about how they treated me. All my life, my father saw me only as a means to a powerful alliance. He wouldn't let me do anything that might damage my value as a potential wife. Several times I pleaded with my mother to teach me to read, or let me look at the bestiary again, but she would never stand up to him, never argue my case. In the end I suppose I grew up thinking I wasn't worth fighting for."

Edmund stroked her cheek. "Oh, *ma belle*, I can only imagine how you must have felt when I left for the Holy Land. I can only say that I would fight my way to the ends of the Earth for you, if that's what it takes to convince you of my love."

She kissed him. "You were right, though. I accepted your loss too easily. I could have found a way to get word to you, if only I hadn't believed I wasn't worth fighting for. And I nearly let you go again. I even…"

She hesitated. This was the hardest thing of all, but if there was to be a full reconciliation, she mustn't hold anything back. "It was true, what you said before you left. I did shrink from you. I always knew in my heart you wouldn't hurt me, but the same lie that I wasn't worth fighting for made me believe I deserved whatever punishment you might deal."

With a groan, Edmund pulled her closer. "Oh, *ma belle*, that's not true. If it takes the rest of my life, I'll do anything it takes to convince you."

The last shred of doubt and fear crumbled, and she looked up at Edmund through a haze of tears. "You already have. By everything you've done for me—the way you put yourself between me and that wolf, how you taught me to read, the way you charged after me when I was with Cannington—you've proved over and again that you believe in me, will fight for me. So I had to come to Oxford and show you that I wouldn't give you up so easily, either."

"Thank all the saints you did."

In response, she wrapped her arms around her neck then and pressed her mouth to his. When she pulled back, she studied his face, and her blood heated when she saw his darkened eyes. "I love you, Edmund. I'll always love you. Promise we'll be together as much as possible. These past days, believing we would hardly ever be under the same roof, have been agony."

Edmund reached up and removed each hair pin from her head rail, placing them on the table. His lopsided smile made her stomach swoop. "There are times I'll be called to fight. I can't take you with me then, but every other time, you have my word. I never want to be parted from you. Where you are is where I belong."

The last pin dropped onto the table with a clatter, and he pulled off her veil, tangling his fingers into her hair. "Now," he said with a chuckle that sent shivers of delight coursing down her spine, "I hope you're feeling rested after your long journey." There was no mistaking the glint in his eyes.

"I do ache rather." She purred into his ear, "I think I should lie down."

He shifted his grip and rose with her in his arms. Too impatient to wait for even the few strides to the bed, she captured his lips in a kiss, reveling in his taste, the delicious contrast between the softness of his lips and the scratch of stubble.

They tumbled onto the bed, and he leaned over her, kissing the hollow in her throat, making her gasp and shiver. Yearning to feel his bare flesh against hers, she tugged at the hem of his tunic and raised her arms so he could unravel the lacings of her gown. She giggled when he snagged them into a tighter knot, then found herself blinking back tears as a thought struck her.

"What's wrong?" Edmund drew away, concern etched on his face.

She gave a soft smile and traced the line of his jaw with her fingertips. "Nothing. It only struck me as strange that we're rushing. There's nothing to rush for. We have all night." She rubbed his lower lip with her thumb. "The rest of our lives."

He smiled then kissed each of her fingertips. "Ah, but a woman as independent as you… I have to make the most of our time together before you take it into your head to go on crusade or single-handedly resolve the dispute for the throne of England."

"And that's why I love you so much. You would let me do it—and make sure that I had all the necessary skills first. And that's why I only want to be independent if I can be independent with you. We can do all these things, but we'll do them together."

Then she pulled him down into a deep kiss, pouring all her gratitude and love into the act. Together. That's how they would be until the end of their lives.

Epilogue

Molbren Castle, March 1140

Edmund stooped over the cradle, marveling at the perfection of his new son's features—from the sweep of dark lashes to the bow of his lips to the miniature fingernails.

"He's beautiful." He brushed the petal-soft cheek with the tip of his finger. "It's hard to believe we made something so fragile and precious." He smiled up at Isobel who, pale but glowing, was propped up against pillows on the bed. After another glance at the baby, reassuring himself that he slept, he sat next to Isobel and pulled her against his chest. "Have you thought of a name?"

"Edmund. And I hope he grows up to be as strong and honorable as his father."

"Edmund." He smiled, already overcome by the tug on his heart created by this new bond, newer, but just as strong and fierce as his love for Isobel and Will.

As if summoned by his thoughts, the door opened a crack and Will peered in. "Can I see him yet?" He tiptoed into the chamber. "Agnes said you might let me if I promised to be quiet."

Edmund patted the space on the bed next to him. "Come and sit with us. He's asleep, but you can look at him from here if you promise not to wake him."

With an eager nod, Will scurried into the room and clambered up to sit in the crook of Edmund's arm. He leaned over the side of the bed, peering into the crib. "He's very small. Has he got a name yet?"

"It's Edmund," said Isobel, "but we'll call him Ned for now. Do you think that suits him?"

"Yes, I like it. And I like Ned. It's going to be fun having him in our family."

Family. Edmund's heart swelled. In under a year he'd gone from a bitter, angry, lonely man to one who was blessed with a beautiful wife and two sons.

"I have news for you both," he said. "A messenger arrived today with a letter from the archbishop. He's upholding the validity of our first marriage and declared Will legitimate."

"Oh, that's wonderful news." Isobel's eyes glistened with tears. "I was afraid he'd reject our suit. After all my worry…" She pulled Edmund's head down for a kiss.

Will wriggled from his grip and whispered to his baby brother, "Mama and Papa kiss a lot. You'll have to get used to it."

Edmund felt Isobel's shoulders shake, and she broke the kiss, giggling into the crook of his neck.

He ran fingers through her tousled hair. "I'll never get used to it, *ma belle*. Never grow tired of having you in my arms, never tire of loving you. Thank you for loving me in return."

Isobel smiled, then relaxed against him and he felt her head grow heavy. "I love you too, Edmund." Her voice was blurred; the words were scarcely out before she drifted into sleep.

And as she slumbered, Edmund sent a silent prayer

of thanks for the wonderful blessing of loving and being loved in return. Thanks for the woman who had rescued him from his anger and bitterness and released him from his fear of love. He had arrived in Molbren intent only on gaining the king's reward, and he thanked God for waking him up in time to the greatest prize of all—Isobel. He had made the mistake of letting her go once, but now they were together and would never be parted again.

A word about the author...

Tora lives in Shropshire in the UK. On childhood holidays her interest in history was fired by exploring castles in Wales and the Welsh borders, and she would make up stories about characters living there. When she started writing, it seemed only natural to turn to the settings that inspired her as a child.

In her free time, when she can drag herself away from reading, she enjoys walking and cycling.

Visit her at:

http://www.torawilliams.uk/

Printed in Great Britain
by Amazon